The Old Deep and Dark

The Old Deep and Dark

ELLEN HART

MINOTAUR BOOKS ✖ NEW YORK

For Jessie and Betty Chandler,
with much love.

And welcome to our family, little Rocket.

THE OLD DEEP AND DARK. Copyright © 2014 by Ellen Hart. All rights reserved. Printed in the United States of America. For information, address St. Martin's Press, 175 Fifth Avenue, New York, N.Y. 10010.

www.minotaurbooks.com

Library of Congress Cataloging-in-Publication Data

Hart, Ellen.
  The Old Deep and Dark / Ellen Hart. — First edition.
    p. cm.

  ISBN 978-1-250-04769-4 (hardcover)
  ISBN 978-1-250-04780-9 (e-book)

  1. Lawless, Jane (Fictitious character)—Fiction.   2. Women
detectives—Minnesota—Minneapolis—Fiction.   3. Murder—
Investigation—Fiction.   4. Lesbians—Fiction.   I. Title.
  PS3558.A6775O43 2014
  813'.54—dc23

                                        2014027207

First Edition: October 2014

10   9   8   7   6   5   4   3   2   1

Cast of Characters

Jane Lawless: Owner of the Lyme House Restaurant in Minneapolis. Partner with A. J. Nolan in Nolan & Lawless Investigations

Cordelia Thorn: Owner and director at the Thorn Lester Playhouse in Minneapolis. Hattie's aunt. Octavia Thorn-Lester's sister. Jane's best friend.

Katherine (Kit) Deere: Actor. Jordan's wife. Chloe and Booker's mother.

Beverly Elliot: Kit's personal assistant. Old friend.

Jordan Deere: Country music artist. Kit's husband. Chloe and Booker's dad.

Chloe Deere: Fund-raiser. Kit and Jordan's daughter. Booker's sister.

Booker Tiberius Deere: Set designer. Kit and Jordan's son. Chloe's brother.

Archibald Van Arnam: Author. Professor of history at the University of Minnesota and well-known Minnesota historian. Friend of the Deere family.

Red Clemens: Longtime janitor at the Thorn Lester Playhouse.

Tommy Prior: Jordan's business manager and friend.

Dr. Daniel Woodson: Cardiac surgeon.

Erin O'Brian: Playwright. Friend of the Deere family.

Avi Greenberg: Jane's girlfriend. Writer.

Julia Martinsen: Jane's ex.

Hattie Thorn-Lester: Cordelia's eight-year-old niece. Octavia's daughter.

Monsters are real, and ghosts are real too. They live inside us, and sometimes, they win.

—Stephen King

He wasn't a boy. He hated it when people called him that, used the word as a way to define him, to minimize him. Okay, so technically, if that's what these judgmental jerks were aiming at, he wasn't a man yet either, but he was way beyond the boy stage. Kids didn't understand love, the romantic kind. The forever kind. He did. He hadn't told anyone close to him that he'd found the woman he was going to marry, mainly because they'd all laugh and tell him he was crazy. He didn't need small-minded, negative thinkers in his life.

Okay, so maybe there were a few hurdles. The age difference, for one. Not that it mattered. Love, as the poets said, would find a way. Kit was the most exquisite woman he'd ever seen. She was Catherine Deneuve, Candice Bergen, and Marilyn Monroe all rolled up into one perfect package, and someday, down on his knee, diamond ring tucked into a small black velvet box, he'd ask her to marry him. It made his stomach clutch and his heart race every time he thought about that moment, when he would make her his own.

Katherine—Kit—Haralson had been crowned Princess Kay of the Milky Way at the state fair two years ago. Eighteen years old, right out of high school. He'd seen her sitting there at the butter-carving booth, posing for her sculpture. She'd been told to keep still, but it was hard with people calling out questions, shouting her name. When the fair was over, she was given the butter statue of herself to take home. He wasn't sure what a dairy farm, where she'd grown up, would do with all that excess butter, although the neighbors would probably ask to see it, so maybe it would be fun for a while—until it melted. After she'd been officially crowned, she'd traveled the state representing the dairy industry. She was a natural beauty, with golden hair and a perfect milk-white smile. And tonight, he was going to meet her for the first time. Since his palms were sweaty, he was definitely *not* going to shake her hand.

It would work like this: During intermission, he would sneak backstage. He assumed that when Kit started acting around town, it would only be a matter of time until she was cast in a play at this theater, a place he knew well. The dressing rooms were behind the stage. Getting to them would be a piece of cake. The hard part, as always, was the waiting.

Tonight, finally, that wait was over. Kit was luminous, acting her heart out. He followed her with eager eyes and when she left the stage, even if it was only for a moment, he felt an emptiness creep inside him. He sat in the dark, mesmerized, gazing up anxiously as the curtain came down and people around him thundered their applause. He thundered right along with them.

Intermission would last fifteen minutes.

Edging his way toward the front of the house as everyone else headed for the lobby, he slipped through a dark velvet curtain held together at the top by a series of safety pins and stood for a moment, watching the crew hustle furniture off the stage. The lead actors were given individual dressing rooms along a back wall. The building was ancient. While the lobby was nothing to brag about, the backstage area, smelling like an old moldy sponge, was a mass of peeling paint, dirty, scuffed floors, battered walls, and a general dankness that totally fascinated him. Thankfully, nobody gave him a second look as he walked briskly into the rear hallway. He bent down and peeked through the first keyhole. Nope. Wrong room. The skinny man inside had stripped to his undershirt and boxer shorts and was searching through a bunch of clothes draped over a chair. Gross.

Moving to the next door, he leaned in and squinted. "Score," he whispered. Kit, her golden hair swept back into a ponytail, was seated at the dressing table, the lightbulbs that surrounded an oversized mirror casting a hard light on her flawless features. Her red lips and white skin reminded him of his sister's porcelain doll. A bouquet of red roses tied with a ribbon spread across the table and claimed all her attention. She removed a tiny pink card, read the message, then smiled a moony smile.

"Hey, what are you doing there?" came a man's voice.

"Me?" He turned around.

Another man came along and grabbed the first man's arm. "We got a problem with the horse prop. Ten freakin' minutes before curtain and this thing goes and busts on me."

As quick as that, they were gone.

After rubbing his palms along his jeans to wipe off the sweat, he gave a soft rap on the door with one knuckle. When he received no response, he tried again. Thinking that his beautiful Kit was lost in reverie, he turned the doorknob and pushed the door slowly inward, all the while rehearsing his words with his eyes shut tight.

"Kit," he began, too frightened to even look at her. "You don't know me. My name is——" When he finally gathered enough nerve to force a smile and open his eyes, he gave an involuntary jerk. "Kit?" he said. This time he spoke her name as a question.

He inched forward. Turning full circle in the center of the room, he found no windows or doors. No closet. No trapdoor in the floor. There was nowhere to hide and no way in or out except for the door he'd just come through.

And yet?

He searched the air around him for the magician's puff of smoke. There could be no other explanation for why the flowers, the ribbon, the card, and his beloved Kit, had vanished.

2

"The old deep and . . . *what?*" said Cordelia, tossing her rinestone-encrusted reading glasses on the restored Chippendale card table she used as a desk. A giant woman and a giant desk, one with huge claw feet, were meant for each other. At least, that's how the antique dealer had sold it to her. As the part-owner and artistic director of the newest theater in Minneapolis—the Thorn Lester Playhouse—Cordelia required an office that reflected her personality and status. Gilded Age, while not a reflection of her bank account, seemed the perfect fit. It was also the general era in which the theater—originally an opera house—had been built.

Across from her sat the University of Minnesota's preeminent Minnesota historian, Archibald Van Arnam, a friend and avid theatergoer. He had, on his own time and at his own expense, offered to look into the history of the theater for her. He'd come to her office at the crack of dawn this morning—nearly ten A.M.—to give her his initial findings.

"Yes, yes," he said eagerly. "That's what they used to call this place. The Old Deep and Dark. Fascinating, isn't it? Fascinating."

5

Archibald, when excited, tended to repeat himself. He was a naturally pedantic man, used to speaking in front of large crowds of disinterested college kids, and thus primed to talk more loudly than was strictly necessary. He was in his early fifties, with the face of an embittered Roman emperor—or a hired thug—the body of a wrestler gone to seed, and a comb-over that was so pathetic, Cordelia couldn't imagine how he could look at himself in the mirror every morning and not dissolve in a fit of hysterics. His eyes were sharp, covered by dark-rimmed glasses, and his crooked teeth were stained from years of too much coffee and too many cigarettes. She'd known him socially as a younger man and figured that some women—at the very least, his three wives—had once found him attractive. He was an inveterate gossip and a natural raconteur—the last a skill that Cordelia felt was becoming endangered in today's Internet culture. In her opinion, Archibald was the perfect dinner guest, always arriving with several bottles of excellent wine, ever willing to entertain.

"Yes, it's interesting," she said, picking up her reading glasses and settling them back on her nose, "but even you have to admit, it's not exactly good news. 'Let's get tickets to the Old Deep and Dark for a show tonight, sweetums.' Virtually every staff meeting I've had this week has devolved into a conversation about branding and positioning our new theater. Do we really want to *be* the Old Deep and Dark?"

"Don't you want to know why it's called that?"

"I don't know," she said, one eyebrow arching. "Do I?"

"The original owner, Elijah Samuelson, the man who built the place in 1903, sold it in 1923. The new owners, Gilbert and Hilda King, intended to turn it into a vaudeville stage, but because of mismanagement, and some say Gilbert's gambling problems, they couldn't make a go of it. Remember, this was right around the be-

6

ginning of Prohibition. Apparently, as the theater was on its way toward insolvency, Gilbert got involved with some unsavory types."

"Gangsters?"

"Bootleggers, though you're probably right. They were likely connected. Lots of mob activity in the Twin Cities back then, you know. Anyway, Gilbert King—he started calling himself King Gilbert—only ran shows on weekends and spent the rest of his time developing a speakeasy. That's what kept him and Hilda afloat until the early thirties."

"Where was the speakeasy?"

"In the basement. People came in through a door along Fifth. They were hustled down a narrow back stairs."

The comment jogged Cordelia's memory. The basement of the theater was essentially unexplored territory. She'd been down there a few times with her sister to check out the rooms, many of them stuffed with old theater paraphernalia. Beyond heating, cooling, plumbing, and electrical concerns, and because extra storage space wasn't needed at the moment, she'd decreed that the basement renovation could wait until the upper floors had been completed. As she thought about it, she did recall seeing a rather beautiful Art Deco bar somewhere in the bowels of the building, but had assumed it was a shell, a prop created in a scene shop for a specific play.

The proscenium stage was located on the third floor of the main building. The costume shop, scene shop, electrical shop, and prop and costume storage rooms fit reasonably well on second. The main floor served as a small lobby, with elevators at the edges, and a ticket booth out front under a large marquee. A two-story addition had been added on to the east side of the building during the late forties. The first level contained two rental spaces, already taken by an independent general bookstore and an Italian deli. Theater offices were on the second.

"Where exactly was the speakeasy?" asked Cordelia, removing a nail file from her sack purse.

"The southwest corner of the main building. King Gilbert had it walled off from the rest of the basement. That is, except for a small door, which, at the moment, is unlocked."

"You've been down there?"

"I've been searching for old theater records. I assume you don't mind."

She waved the comment away. "And thus, because of the illegal nature of the speakeasy, the theater became known as the Old Deep and Dark?"

"No, the building wasn't called that until Gilbert and Hilda were murdered."

Her eyes widened. "Murdered?"

"It was 1933, the year Prohibition ended. Supposedly, King Gilbert got in over his head with the wrong guys. Those guys cornered him and Hilda behind the bar one night and blew them away. It was a fairly typical gangland shooting. One goon stood upstairs outside the door on Fifth, while two more crept down the stairs and opened fire with Thompson submachine guns. A couple of bystanders were wounded. Thankfully, both survived."

"Wonderful. Just . . . exactly what I wanted to hear."

"I believe Gilbert was hit with at least fifteen rounds. Seven slugs passed through Hilda. What was left of them was buried at Lakewood a few days later." He adjusted his bifocals. "I'm afraid there's more."

"Of course there is."

"The building's haunted. For the past eighty years, folks have seen faint images of Gilbert and Hilda on the stairs, in the elevators, onstage during shows. They've heard voices and footsteps, creaking floorboards when nobody is around. Windows in the offices are found open in the middle of winter." Leaning closer to her, he dropped his voice. "Apparently, they don't get along."

"Excuse me?"

"There's a lot of bickering. You've got a ghost light on the stage, right?"

"Of course. It's an actor's equity thing, a safety feature. It's not supposed to work for actual ghosts."

"Why are you smiling?" asked Archibald.

"Every theater should have a ghost," declared Cordelia. "It's tradition."

"Yes, well," he said, clearing his throat. "If you believe in that sort of thing."

"You don't?"

"I believe in the romance of any given theater being haunted, but no, I don't believe in actual ghosts." Flipping past a couple of pages, he continued. "To move on with our mini-history tutorial. After Gilbert and Hilda died, the theater sat empty for many years. It was the Great Depression and nobody had the money to restart it. Eventually, two Chicago-based entrepreneurs bought the property for a song and turned it into a movie theater. They slapped a neon marquee on the front, added elevators in the front lobby, built the addition, and operated it until 1964, calling it the Downtowner. It was sold again in 1967. The third-floor movie theater was dismantled and the space was used as a general auditorium. It continued to deteriorate. A couple of theater groups rented it after that. One from 1975 to 1987. One from 1998 to 2006. It sat empty for the rest of the time."

"And then my sister and I bought it," said Cordelia, trying to hurry him along. She had another meeting scheduled for eleven and wanted to get some breakfast before it began.

"Speaking of your sister, where is Octavia?" asked Archibald, closing the folder. "I was hoping she might sit in on our discussion this morning."

"Italy," said Cordelia, repositioning her turquoise necklace across her impressive décolletage. She knew the necklace was gaudy, which was why she liked it. "She's trying to disentangle herself from husband number fifteen."

"Fifteen?" he repeated, looking shocked. "So many?"

"Well, eight? Twelve? I can't keep track. This one's a real bloodsucker, that's all I know."

"When will she be back?"

"Next month. Next week. Tomorrow. She is a will-o'-the-wisp until we start rehearsals."

"With a name like hers—so famous on the New York stage, in movies—"

"She obviously has the lead in our first production."

"And you'll direct."

It gave Cordelia a bad case of indigestion to even think about directing her sister. Not only was Octavia a black hole when it came to emotional hand-holding, she didn't take direction well. Since the renovations and the need to get the theater organization on firm footing had run into a few snags, the opening production couldn't be mounted until spring.

Archibald moved to the edge of his chair. "I've heard some scuttlebutt."

"About what?"

"You're thinking of offering one of the starring roles to Kit Deere."

Cordelia generally hated leaks, though in this case, since she'd been the one who'd leaked the story, she hoped the rumors would work in her favor by putting a little pressure on Kit to take the part. She was reasonably well known in the national theater community. Locally, however, she was nothing short of theatrical royalty. That and the fact she was married to country music singer Jordan Deere made her box office gold. "Have you heard from Kit or Jordan recently?"

"I hear from them all the time."

Another one of Archibald's more annoying traits was his tendency to collect people who fascinated him for one reason or another. On the other hand, since Cordelia was one of "the fascinating" he'd collected, she gave him points for taste. He'd started out his career as a Roman history scholar, but had realized in his midforties that there was more bang for his career buck if he switched his interests to Minnesota. He'd written the definitive volume on Minnesota theater history, devoting an entire chapter to Cordelia—and one to Kit.

"I've also heard you want to hire Booker Deere as the head set designer," said Archibald. "Any truth in that?"

"My lips are sealed," said Cordelia, rising from her chair, hoping Archibald would get the message and do the same.

"Am I being dismissed?"

In high heels, at nearly six foot three, she towered over him, though she wasn't interested in intimidation—at least, not this morning.

"One more question before I go," he said, shuffling papers back into the folder. "You're giving me full access to all areas of the building, right?"

She saw no reason to deny the request. "Everything but our current office space."

He smiled, tucked the folder under his arm. "I'd like to continue our little meetings, just to keep you abreast of what I'm learning."

Cordelia walked him to the door. "Just so that we're clear. You intend to write the text for the pamphlet that we'll use for publicity purposes, yes?"

"As long or short as you'd like."

"You'll need to talk with our marketing director, Marcus Yeboah."

"I have a meeting scheduled with him later today."

"Good man. I owe you."

His smile broadened. "I'm easily bought off with comps."

"Consider that a given."

3

The late autumn air was sweet with the smell of wood smoke as Booker made his way from the back veranda of his parents' summerhouse on Frenchman's Bay down to the flagstone patio closer to the beach. He'd arrived on a flight from New York shortly after seven, and had just finished stowing his bag in one of the upstairs bedrooms when he looked out the window and noticed his sister, Chloe, standing down by the fire pit. He hadn't seen her in almost a year, though they texted and phoned occasionally. The next few days were supposed to be a family reunion of sorts. His father had been the instigator, writing in his e-mail that it had been too long since they'd all been together. Since Booker had another reason for visiting the Twin Cities, he'd e-mailed and said he would be able to make it.

Nothing was ever simple when it came to his mom and dad, so he assumed that the stated reason was only a part of the story. He doubted his parents were getting a divorce. They were too content with their lives to shake up their worlds so radically. His mother was fifty-seven, which meant it wasn't a baby announcement. Chloe could be pregnant, of course, though that would require nothing more than a text from someone in the family and maybe a phone call from Chloe. His mother was flying up from New Orleans tomorrow, where she'd been starring in a play for the last couple of months. His father had been staying at the Lake Minnetonka house all summer—Booker wasn't sure why. That piece of information was what had heightened his sense that something was up. His dad's life was generally too peripatetic for him to remain in one place for such a long stretch. His career, even at fifty-nine, was still going strong. Booker couldn't see any end in sight—for either of his parents. Unless it was a physical ailment. Cancer. Alzheimer's. Tooth decay might have the most devastating immediate effect on their careers, since their bright, broad, icy white smiles were fundamental parts of their home-and-apple-pie images.

Booker loved his parents, he supposed. It wasn't something he thought about much anymore. They didn't really know him, partly because they hadn't had the time or inclination to ask leading questions, and partly because he tried hard not to present them with any obvious problems that would take them away from their more immediate interests: themselves. Mostly, though, they couldn't possibly know him because he'd purposely stayed under the radar. He'd seen what their attention had wrought in his sister's life— she was three years his senior—and he wanted no part of it. "Mom and Dad don't understand me" might be a familiar refrain, which didn't make it any less true. In Booker's case, it had been his goal.

Booker and Chloe had been two kids swimming—drowning?— in a sea of seeming perfection, expected to live up to standards that were nothing more than chimeras. In many ways, they were still those kids, still fighting their way to a safe shore. Jordan and Kit Deere weren't bad people. Far from it. They could be generous, good-natured, occasionally even kind. They weren't big on consistency, however. Booker was never quite sure, when he came out of his bedroom in the morning, what mood he'd find them in.

They had many. Often, when they were gone, Booker felt more at ease because he didn't need to check which way the wind was blowing every few minutes. In Booker's opinion, his parents' failings all stemmed from an inability to perform even the rudiments of introspection—of self-examination. They saw no further than the adoring reflections of themselves in other people's eyes. They were cursed by mistaking those reflections for reality.

Coming down the steps to the patio, Booker saw that Chloe had a thick stack of typing paper wedged against her stomach. She'd built a fire and was tossing pages in, one by one. Wearing a baggy sweater, black leggings, and a pair of wedge sandals, she looked about as angry as he'd ever seen her. On a bench by the edge of the flagstones was a bottle of red wine and a half-filled wineglass. "Hey," he said, holding open his arms as he walked toward her. "Remember me?"

She brightened instantly. "Booker," she said, rushing to him. "God, I'm so glad you're here." She squeezed him tight with one arm, holding on for almost a minute. "You're the only thing that's going to make the next few days bearable."

"That bad?" he said, kissing her hair. Hugging her felt like hugging a sparrow. He could easily feel every bone in her back. She maintained to everyone in the family that she was in great shape. He knew she got a lot of praise for her slimness, the last thing she needed.

She tilted her lovely, heart-shaped face up at him, looking so much like their mother that it was almost uncanny. "Why do we live on opposite ends of the country? Sometimes I miss you so much it's like . . . like I'm missing a limb."

"We've had this conversation before. Do you want to live in New York City?"

She scrunched up her nose. "You should move to L.A. It's not so bad."

15

"With all the beautiful people? I think not." He gave her another kiss, then backed up and pointed to the papers. "Burning your X-rated diary?"

"It's his goddamn manuscript." Her fury seemed to boil up again as she looked back at the house.

When he turned, he saw a dark figure in one of the second-story windows. "Is that Dad?"

"We're being observed," she said, continuing to ball up pages and slam them into the flames.

"Why are you doing that?"

"Haven't you read it? His novel?"

"Oh, that. Actually, no. It was waiting for me when I got back from Atlanta. I tossed it in my duffel before I left the apartment. Figured I'd read it while I was here."

"I suggest you read it fast. It's the whole point of this family meeting. I can't believe our parents are such utter douchebag liars. God but I hate them."

He sat down on the bench, drank what remained of the wine in her glass, then refilled it. "Lies about what?"

"That manuscript is the end of the world. My world."

This was a little much, even for her.

She began to toss clumps of pages into the fire, as if she couldn't burn them fast enough. She bit down so hard on her lower lip that it began to bleed.

"Could you focus for a second? Give me a few specifics?"

"What I want appears to be of no concern to anybody but me."

"You'll need to speak less cryptically if you expect me to sympathize."

"Oh, you'll sympathize all right. This will affect you as much as it does me. Read the goddamn manuscript. Then we'll talk."

He wanted to press her to explain, but knew it wouldn't do any good. Behind Chloe's sweet face was the most fiercely stubborn

16

human being he'd ever known. Deciding to take another tack, he asked, "Who else is here?"

"Tommy."

Tommy Prior was their father's manager. He'd started out as a lawyer with a special interest in finance, intellectual property, and entertainment law before branching out and taking Jordan on as a client. He'd become a close friend, almost a member of the family. Booker had many fond memories of the time he'd spent with Tommy as a kid. He'd been a surrogate parent of sorts.

Thomas Cole Prior was a quiet, smart, good-natured man. Sadly, in the last few years, he appeared to have lost his energy for managing the career of a highly acclaimed country music singer. Booker saw Tommy as the kind of guy who would much rather spend his time camping in the woods, where he could do what he loved—hiking, swimming, hunting and fishing—than spend his days in a corporate boardroom. Unlike his parents, Tommy was self-reflective, possibly too much so. His growing addiction to alcohol was hard to watch. He'd used martinis for years to loosen himself up at parties. It seemed to help, though in the end, it was a solution with disastrous consequences.

From what Booker had been able to piece together, Tommy had made a serious business error that had ended up costing his dad a bunch of money. The fact that he was still employed, that they were still friends, highlighted another one of his father's good points. Jordan Deere was loyal to the people he cared about. Perhaps, it might be suggested, loyal to a fault.

"Have you spent any time talking to Tommy?" asked Booker, curious to know how he was doing. His drinking could add another element of rollicking good fun to the weekend.

Chloe stood for a moment staring intently into the fire, then shook herself and pulled out of her trance. "A little."

"He still on the sauce?"

"Not while I was making him breakfast. But, yeah, I think he's still drinking. He seems depressed. He sat there at the island this morning and tasted the omelet. Said it was wonderful. But then he never took another bite. He eventually drifted off with a cup of coffee heading toward the bar in the family room. I'd say his trip to rehab last winter didn't take."

"It's a hard demon to fight," said Booker, taking another few sips of his sister's wine, glad that of all the problems in his life, that wasn't one of them.

"Hey, share," she said, dumping one last chunk of the manuscript into the fire, then sitting down next to him and lifting the glass out of his hand. Eyeing him briefly, she said, "You look good. Better than you usually do."

"Gee."

"I didn't mean it as a slam."

He was surprised that she'd noticed. He'd been working out. He was such a complete nerd that it came as a surprise to him when his body responded to lifting weights. He'd put on twenty pounds in the last year, all muscle. He did look good, which gave him a new sense of confidence. Still, he would never be physically attractive, no matter how hard he tried. He'd grown a beard in his late twenties, which covered up the worst of his acne scars and erased his weak chin. Orthodontia had taken care of his teeth. He might not be the same ninety-pound weakling he'd been in high school, a kid hiding in black clothes, projecting what little menace he could muster, but he'd never fit the heavily advertised Deere model: beautiful Americans living beautiful American lives. Booker had always been a square peg trying to wedge himself into a tight round hole, which meant he understood futility from the inside out. "Since we're commenting on looks," he said, moving a few feet away and studying her. "You look different."

"You're such a *guy*."

"No, tell me. I can't put my finger on it."

"My hair, dumbass. The bangs. They're trendy."

"You're such a slave to fashion."

"Shut up," she said, a little too forcefully to be playful.

It seemed like it was time to ask how she was, always a touchy subject. After what she'd been through in junior high school, everyone was always looking for the cracks, the clues, the secretive behaviors—for anything that might help them understand where Chloe was at the moment. Living under a microscope was what had driven her out of the house as soon as she turned eighteen. Booker had left for similar reasons, though his problems had been different. He had to come up with an opening, a question that wouldn't seem too direct. "What's up with you these days—other than the mystery of the burning pages?" He hadn't realized how twitchy she'd been acting until the twitching stopped.

Her shoulders still looked tense, but it was an excited kind of tense. "Wondrous and terrible things," she said, almost, but not quite, smiling.

"Can you be a little more specific?"

"Give me some time and I promise, you will know all."

"You've never been big on clear, easily understood information."

Her expression turned from excitement to a sulk.

He pushed on. "So," he said, clasping his hands casually around one knee, "how's the meditation practice going? Last time we talked, you were pretty high on it."

"Been too busy."

"You're still working for that foundation, right? Doing fund-raising?"

"Yeah. And I've joined a political campaign," she said, examining a cut on her index finger. "I'm trying to get this guy elected to the House."

"In Washington?"

"No, in Moscow."

"Who is he?"

"Name's Wentworth. When he found out I was Jordan Deere's daughter . . . well, let's just say, the name occasionally comes in handy."

"If you ask me, you're amazing all by yourself."

"Eye rolling," she called, jabbing a finger at her face.

Since the fire was beginning to burn down, he got up and tossed another log into the pit. It gave him something to do while he figured out what he should say next.

"Mom's flying in tomorrow," said Chloe. Her way of changing the subject.

He was grateful. "I heard. Will Beverly be with her?"

Chloe flashed an evil grin. "What do you think? Badass Beverly."

It was what they'd called her when they were kids. Beverly had put in sixteen years as their keeper, the resident adult when their parents were out of town. The problem was, she'd also been put in charge of the ranch outside Nashville, which took most of her time. They both liked Beverly well enough. She was fair and gave them lots of freedom. When they got too old and she wasn't needed anymore, she became their mother's executive assistant.

"When it comes to Mom, she's superglue," said Chloe.

"Kinda sad."

Pressing a hand over her mouth, she stifled a giggle. "I still can't believe Mom has no idea."

"That Beverly's in love with her?"

"It's so obvious."

"Not to a woman who thinks *everyone's* in love with her, that it's a natural state of being."

Chloe stood and walked back to the pit, warming her hands over the flames. In an instant, her mood darkened again. "This is all just bullshit, you know that? The harm that book will do? Somebody's got to stop Dad."

"From what?"

She didn't answer. "I feel like packing up my bags and calling a cab."

"You can't leave me here alone. With *them*." He clutched his throat, made a strangling noise.

Returning to the bench, they sat for a few minutes, passing the wine bottle between them.

"We're in for some major family drama these next few days," said Chloe, her eyes scanning the house. "I can't be the only one who thinks that novel is the end of the freakin' world. When Mom get's here, trust me. It will be all-out thermonuclear war."

He gazed into the dying fire, feeling a chill breeze roll off the lake. October was almost over. November was just around the corner. All he wanted was to crawl under a warm blanket and go to sleep, but he figured he'd better put in some time with that manuscript tonight.

"I suggest we watch each other's backs," said Chloe.

"Deal," he said, holding up his hand.

Instead of slapping it, she handed him the empty wine bottle. "I'd make a toast if there was anything left."

"And what would the toast be?"

She considered it. "To our beloved Deere family values. Let's hope we're not all dead by the end of the weekend."

4

Just after midnight, Booker set the half-finished manuscript next to him on the bed and groaned. Chloe hadn't exaggerated about the contents, although his reaction wasn't the same as hers. He found the situation almost, but not quite, hilarious. Some of the narrative details had obviously been changed. Still, if the essential story was true, the ground he'd been walking on his entire life had just shifted. After rolling out of bed, he threw on his bathrobe, opened the door and looked out into the darkened hallway, listening for signs of life. He'd purposefully taken the small bedroom at the far end of the second floor hallway, sacrificing space for privacy. Once everyone arrived, it would be a valuable commodity.

As he tiptoed toward the back stairs, he became aware of the soft growl of a conversation coming from his father's study. Listening at doors was a venerated Deere family sport. Seeing a partially open doorway was an invitation to pull up a chair and get comfortable.

Easing down on the top step, leaning his back against the wood railing, Booker closed his eyes to concentrate. His dad appeared to be in a quiet yet heated conversation with Tommy.

"Why don't ya just shoot yourself in the balls," said Tommy, his voice gravelly and slurred. He would never have used those words if he'd been sober.

Tommy was a Minnesotan by birth, pronounced his Os a bit too broadly, his As a bit too flat, but when he'd had a few too many, he tended to assume Jordan's Kentucky drawl.

"Save all of us a whole buncha grief," he continued. "Your wife. Your kids. Your fans. Your label. We should be planning your next tour, not spending our time on that goddamned manuscript."

"I don't know why I even talk to you when you're like this," said Jordan.

"You know I'm right. This is career suicide. I've worked my whole life to getcha where you are."

"Sounds like I didn't have much to do with it. That right, Tommy? It was all your doing? My talent, my hard work——"

"You *know* what I think. How I feel. And come on. I've put in my time with you. Put up with the crap in *your* life. Now I need a little puttin' up with."

Booker heard the clinking of ice against glass.

"Pour yourself another one, buddy," said Jordan. "It's on the house."

"Asshole," came Tommy's angry response.

"So," said Jordan, his voice oozing impatience. "I asked you a direct question and I want an answer."

"Ask again. I promise, I'll listen this time."

"Do you know anything about those notes I've been receiving? Yesterday it was 'J.O.R.' Day before it was: 'J.O.R.D.' Day before that it was——"

"It's nonsense. Somebody's playing a joke."

"Today's was simply 'J.O.' And there's always this . . . thing . . . at the bottom. Look at it. You tell me what you think it is."

Booker could hear a paper rattling.

"It's just a smudge of ink," said Tommy.

"No it's not. It's a crow. You know how I feel about crows."

"Forget it."

"Is it your kind of joke, Tommy? Your little way of telling me something?"

"I love you, man. You know that."

Jordan didn't respond.

"That's why I'm trying to get you to see reason. The big picture."

Patiently, Jordan replied, "I see the big picture. More clearly than I ever have in my entire life. That's why I came to Minnesota for the summer."

"Right. To work on your writing career." He snarled the last word. "You wanna commit suicide, okay. Go for it. Just leave the rest of us out of it." When he spoke again, his voice sounded thick, quivery, as if he was holding back tears. "So where does that leave me?"

"Where do you want it to leave you?"

"Remember," he said, over enunciating the word and yet still slurring so badly that it was almost indecipherable. "We both know where the bodies you *failed* to mention are buried."

"You know, Tommy, if I were you, I'd stop pointing out what a liability you are to me. It's not real smart."

"What are ya gonna do about it? You can't unring a bell."

The floor creaked.

"Think I better help you to bed," said Jordan.

"I don't need your help. Just need some fresh air."

A moment later, Tommy tumbled out of the room holding a bottle of scotch by the neck, knocking into the wall across from the door and nearly upending a narrow table and a vase of flowers. "Sweet dreams, my prince," he mumbled as he passed by Booker, never seeing him as he careened down the stairs.

5

Jane stood next to a tall filing cabinet, pawing through the first few folders in the top drawer, searching for a specific form, one she needed to fill out and get into the mail before the end of day. She was tying up loose ends with the intent of focusing all her attention on her restaurant until the new year.

Jane had worked for fifteen months to earn her PI license from the state of Minnesota. Once she was legal, she'd formed a business partnership with a friend and retired homicide cop, A. J. Nolan. As an incentive to get Nolan back to work after a difficult surgery, one that had left him in a wheelchair, Cordelia had offered them office space on the second floor of her new theater. Thus, Nolan & Lawless Investigations was born.

Nolan worked the job more or less full-time. Because neither of them relied on the income the business generated for their livelihoods, they were free to choose their clients. Most PIs were forced to do grunt work—tracking down personal assets, doing background checks, sitting in endless parking lots waiting to take pictures of some cheating husband or wife leaving a paramour's apartment. Not the kind of work that Jane, now in her midforties, or Nolan, in his midsixties, wanted.

Jane was a restaurateur by training and by passion. The Lyme House on Lake Harriet in south Minneapolis was the culmination of her childhood dream. She'd named it after the town in which she grew up—Lyme Regis, on England's southwestern coast. She'd lived in England with her family until she was nine, returning again for two years after her mother had died. In her late thirties, however, shortly after her partner of some ten years, Christine Kane, had succumbed to cancer, Jane began to feel an itch to move beyond the confines of a 24-7 restaurant life. Her father was a criminal defense attorney, and the gift of his DNA, as well as the interest she'd taken in his cases when she was a child, were beginning to tug at her. Melding these interests had created some difficult hurdles, but for now, Jane felt satisfied that the two were coexisting reasonably compatibly.

Sometimes she wondered why she hadn't pursued a law degree. It was what her father had wanted. The problem was, unlike her dad, Jane wasn't a fan of the U.S. criminal justice system. She didn't think voting on the truth was a particularly persuasive way to locate it, especially when lawyers were allowed to play so many legal games, mostly behind the scenes, aimed at suppressing relevant information. Even under the best of circumstances, with all the facts placed clearly on the table, putting a life or death decision in the hands of twelve fallible human beings seemed an immensely tricky proposition. Justice might be the goal, but once hobbled by poorly informed opinions based on facts that had been shape-shifted into a compelling, though fundamentally misleading narrative, truth was what suffered the most. As Jane's father often said, the lawyer who was able to spin the best story from the permissible evidence generally won. Finding criminals, solving the puzzle, proving guilt, compelled Jane, though once they were delivered into the legal system, the whole process gave her a huge headache.

Just as she located the form she was looking for, her cell phone buzzed inside her jacket.

"Hello," she said, sitting down behind her desk. She began pulling drawers open until she found a pen.

"Janey, hi. It's Peter. You got a minute?"

"Hey, kiddo. How was the plane ride?"

"Uneventful. That's about the only good thing you can say these days."

"And New York?"

"Sigrid and Mia are in heaven. I'm nervous."

"You've got meetings today, right?"

"This afternoon."

Peter had been asked to shoot a documentary on the Latin American Spring—all the protests in Brazil, the change that was right on the cusp. Since he would be gone for more than a year, living and working out of Rio, his wife and daughter had agreed to accompany him. They considered it the chance of a lifetime. Though Jane would miss them, she heartily agreed. "What happened with your house?"

"Sigrid's brother, Matthew, finally signed on to stay there. We gave him a great deal—free rent, as long as he cuts the grass and shovels the snow. And pays the utilities."

She leaned back in her chair. "Sounds like you've got all your bases covered."

"Dad already gave us the you-have-to-be-careful lecture. I can hardly believe this is happening."

"That makes two of us."

"Listen, Janey. You have to take extra care with Dad. I know his breakup with Elizabeth was three months ago, but I think he's still feeling the effects. He seems so lonely. And how does he solve that? He works more, which is the last thing he should be doing at his age."

27

Jane's father had just turned seventy. He had heart problems, though from what his doctors told him, he was in generally good shape. He'd always been a workaholic, which was probably where Jane got her own workaholic tendencies.

"With Elizabeth taking a job with another firm, he's been trying to fill in when he can," continued Peter.

"I know," said Jane. "Why don't they just name another partner?"

"Apparently it's a long process. Anyway, will you make extra time for him? I worry, you know?"

"I'm on it."

"Well, I guess this is good-bye. Like I said, we'll e-mail and Skype. Mia says she'll learn everything she can about Brazilian cooking so she can teach you when she gets back. Oh, and tell Cordelia we'll come home bearing gifts. She should let us know if there's anything specific she wants. That includes Hattie, too."

Hattie was Cordelia's eight-year-old niece. She'd lived with Cordelia most of her young life. For the last couple of years Hattie had been into collecting bugs, an interest that horrified her aunt, especially when her secret bug collection had orchestrated a jailbreak and infested their loft. Recently, under pressure from Cordelia, she'd moved on to archeology. "Bring Hatts back a pre-Columbian twenty-four karat gold necklace. That would make both Cordelia and Hattie happy."

His laugh was deep and rich, a sound Jane loved. "She'll probably have moved on to particle physics by the time we get home."

"Probably," agreed Jane. "My love to all of you."

After saying a somewhat emotional good-bye, she felt the phone buzz. Glancing at the incoming text, she saw that it was from Avi Greenberg, her girlfriend. She read it, smiling:

Hate Chicago. I know, stop whining. Third meeting
w/ editor on new book. Didn't go as well

as hoped. The hotel is okay. Quiet. Boring
Lonely as hell. Y don't you come down 4
the weekend? Am having dinner w/ Julia tonight.
She's been the only bright spot. All for now.
Miss you.

The mention of Julia's name gave Jane a brief jolt. She had no idea that her ex was in Chicago. As she thought about it, the questions she'd had about why Avi needed to travel there to work on her revisions were all tied up neatly with that one simple word: Julia. She owned the press and thus had pulled the strings, urging, or perhaps ordering, Elaine Ducasse, the senior editor at Ducasse & Ducasse, to not only acquire the book, but to insist that Avi come to Chicago to work on the revisions. What a coincidence that Avi's arrival coincided perfectly with the few days Julia happened to be in town.

Ever since Julia had learned that Jane had a new love in her life, and that this new love was an aspiring writer, she'd been playing her little games behind the scenes. Avi's newest novel was wonderful, in Jane's opinion, and well worthy of publication. That had never even been a question for Jane. What was in question were Julia's motives. Did she want Avi for herself? Did she simply want to mess with Jane, cause her a few sleepless nights for old times' sake? Either was possible, as were other scenarios Jane had no desire to contemplate. Having a sociopath in your life was truly the gift that kept on giving.

As Jane stuffed her phone back in her pocket, Cordelia appeared in the doorway. Sauntering over to a folding chair, she sat down and crossed her legs, pulling her skirt demurely over her knees. "Something wrong?" she asked as Jane studied the form in front of her.

"Just . . . business." She signed her name at the bottom.

"Don't you want to know why I'm here?" asked Cordelia.

"I assume you're going to tell me."

Leaning close to the desk, she whispered, "Ghosts. The theater's lousy with them. Isn't that fabulous?"

"It certainly makes *my* day," said Jane, folding the form into thirds and slipping it into an envelope.

"I already knew about the cat."

"A ghost cat?"

"It bit me a couple times. Landed in my lap once. But the real news is . . ." She glanced dramatically over each shoulder. "Gilbert and Hilda King. They were murdered. In the basement."

Jane looked up. "Murdered?"

"In the basement."

"Who were Gilbert and Hilda King?"

"They used to own the theater. It was a gangland hit. Because of Gilbert's gambling debts. Or, maybe because of the speakeasy."

"What speakeasy?" Jane was beginning to get lost in all the unconnected details.

"The one they ran out of the basement. Back in the twenties and early thirties. Have you ever looked around down there?" she asked, sotto voce.

"No."

"I have. It's mostly stuffed with a hundred years of theater detritus. But—and this is straight from Archibald Van Arnam—the speakeasy is still there—the room, the bar, the stairs up to the street."

Jane knew Archibald, mainly from Cordelia's legendary dinner parties. She also knew never to call him Archie. Apparently, according to Cordelia, he'd been called that as a kid, something he'd loathed. When he'd become a professor, he'd shaken it off like a dirty and disgusting old coat, becoming Archibald, a name worthy of his new persona. If people made the mistake of calling him Archie, they were met with such a withering stare that they never did it again. When Archibald had suggested doing a little research on the theater without the need for compensation, Cordelia had been over the moon.

Pulling a couple of small flashlights out of her blazer pocket, Cordelia continued, "I thought we should go down and do a little reconnaissance."

"Now?"

"Something wrong with now?"

"It's just . . . I need to get back to the restaurant. We're bringing out that new tasting menu—"

"This won't take long. You know me and basements. They're full of creepy crawlies." She shivered.

"Maybe you should get Hattie to down there with you."

"She's at school. You'll have to do." Standing erect, she handed Jane one of the flashlights. "This will be an adventure, a ride on a time machine back into the gangland past."

"What if we run into Gilbert and Hilda?"

Cordelia's eyes gleamed. "All the better."

6

Archibald would never forget the first time he'd met Jordan Deere.
It had been a warm September evening in 1980, long before Jordan became famous. Archibald had been standing on Hennepin
Avenue after the theater had closed up for the night, waiting for a
bus to take him back to his apartment near the university. During
the last two years of his undergraduate study, he'd run the Piccolo
Theater box office for $4.10 an hour, a buck over minimum wage.
He thought it was a perfect part-time job, allowing him a chance to
expand his interest in the theater and at the same time assure him
that he'd have plenty of free time for his studies. He made a point
to get to know Kit, of course. Everybody wanted to meet her.
Not only was she glamorous in an old-fashioned Hollywood kind
of way, but she was friendly and funny, and occasionally even
went out for drinks with the theater staff after the place shut
down for the night.

That evening, as Archibald was lighting a cigarette, he saw Kit
come around the corner with a guy's arm around her waist. Kit
introduced Archibald to Jordan and then asked if he needed a ride
home. Since it was late and he had a test in the morning, he took

her up on the offer, which allowed him to study Kit's newest boy-friend more closely.

Jordan explained that he'd been born in Maryland, raised in Kentucky, and was currently in Minnesota playing guitar and singing at his uncle's bar in Saint Paul. He wasn't reticent about the fact that he intended to make a career in country music. With his Irish looks—strong chin, slanting blue eyes, rosy cheeks—he reminded Archibald of a Catholic choirboy: beauty and innocence combined in almost perfect harmony. Kit was clearly smitten. While Archibald hated country music on principle, he liked Jordan. The guy had a Kentucky twang and an easy way about him that made people forget—well, almost forget—how startlingly good-looking he was. Less then two months after that first meeting, Jordan and Kit had been married in a ceremony that seemed as if it included the entire Twin Cities.

Seven months later, Chloe was born. No one commented on the timing. At least, not in front of Kit.

Archibald had been working on his friendship with Kit ever since he'd begun running the box office at the theater, and after the marriage, his friendship with Jordan grew as well. He was touched and deeply honored when they asked him to become their second child's godfather. Booker Tiberius Deere had been born three years after Chloe. The name Tiberius had actually been Archibald's suggestion. Archibald had moved on to a doctorate by then. Roman history had always been his primary interest. Booker loved his middle name so much that in his early teens, he'd insisted people call him Tiberius. It hadn't lasted, which had always made Archibald a little sad. He'd been closer to Chloe than Booker, though he loved them both like a father.

Nobody, in Archibald's opinion, had ever known what Booker was thinking when he was a kid. He didn't smile much, kept his head down and his opinions, whatever they were, to himself. Archibald had tried to crack through his defenses by spending time with him, even taking him once on a trip to Italy, mainly to get his mind off the hubbub in the house over his sister. Chloe had always been an emotional handful. Then again, at least you knew where you stood. With Booker, Archibald never felt confident that he'd grasped the boy's essential nature, and that nagged at him.

Thirty-four years after saying their wedding vows, the Deere family was now standing at a precipice. If Jordan had his way, it wouldn't be long before everything that Kit and Jordan had built would all come crashing down.

That was why, on this chilly late October morning, Archibald—instead of Jordan—had driven out to Flying Cloud Airport in Eden Prairie, and was waiting for the Deeres' Learjet to land. Kit and Beverly were flying up from New Orleans, no doubt talking of little else than the meeting Jordan had forced on the family. By this point, everyone knew more than they ever wanted to know about the Deeres' marriage—and they also understood what was at stake if the union blew apart.

Looking out a broad picture window, Archibald gazed toward the landing strip and then up at a hard gray sky. His plan was to take the women to lunch and eventually deposit them at the lake house. He hoped to add a cheerful note to an otherwise gloomy day.

Hearing a commotion behind him, Archibald turned to find Jordan, his jaw set hard, steaming toward him. His looks had changed subtly over the years. His eyes had grown more hooded and dark, his skin tanned and weathered, and his smile crooked. He was focused on the door out to the landing strip and didn't seem to notice Archibald until he was almost on top of him.

"Oh," said Jordan, stopping abruptly. "It's you." He removed his sunglasses.

A small crowd had begun to gather behind them.

"Jesus," said Archibald, stepping back to take in Jordan's frayed jeans and ratty canvas field jacket. "You need to find yourself a tailor—and a barber."

Jordan hung his glasses on his shirt, then sunk his hands into his pockets. "I was going to call you later today. Did you—"

"I read it, yes. Last week."

"You're coming to the house tomorrow, right?"

"I am."

"So? Give me a preview? What did you think?"

"It's a compelling story."

He seemed relieved. "You don't know how much I needed to hear that."

"But it will never be published."

Jordan's eyes narrowed. "Meaning what?"

"Meaning you're not that stupid."

"Look, I'm not going to publish it under my own name, if that's what you're afraid of."

"Doesn't matter. People will find out. They always do. There's no way you, Jordan Deere, can publish that novel anonymously. I can't believe you're even considering it."

"All I know is that I've spent the last two years working on it, and every day this summer finishing it."

"Who else has a copy?"

Jordan seemed surprised by the question. "I sent one to everybody in the family."

"Lord. Your kids deserve better than that. Don't you think you should have spoken to them personally before they read the book?"

"What are you saying?"

"That you're a bigger fool than I thought you were."

"I don't need to explain myself to you," he said, walking past Archibald up to the window.

"Fine. But if you gave me that manuscript thinking I could help you find a publisher, I can't help you."

"You mean you won't."

"Okay, *won't*. I refuse to do anything that would hurt Kit and the kids."

"Like they say, the truth hurts. But sometimes it's also necessary."

"Truth is profoundly overrated," said Archibald, disgusted by Jordan's use of such a self-serving cliché.

A small jet dropped out of the low gray clouds. The sound didn't hit for another few seconds.

"That's our plane," said Jordan, watching it descend toward the runway.

"Are you planning to take Kit and Beverly home with you?" asked Archibald, annoyed that he driven all this way for nothing.

"I'm not sure," said Jordan, unhooking his sunglasses and slipping them back on. "Give me a second, okay?" He rapped Archibald on the shoulder, then pushed out the door.

As the plane came to a stop, Jordan moved beyond the chain-link fence and waited for the top section of the hatch to come up and the stairs to come down. And then he disappeared inside.

Archibald scowled at his watch. He found a chair and sat down, rattling through the morning paper, feeling as if he'd just had a conversation with a brick wall.

Inside the cabin, Kit stared out the window, fingering a gold chain necklace and watching her husband make his way across the blacktop. "Figured he might show," she said, turning to look at Beverly, who'd taken off her seat belt and was stuffing a Sudoku puzzle magazine into a leather bag.

Kit hated to say it, but because of the miracle of modern cosmetic surgery, she looked a good ten years younger than Beverly even though they were the same age. She'd encouraged her friend to get some surgery done herself, but Beverly wanted no part of it. She would point to her helmet of short, blunt-cut gray hair, to the crow's-feet at the edges of her eyes, and she'd laugh, saying she'd earned them, like they were merit badges.

Kit, of course, didn't view wrinkles that way. Still, she knew enough about Beverly and her ways to stop pushing. Trying to make Beverly Elliot into something she didn't want to be had always been a losing proposition. Like the time Kit had wanted Beverly to attend a cocktail party with her at the governor's mansion in Nashville. Jordan had planned to attend but at the last minute he had been called away. Kit didn't want Beverly to feel out of place, so she offered to take her shopping, buy her something dressy, something fun and fabulous. Beverly wouldn't hear of it. She maintained that she felt uncomfortable in fancy clothes. She liked plain styles, mostly slacks and sweaters in the winter, and cargo shorts and T-shirts in the summer. Like a lot of Minnesotans, she was terminally casual. Well, so be it, thought Kit. Beverly was who she was, and Kit admired her conviction and self-confidence, if not her crow's-feet.

"I thought Archibald was picking us up," said Beverly, her restless eyes darting around the cabin. "I'm sure Jordan's here because he wants to test the waters. See what you thought of the book. He's never been big on patience. If he wants something, he wants it now."

That wasn't entirely fair, thought Kit. But then Beverly and Jordan had never really gotten along. There were good reasons, of course, and yet Kit had always wished it had been different. Kit loved both of them without reservation. They were, in the deepest sense, her soul mates. Sure, she was furious with Jordan at the moment and intended to make his life a living hell for as long as it took to get him to change his mind. In the end, she knew he would.

37

He wasn't reckless. She simply had to make him see he was about to jump off a cliff and drag the rest of family over the jagged rocks with him.

After the hatch opened, Jordan jumped up the steps. In an instant, he was in the cabin, his height and size dwarfing everything around him. He took Kit in, smiling a sheepish smile as he moved toward her.

She tried not to return the smile, though it was impossible.

"I thought maybe you'd station a guard at the door," he said. "Not let me in."

"Bull," said Kit, nowhere near as refined in real life as her image suggested. "Give me a hug and a kiss." Across from them, Beverly remained in her seat, glowering.

Turning around so that she wouldn't have to see Beverly's puckered face, Kit luxuriated in the feel of Jordan's strong arms around her. She loved men. Absolutely adored them. Couldn't ever seem to get enough male attention, even at her age, which had been a periodic problem in her marriage. As she pulled back, she saw Jordan wink at Beverly. He did it to annoy her. It always worked.

"So, what do you think?" asked Jordan, holding Kit at arm's length.

"About that book?"

"What else?"

"I think you're out of your freakin' mind." She pulled away, needing to put some distance between them. "All I can say is, I'm glad the kids haven't seen it."

A muscle in his face twitched. "I sent a copy to everyone. Even Badass Beverly over there." Another wink.

Kit was almost too stunned to speak. "You're . . . a madman. Don't you think I should have had something to say about that?"

"No. It's my book. My story."

"It's never going to be published. No way in hell."

"I'll tell you the same thing I told Archibald. I plan to publish under a pseudonym."

She couldn't help but laugh at his painful naïveté. "Where is this coming from? This need to air all our dirty laundry. Not only will it hurt our kids, but it will damage our careers. Hell, damage them? We might as well take a sledgehammer to them."

He glanced over at Beverly, then back to Kit. "Okay, so maybe some stuff does come out. We can manage it."

"The media will eat us alive. If it's a slow news week—"

Jordan's expression hardened. "I've already made up my mind."

"Well, unmake it."

"That's why I called this family meeting."

"I thought it was a reunion."

"Whatever it is, there will be only one topic under discussion. I was hoping we could talk first. I mean, there are . . . things . . . I didn't address in the book. I thought maybe you'd like to get everything out on the table with the kids."

"That is never going to happen. Never."

He held up his hands. "Okay, it was just a thought."

"You called this meeting so that you could issue an edict."

He threw his arms in the air. "Why is everyone fighting me?"

"Really? Everyone? Maybe that should tell you something."

Coming close to Kit's face, Jordan said, "This isn't your call. It's not a business decision. We're not taking a family vote. This is *my* life."

"How can a man who has experienced the world the way you have still remain such a simpleton?" asked Beverly, rousing herself to stand and face him.

"Oh, sit down and shove a sock in it," he growled, his Kentucky accent more pronounced when he was mad.

"You are such a pathetic little boy," she continued. "Throwing tantrums when you don't get what you want. Well, suck it up. Nobody gets everything in this life."

"That right, Beverly? And what is it that you want?"

"One day you'll go too far." She shoved a finger in his face. "One day."

"And then what? More truth will come out? We couldn't have that."

"Stop picking at each other," demanded Kit. "Beverly has nothing to do with this. We need to stay on point. And the point is," she added, sitting down and looking around for her overnight case, "I'm not on board with what you're proposing. You fight me on this and you'll lose. We made a deal. Long time ago. We *both* have to agree. I don't. There will be no book. End of discussion."

Jordan gazed down at her, said nothing for several seconds, then moved back to the hatch. Hesitating, as if he wasn't sure what his next move should be, he gave himself a few seconds. Finally, his eyes hardened into a decision. "There's one more thing I came to say."

"Then you better say it," said Kit, bending down to look under the seat. As far as she was concerned, the conversation was over. There would be no family horror show.

"I want a divorce."

Her head snapped up.

"Our marriage," he said. "It's over. But don't worry. You and the kids will be well taken care of. I'm not vindictive. I still love you, Kit. Always will. I hope we can end this amicably."

Dazed, Kit stood, arms at her sides. "A divorce?" she repeated. He hadn't laid a finger on her, and yet she saw stars, specks of bright light swimming in the air around her. "You can't be serious."

"If you want to talk some more, I'll be around the house all afternoon. And look, I'm sorry, Kit. I really am. But this is for the best."

As he disappeared out the hatch, Kit dug out her cell phone. She did want to talk, but not to him. She searched her address book until she found the name she was looking for. Come on, Cordelia. Pick up the damn phone.

7

The theater basement was as dreary as Jane assumed it would be. Cleaned up, with the walls repaired and the floor covered in something more friendly than ancient, cracked concrete, it would provide a good space for all sorts of theater needs. As it was, it was poorly lit, and seemed depressingly dank.

Waiting at the bottom of the steps while Cordelia took a call, Jane dug her own cell out of her jacket, seeing that she had two more texts, both from the manager at her restaurant. This day was not turning out the way she'd planned.

"So glad to hear from you," cooed Cordelia into her phone. "Are you in town? What?" She listened. "Actually, Jane's with me. Why don't I ask her?" Holding her hand over the phone, Cordelia said, "It's Kit Deere. She didn't give me the details, but she's in a bit of a legal bind. She's wondering if your father would have a minute to talk to her. Today. As soon as possible. Could you call him?"

"I suppose," said Jane. "But I have no idea what his schedule is."

"Just try. It sounds important. She thought if the request came from you, it might, you know, cut more mustard."

Jane moved a few paces away and placed the call. Three rings later, her father picked up.

"Hey, honey," he said, his rich baritone sounding more than a little harried. "What's up?"

She put Kit's request to him.

"Kit Deere? My Lord. Haven't seen her in years."

"I didn't realize you knew her."

"She's suggesting we meet this afternoon?" He hesitated. "Well, I suppose I could make it happen. Give me a time and a place."

Jane relayed the question to Cordelia. After explaining it to Kit and listening to her response, Cordelia said, "Can't be any earlier than four-ish. She has some stops to make this afternoon."

"Where does she want to meet?"

"My house?"

"You mean Octavia's house."

"No need to split hairs, Janey."

After Cordelia's loft in downtown Minneapolis had suffered a severe bedbug infestation last spring, Octavia, who'd been staying with Cordelia at the time, went out and bought a grand mansion on Mount Curve in Minneapolis, not far from the theater. She invited Cordelia, Hattie, and Hattie's Nanny, Bolger Aspenwall III, to move in with her. To Jane's amazement, Cordelia and company had accepted and so far, seemed to be making no effort to leave. It was an odd arrangement because Cordelia and Octavia were the original oil-and-water sisters—occasionally oil and nitroglycerine.

Jane gave her father the details.

"If I can't make it," he said, "I'll call you, but let's proceed on the assumption that I can. Do you know anything about Kit's difficulties?"

"Nothing," said Jane.

"Will you be coming with them?"

She hoped she'd be back at her restaurant long before four o'clock. "Not sure. But let's get together soon for dinner. Maybe a movie."

43

"I'd love that."

After saying good-bye, Jane nodded the go-ahead.

"It's a go, Kit," said Cordelia into her cell. "We're all set." She repeated her new address. "When you and Beverly get to my house, ring the bell. The house man is usually around." In case he wasn't, she explained where they could find the hidden front door key. "Go in and make yourselves comfortable. We'll be there as soon as we can."

Jane assumed Cordelia was using the royal "we."

Listening a moment more, Cordelia said, "Yeah, I'm looking forward to seeing you, too. We have a lot to catch up on. Kiss, kiss, darling." After cutting the line, she stood for a moment looking down at the phone in her hand. "Wonder what's going on. She sounded upset. No, that's not quite right. More . . . irate. This will definitely not be the time to ask her to consider taking a role in our first production."

They continued down the narrow corridor. The basement was a warren of rooms, some big, some smaller, most relatively empty, though several were stuffed to the gills with old theater props. A few of the doors were closed and bolted. Every ten feet or so along the hallway, a bare bulb gave off its weak, cobweb-encrusted light. Not enough to read by, but enough to cause the small hairs on Jane's arms to prickle.

At last, Cordelia stopped in front of an oversized door with a rusted padlock hasp—sans padlock.

"I've actually been in here once before," she said, her silver bracelets tinkling as she pulled the heavy door all the way open. "I thought the bar was a theater prop." She felt along the wall, saying, "I think there's a wall switch."

A second later, several wrought-iron chandeliers flickered to life over their heads.

"Wow, that is one big bar," said Jane. It must have been twenty feet long, covered in the dust of decades, but with the Deco design features still visible in the carved oak.

"Look at that," said Cordelia, pointing to a row of bullet holes that began at the far end and moved toward them. Her high heels clicked against the black and white floor tiles as she moved behind the bar and pointed to the shattered mirrored shelving that, once upon a time, had probably held the liquor bottles. "More bullet holes."

Jane counted them. Fifteen along the front of the bar, in one long wavy row. At least eight into the glass at the back. "Can you move that poster away?" she asked, sitting down on a rickety wood bar stool. It seemed that someone had decided to store an extra-large 1970s promotional poster against the back wall, one that advertised the play *Enter Laughing*.

"Yuck, but I hate spiderwebs," said Cordelia, pushing the poster only a few feet before she shuddered and backed away.

"What's that?" asked Jane. She'd expected the wall—and the bullet holes—to continue. Instead, the lath and plaster stopped, replaced by a bricked-up section that looked far newer.

"Strange," said Cordelia, hands rising to her hips. "Why would someone cut a hole in the wall and then brick it up?"

From behind them, a soft voice asked, "Can I help you, ladies?"

Jane turned to find a red-haired man in a dapper Harris tweed suit, white shirt, and yellow silk tie standing in the doorway. The look on his face was friendly, open, even curious.

"Oh, Ms. Thorn," he said, breaking into a grin, revealing a gap in his front teeth. "Didn't recognize you."

Cordelia's hand shot to her chest. "Heavens. You scared me. What are you doing here?" she asked, wiping the sticky cobwebs off the front of her navy-blue wool blazer. "I thought you weren't coming in until next week."

Moving farther into the room, the man stuck out his hand to

45

Jane. "Phil Clemens," he said. "My friends call me Red." He pointed to his hair.

"Jane Lawless."

"Red's signed on to be our senior maintenance manager," said Cordelia.

"Janitor," he said with a wink. "I've worked in this building, at one job or another, since I was a teenager. When I saw that the place had been bought and was being rehabbed, I came in and offered my services. Nobody knows this place better than I do. I was telling Ms. Thorn here that I'm the unauthorized great-great-grandson of Samuel Clemens." He grinned again, looking from face to face to catch their reactions.

"Unauthorized?" repeated Jane.

"So what do we have here?" he asked, nodding toward the bricked-up wall. "That's an odd one. Don't remember seeing it before. Guess maybe that poster was hiding it."

"Why don't we take a closer look?" said Jane.

"You want me to break through the wall?" asked Red.

"Why not?"

"Give me a sec."

After he'd left the room, Jane crooked her finger at Cordelia, drawing her in. "You think that guy's got, you know, all his oars in the water?"

"Oh, for sure. I had him checked out. He's worked as a janitor for every theater group that's been in this building since the beginning of recorded time. Received high marks from everyone."

"What about the unauthorized grandson thing?"

Cordelia waved it away. "Everyone's allowed a few eccentricities." She returned her attention to the brick wall. "What do you think's behind there?"

"A dead body," Jane deadpanned, folding her arms and wondering when she could— politely—take off.

Red returned carrying a sledgehammer. "The right tool for the right job," he announced, moving back behind the bar and motioning for Cordelia to step away. After taking off his suit coat and removing his wire-rimmed glasses, he took a couple steps back, planted his feet and then whacked at the bricks until the middle section crumbled inward. Peeking inside, waving the brick dust away from his face, he said, "Anybody got a flashlight?"

Jane continued to sit at the bar as Cordelia edged in front of him, shining a beam into the darkness. "I'm not sure what I'm seeing. Looks like a heap of crumbled bricks and mortar on top of a ripped black plastic bag."

Red took a couple more whacks, filling the air with even more dust.

Cordelia squinted back into the hole. "Is that—" She worked the light until her entire body froze. "Someone better call 911."

"Why?" asked Jane.

"The police will want to see this."

"See what?"

"A skull."

"A *what*?"

"If I'm not mistaken, there's a nice round hole smack in the center of the forehead. Not to put too fine a point on it, but the body count around this place appears to be rising."

Up on the third floor, in the lobby outside the theater, Booker stood in front of the great arched window and looked down at the street, watching two uniformed police officers emerge from a squad car and enter the building under the marquee. His natural instinct when seeing a cop was to walk—swiftly—in the opposite direction. It was a habit from his youth, one that didn't serve him particularly well as an adult.

Because he'd stayed up most of the night reading his father's so-called novel, he was tired. Thus the idea of doing anything quickly didn't appeal. The book was so poorly written, so amateurish and overwrought, that if it hadn't been for the periodic revelations, he would have tossed it in the wastebasket.

Booker was aware that his sister wanted to discuss the book with him, though what he wanted, from the moment he'd stepped out of the shower until he'd jumped in his rental car, was to get away from Frenchman's Bay. He needed a beer, or maybe a joint— something to undo himself a little. Without any real plan, he'd simply driven into town and ended up here. He'd been thinking that he should take a look at the theater before he met with her highness, the Empress Cordelia. Her shiplike physical size and persona had a way of dominating conversations. He wanted to form his own conclusions about the place before she could tell him what he was supposed to think.

Booker had known Cordelia since he was a kid. As a teenager, he had thought she was weird, though in a generally good way, always flouncing around in outrageous costumes, the center of every summer party his parents had ever given. In his late teens, he'd come to respect her achievements, even found that he liked her. She was the one who'd suggested he check into Boston University. He'd been thinking about pursuing a degree in stage design and dithering about which college would best suit his needs. Cordelia explained that BU was where she'd worked on her graduate degree, that it had one of the best theater programs in the country, and that, as a bonus, he'd be living in one of the most culturally progressive cities in the nation. She knew how sick to death he was of Nashville.

In the end, Booker had taken her advice. After receiving his BFA in theater studies, instead of entering the graduate program as his mother had wanted, he'd moved to New York and worked his way through every grunt position he could find, getting the hands-on theater experience he needed. During that time, he began to grow up.

Turning at the sound of footsteps, Booker came face to face with a woman he hadn't seen in fifteen years, not since she'd graduated from the arts high school in Nashville, the same one he'd attended. He'd known he might run into her at some point during his visit because it was her play that the Thorn sisters had chosen to produce for their initial offering. He wished he'd worn something other than a pair of frayed jeans, an untucked cotton shirt, and a navy-blue hoodie.

Surprisingly, Erin O'Brian hadn't changed all that much. She still had the same strawberry-blond hair, the same light spray of freckles across her nose and cheeks. The glasses had been replaced by contacts. Like him, she'd never run with the popular crowd, though she'd been pretty enough to be included. She'd been one of Chloe's friends, two years older than him. While he rarely paid attention to the people his sister brought home, he had noticed Erin. In fact, even before he bumped into her at the house, he'd begun a quiet campaign of scoping her out at school.

Booker understood that some might have found this behavior unacceptable, even obsessive, though he didn't see it that way. Whatever the truth was, he had enough smarts to keep his feelings to himself. He saw no point in expressing himself only to get shot down by Erin—or be shuffled off to a therapist, his parents' favorite child-rearing practice. Booker had never expected to see Erin again after high school, though memories of her had grooved themselves deeply into his brain.

When she smiled at him now, approaching him somewhat hesitantly, he felt the same frisson of sexual tension he used to feel when spying her in the school lunchroom or eavesdropping on her and Chloe studying together down in the basement family room. The only time they'd ever had a real conversation was sitting in the bleachers one late spring afternoon, watching the school track team practice. It was a surprisingly intimate conversation right from the start, as if they didn't need to make the usual smalltalk before they said what was on their minds. He couldn't remember now what they'd talked about, just that she had a way with words and a way of approaching life that completely fascinated him. And she had dreams. Wild, fierce, risky dreams for her future. He'd been deeply affected by that. He gave himself extra points because he was as taken by her mind as he was by her looks. It made him feel better about himself for about fifteen minutes.

"Do you remember me?" she asked, stepping up to the window but keeping her distance.

"Erin O'Brian," he said, returning her smile. "Of course I remember you."

She played with a button at the top of her sweater. "I hear you may help stage my play. Feels like a small world sometimes, doesn't it?"

"I haven't taken the job yet."

"No? Because?"

He shrugged, returned his attention to the park across the street. "I love New York. It's my home. If I accept the position, I'd have to move here."

"The Twin Cities not cosmopolitan enough for you?"

He didn't want to tell her the real reason, the fact that moving to Minneapolis would put him closer to his parents for part of each year, something he absolutely did not want. "Just . . . a lot of things to weigh." When he looked at her again, he saw that she was preoccupied, only half listening. "I've followed your career," he said, marveling that she wasn't a girl anymore. "I saw your first play when it was produced in Houston."

"Did you?" she said absently. "Did you like it?"

"Very much. Saw your next play in Chicago. I thought that one was even better."

Her hand drifted to her stomach. "I wrote that right before I got married. It was a happy time for me. There's a lightness in the play. I've never been able to capture that again."

Booker hadn't heard she'd gotten married. "Who's the lucky guy?"

Her mouth twisted. "Turns out, neither one of us was very lucky. We divorced last year."

"I'm sorry." And he was. The thought that she'd been in pain, perhaps still was, upset him.

"It's the way the world works. I've found some small success as a playwright, while my personal life is pretty much a mess."

"Where are you living these days?"

"Seattle. I like it there. Like the cloudy days. You ever been?"

"Once. The clouds depressed the hell out of me."

She glanced over at him, the hint of a smile playing at the corners of her mouth.

"How long will you be in town?"

Looking back out at the street, the smile faded. "I'm not sure. A few days. Maybe more."

"To meet with Cordelia."

"What? Oh, right. Yes, Cordelia."

He had the sense that he'd just been lied to. "Chloe's here. I'm sure she'd love to see you. Why don't you stop by the house?"

"I should do that," she said. "What about you?" Her tone sounded more polite than truly interested.

"My father called a family powwow. We're supposed to have dinner together tonight."

"I hope it's nothing serious."

"Yeah," he said, his voice trailing off. When he came out of his reverie, he saw that she was looking him full in the face. This time, she actually did seem concerned.

"I always liked your parents," she said. "Your dad was so sweet and funny. And your mom doted on you and Chloe."

Booker supposed it may have looked that way. Maybe it was partly true. Booker felt certain his parents cared about him, but also certain that they had never wanted him to bother them with anything too difficult. They'd already had their hands full with Chloe.

"Listen," he said, glancing at his watch. "I need to get out of here, but I was wondering. Would you like to have lunch? Maybe tomorrow? It would be great to catch up. Where are you staying?"

She wrapped her arms around her waist. "It would have to be a late lunch."

"Sure. Fine."

"I'm staying at the Heidelberg Country Club on King's Bay. It's—"

"I know where it is. It's about twenty minutes north of our summerhouse. But it's a private club. How did you get a room?"

"A friend booked it. What if we meet at the Rhineland Grill in the main Gasthaus?"

"Perfect."

"Two?"

"That sounds great."

This time her smile encompassed the whole of him. "You've changed."

"God, I hope so."

She laughed at his vehemence. It was a bright, beautiful sound.

"Tomorrow," he said, reluctantly backing away.

8

Shortly before five, Kit tipped the small bronze statue of a greyhound back and removed the hidden key. From the empty state of the rounded driveway in front of the house, she assumed she and Beverly were the first ones to arrive.

"I thought Cordelia said there was a butler," said Beverly, standing under the massive stone portico, banging impatiently on the front door with the brass door knocker.

Even on her best days, she was a glass-half-empty kind of person. She also had one of the most loving hearts Kit had ever known. They'd been fast friends since second grade. "Cordelia called him her house man," said Kit. "Here we go." She unlocked the door.

Inside, they found themselves in a gothic-inspired manor, complete with a broad open staircase that rose to a second-floor mezzanine and a churchlike series of stained-glass windows in the main hall to their right. They were met almost instantly by a small girl shuffling out of a back hallway. She had on oversized high heels, a white feather boa wound around her neck, and a clipboard propped against her hip.

"Hi, Hattie," said Kit, bending down and smiling. "I'm Kit

Deere. Remember me? It's been a couple of years since I've seen you. This is my friend, Beverly."

Hattie squinted up at them. "Will you take a survey?"

Kit and Beverly exchanged amused glances.

"Survey?" said Kit.

Adjusting her boa, Hattie plunked down on a bench by the door. "Yeah. Just a few questions. Won't take long."

"Well," said Kit, looking around, feeling like she'd entered a time warp that had deposited her in the Middle Ages. "Sure. Why not?"

Something about the interior of the mansion recalled scenes from the movie *The Magnificent Ambersons* for Kit, although this place was on a much grander scale. The house, no doubt an excessively expensive monstrosity, was dramatic, but gloomy.

"Okay," said Hattie, pulling a pencil out of her shirt pocket. "This first question is about bedtime. What time do you think an eight-year-old girl should have to go to bed?"

"Oh, now that's a hard one," said Kit.

Beverly sat down on the bench opposite the little girl, removing her athletic shoe and rubbing her foot. "Seven?"

"Seven P.M.?" repeated Hattie, her small brow furrowing.

"No," said Kit. "I'd say nine. On a school night."

"What if it's not a school night?" asked Hattie.

"Then, oh, maybe nine fifteen."

Glaring up at her, clearly unhappy with the responses, Hattie said, "How much allowance do you think an eight-year-old girl should get per week?"

"Fifty dollars," snapped Beverly, looking absolutely serious.

"Really? *Fifty* dollars?"

"Not a penny less."

This time, Hattie's eyes lit up. "Will you tell Auntie Cordelia that?"

"Be happy to," said Beverly. "If," she added with a conspiratorial look, "you let me borrow your boa."

"Oh, for sure," said Hattie, whipping it off her neck. She paused before she got up. "Do you really think seven is the right bedtime?"

"Nah," said Beverly. "I was just teasing you."

Hattie jumped up, ran across to Beverly and snuggled down next to her. "I like you."

"And I like you," said Beverly. "You know, I used to take care of Kit's two kids. Booker and Chloe. Have you met them?"

"Nope." She shoved the pencil behind her ear. "Do you like chickens?"

"Chickens?"

"I like the Orpington Red and the Plymouth Rock chickens best. Have you ever seen a white feathered Frizzle?"

"Not that I recall."

"Curly feathers," she said matter-of-factly, as if it was something everyone knew. "I want to raise chickens in our rose garden. Auntie Cordelia said it's not legal for them to live in the city, but she's wrong. I have a friend who has three chickens in her backyard. In a coop. Her dad built it. Her mom gathers eggs every morning. Wouldn't that be the coolest?"

"Well," said Kit. "I guess. If you like eggs."

"Will you talk to my aunt, tell her she should let me have a chicken? Just one. We could work up to more. I'd take care of it, I promise. Take it for walks. It could even sleep with me when it gets cold out."

Beverly looked over at Kit. "I'll see what I can do."

"I've got a way big telescope," Hattie continued, spreading her arms wide. "I'm not just interested in biology, you know. Auntie Cordelia keeps it in her office at the theater. If I'm there at night, we take it up on the roof. I know a whole bunch of the constellations. I've also got this great big book on Egypt. The pharaohs."

Squinting up at Kit, she added, "Have you ever seen the pyramids?"

"I believe I have, but I'd love to look at your book." She moved Beverly's backpack off a softly padded small chair in the front hall and sat down.

"Now?"

"I'm waiting for someone, but until he gets here, sure."

"Hattie?" asked Beverly. "Can you tell me where I could find a bathroom?"

The little girl stretched her arm as far as it would go and pointed to a hallway. "There. It's on the right. You can't miss it." Turning back to Kit, she said, "Do you have any bubble gum?"

"I'm sorry, but I'm fresh out."

The little girl looked so crestfallen that Kit said, "Maybe Beverly has some. It might not be bubble gum. It could be just plain gum."

"I like plain gum, too."

She dug through Beverly's backpack at her feet. As her hand sank into the middle section, her fingers struck something cold and hard. "Just another second," she said, smiling at Hattie. Pulling the backpack into her lap, she looked inside. The cold, hard object was Beverly's handgun, the one her father had given her before he died. He'd wanted to present it to his son, but since the kid was both a vegan and a Buddhist by then, it went to Beverly by default. She'd been happy to have it, often taking it to shooting ranges to keep up her skills. Kit was a little surprised that Beverly was traveling with it. Generally, she kept it in a locked case at her home in Nashville. Zipping the backpack back up, Kit shook her head. "Sorry, no gum."

"Rats," said Hattie, heaving a dramatic sigh. "Oh well, I guess I'll go get my book on Egypt." Kicking off the high heels, she rushed up the stairs, nearly bumping into a young man who was on his way down.

"Hatts," said the man, catching her by the shoulders. "I've been looking all over for you."

"I was right *there*," she said, pointing to the bench by the door.

"You have a dentist appointment."

She made an exasperated face. "Do I have to go?"

"You don't want all your teeth to turn black and fall out, do you?"

"You shouldn't try to scare me. It's not nice. Besides, we've got guests."

"I can see that. Let me go down and introduce myself and then we need to hit the bricks. Go get some shoes on, okay? And brush your teeth."

"If I'm going to the dentist, why do I need to brush my teeth?"

"Hattie," he said, giving her a stern look.

"Oh, all right," she grumped, chugging up the remaining stairs.

When the man reached the bottom, he introduced himself as Bolger Aspenwall, Hattie's nanny. "It's a great pleasure to meet you in person," he said to Kit.

"You're the one getting his M.F.A. in directing at the university."

"Guilty. Listen, I just had a call from Cordelia. There's been some sort of crisis at the theater and she's running late. She said that Mr. Lawless should be here any minute. She asked me to tell you to feel free to treat the house as your own. There are cold drinks in the kitchen refrigerator. If you need something stronger—"

What Kit needed was a map of the place. "Not necessary." She wasn't against a little chemical optimism, though at the moment, she needed a clear head.

Bolger suggested a quick tour. As they were about to head into the bowels of the mansion, Beverly came out of the hallway and Kit introduced them. And then the doorbell rang.

As Bolger opened the door, Kit refastened one of her earrings, then smoothed a hand over the front of her dress, feeling uncharacteristically nervous.

Ray's smile was as warm as she remembered. He was older, less robust than his younger self, but still handsome—and still a commanding presence with his neatly trimmed white hair, silver-rimmed glasses, and impeccable three-piece suit. She'd been planning to take his hands in hers, squeeze them amiably, but instead, he came forward and drew her into his arms.

"It's been too long," he said.

She closed her eyes and luxuriated. There'd been a time in her life when she'd had Ray Lawless squarely in her sights, though in her heart she knew it would never happen. He was always either solidly with a woman or dating someone, and he wasn't the kind of guy, alas, who liked a little frolic on the side.

"Sorry I'm late," he said, tilting his head apologetically.

Kit remembered now why she'd been so drawn to him. It was his unflappability, his self-possession. He might deal constantly with issues of life and death and yet he seemed to personify the calm at the center of the storm.

Bolger offered to walk them to the sunroom.

Before she left the foyer, Kit pulled Beverly aside and whispered that she needed to speak with Ray alone. She could tell that her words upset her friend. "I'm sorry," she said. "This is going to be a tricky conversation for me."

"But I can help," insisted Beverly.

"Of course you can. Just not right now." She patted her shoulder, glanced furtively down at the backpack, then turned and walked away.

9

The sunroom was a revelation. It was a small slice of India, reminding Kit of a friend's home she'd stayed in once in Jaipur. The design features were intricate, ornate and busy, with a mix of patterns, silks, and brass accents. A series of tall mullioned windows let in the afternoon light, a welcome note of brightness in an otherwise dark house.

"Cordelia redid this room," said Ray, standing in front of the fireplace. "She found the statuary, the bowls, boxes, and baskets, mostly on eBay."

"Cordelia has always been a decorating alchemist."

"Both sisters tend to think they know what's best when it comes to renovation."

It was small talk, thought Kit, all necessary. Ray must have sensed that she was having trouble jumping right in. She sat down on the sofa, trying to find a comfortable position amongst the pillows.

Ray lowered himself down on a carved wood chair. Sitting back and crossing his legs, he said, "So, how can I help you?"

"Well, you see, I know you're not a family lawyer, but I need your advice. Jordan's asked for a divorce."

"Oh. I thought, I mean, it occurred to me——"

"You assumed it was another problem with Chloe."

"I wasn't sure. I don't like to jump to conclusions." Studying her for a moment, he said, "Okay, so let me ask you something. If it's too personal, I entirely understand. Has Jordan been unfaithful?"

The question was so ludicrous, she had to stop herself from laughing out loud. "Ray, I hope you won't judge us, but Jordan and I have had an open relationship from the very beginning."

He nodded—and kept on nodding. "I see."

"I know people don't expect it from us—with our squeaky clean image and all. I mean, we love each other, but we've never been exclusive."

"Uh-huh."

Time for Ray to pause for a little attitude adjustment, thought Kit. When he looked at her with new interest, she found herself thinking deeply wicked thoughts. She wondered if he was involved with anyone at the moment. "Let me put a hypothetical question to you," she said, playing with a tassel on one of the pillows. "What if Jordan had written something—something I don't want anyone to see. And what if he insisted on making it public? Is there any way I could stop him?"

"Again, this isn't the area of my expertise," said Ray, adjusting his glasses. "Is it true? Whatever it is that he's written?"

"Some of it."

"But not all."

"No, definitely not all."

"So you're saying it's libelous?"

"I guess . . . right. It's libel. But if I sue him, will the content become public knowledge?"

"That's a hard one," said Ray. "You would normally expect a certain amount of privacy, but with people as public as you and Jordan, it might prove difficult. I assume you have reporters sniffing around all the time looking for dirt."

"So there's no way to prevent him from going public with it?"

"You'd need to put that question to a libel attorney."

She shifted in her seat. "Then a different question. Jordan and I keep separate bank accounts. It's been that way from the start of our marriage. He makes millions, so he pays for all of our living expenses—the houses, the cars, the clothes. What I've earned has been invested. I took a huge hit in the stock market like everybody else a few years back. I pulled much of my money out, which was probably a stupid thing to do. I'm not poor, but I'm hardly wealthy, the way I am with Jordan as my husband. So the question is this: Will the fact that we've kept our finances separate hurt me in a divorce?"

"Where's your legal residence?" asked Ray.

"Tennessee."

"Again, you'd need to consult a divorce lawyer from your state. There's no real way I can answer that for you."

"But can't you give me an educated guess?"

He held her in his blue-eyed stare. "It could be a problem. Have you and Jordan considered counseling?"

She couldn't help herself. The idea made her giggle. "Not going to happen."

"At least you haven't lost your sense of humor."

"If I have anything to say about it, I'm not going to lose anything."

"That sounds ominous."

She offered a smile. Nothing more.

"Look, I'm not trying to rush you, or change the subject, but I'm starving. I didn't have any lunch today and all I had for breakfast was toast and coffee. I don't suppose we could continue this conversation over an early dinner."

"Why, Ray, I'd love that," she purred. Her first thought was Beverly—how she could ditch her. Her second thought was the dinner Jordan had planned at the lake house. It suddenly occurred to her that she could use one to take care of the other.

As they came out of the sunroom, Beverly, who'd been sitting in a chair in the hallway, stood up. Ray continued on to the front foyer, while Kit pulled Beverly aside. "I need you to do something for me."

"Sure. Anything."

"Drive back to Frenchman's Bay and tell Jordan I won't be joining the family for dinner."

"Really. Why? He's going to be upset."

"And I should care . . . because?"

The evil gleam in Beverly's eyes told Kit that not only would Beverly go, she'd enjoy being the bearer of bad tidings.

"How will you get home?" asked Beverly.

Archibald had dropped them off at a rental car company earlier in the afternoon. Both Kit and Beverly had cars of their own back at the house, but because they were staying in town, at least for a few hours, they'd needed a set of wheels to get them around, and then later, out to the lake.

"Ray said he'd drive me, so go ahead and take the rental. We're going to grab a bite to eat and talk a little more."

Beverly bent closer. "Did you get any answers?"

"A few. I'll tell you all about it later tonight."

She nodded. After saying her good-byes to Ray, she took off out the front door, though not before offering Kit a conspiratorial wink.

As Ray helped Kit on with her coat, Cordelia burst in, with Jane close behind.

"I need a stiff drink," she cried, her cheeks flushed, her auburn curls corkscrewing around her face. She tore off her cape and tossed it over a chair. "What a day. What . . . a . . . freakin' day!" Glancing at Kit's coat, she said, "You going somewhere?"

"Well, I—"

"Come with me," she ordered, seizing Kit's hand and dragging her off toward the back of the house.

Kit glanced over her shoulder, giving Ray a helpless look.

"A glass of wine might be nice," he called after them.

"You know, Dad," said Jane, trying not to get swallowed up by the feather cushion on a wing-back chair in the main hall. "Cordelia didn't mean wine. She meant black cherry soda."

Ray shook his head and groaned. "Should have known. Maybe Kit can persuade her to offer the rest of us something a bit more palatable." He struggled to get comfortable on his own feather cushion. "What's Cordelia so upset about?"

Halfway through the afternoon, Jane had given up any hope of returning to her restaurant. The uniformed cops who'd initially come to the theater had eventually called in a cold case team. She should have simply left, but like Cordelia, she was both repelled and fascinated by the scene.

Jane took a few minutes to explain about Gilbert and Hilda King—about the speakeasy in the basement of the theater, the gangland shooting, and the bricked-up wall.

"At one point, I jokingly said that we'd probably find a dead body behind it."

Her dad grimaced.

"There was a bullet hole right in the center of the skull." She didn't mention Red Clemens or the fact that he'd appeared— conveniently?—out of the blue right when they'd discovered the brick wall. When the police first came in, Jane looked around for him, thinking that, since he'd worked at the theater for so many years, he might be a source of information. She never saw him the rest of the afternoon.

"Any idea who the skull belonged to?" asked her father.

"A guy on the forensics team thought it was a man, though he said they'd have to perform some tests to determine the sex, age—and when the person was likely shot. They found a gold signet ring. It was large, heavy. Looked to me like it had belonged to a guy. The lead cold case investigator thought the body had been back there at least twenty years. Maybe more."

"Since you're now a licensed PI," said her father, "let me take a wild guess and say that Cordelia wants you to figure out who was murdered and why it happened."

Jane sighed. "She did drop a few broad hints."

"You're not interested?"

"Dad," she said, knowing she sounded impatient—no doubt on the way to pissed. "I've spent the last month clearing the decks so that I could spend the fall concentrating on my restaurant."

"And your girlfriend."

"Yes, Avi's part of why I want more free time." She drummed her fingers against her thigh. "So, what about you? Did you and Kit have a chance to talk?"

"We did."

"And? Is everything okay?"

"It's a legal matter I'm afraid, one I can't talk about."

"She sure looks great for a woman who must be close to sixty. I didn't realize you two were friends."

"Hardly friends," he said. "I helped the family with a couple of legal problems many years ago. Kit . . . well, as you can imagine, she's a hard woman to forget."

Cordelia entered the great hall carrying a tray, with Kit bringing up the rear. "I've opened a bottle of Pinot Noir," she said, setting the tray down on the coffee table. "And for those of us who require something stronger, I have a complex little black cherry soda with a velvety mouthfeel, decidedly jammy notes, and a long, elegant finish. I suggested to Kit that once we've spent a few minutes relaxing with our various poisons, we should take our merry little party over to Jane's restaurant, where dinner will be served."

Jane watched her father and Kit share a glance. She wondered what that was all about.

"Sound like a plan?" asked Cordelia, draping herself over an antique fainting couch. When nobody responded, she held the back of her hand to her forehead and said, "Don't everyone talk at once."

10

Booker no longer had any idea where to buy decent weed in this town, so instead of wasting his time trying to figure it out, when he got back to the house, he changed into his swimsuit, grabbed his bathrobe and a towel, removed two bottles of Corona Extra from the fridge, and headed up to the heated pool. He'd never much cared for lakes, didn't like all the tiny lake creatures nipping at his legs, nor the tangled patch of slimy weeds about twenty feet out from the beach. If that made him a pansy, so be it.

From his position on the diving board high above the house, he looked down on the red-tiled roof of the boathouse, where Tommy usually stayed when he was in residence. As he stood motionless, with his eyes closed, he could still feel the hot summer sun of his youth, see the crazy mix of colored beach towels hanging up to dry along the retaining wall. It felt happier in retrospect than it had been in reality. Turning to look out at the bay, he saw that it was one those special, golden autumn evenings on the lake, when all the world looked like a Flemish painting—one with a few jarring modern touches. A Yamaha jet boat, two Jet Skis, and a party barge were all tethered to the dock. The thirty-foot sailboat was kept at the Frenchman's Bay Marina. Booker had no idea how much his father had spent on water toys in the last thirty years, though he suspected the amount could easily support several small countries.

Perspective was what Booker craved. If he really had cut his parents out of his life, why did he care about all their deceptions? And, as he was surprised to find, he did care.

After chugging an entire beer, Booker dove into the water. The frigid shock to his body pulled him away from his thoughts, and it also caused him a moment of intense fury. "Jesus," he screamed, roaring up out of the center of the pool, scraping water from his eyes. "You're a freakin' sadist!" His dad liked to keep his pool water ridiculously cold.

Without much enthusiasm, Booker swam a few laps, though his system never entirely acclimated to the ice water. Eventually, he gave up. He toweled himself dry, chugged the second beer, then headed back down to the house. He wanted to take a shower before the first "family reunion" event. If he hadn't taken the swim, the beer might have been enough to achieve a minimal mellow. Instead, he felt wide awake with a pounding headache.

As he came through the side door, his sister burst past him. "Hey," he called, watching her wipe tears off her cheeks before plunging into her bedroom and slamming the door. Hearing voices, he tied his robe and hurried down the hall. "What's wrong with Chloe?" he demanded, coming into the kitchen.

Archibald and Tommy were seated at the center island, both intently examining the insides of their wineglasses.

Beverly leaned against the back counter, a study in grim determination. "Hello, Booker," she said. "It's been a while. Good to see you."

"Yeah. Good to see you, too." Glancing up at the clock above the sink, he saw that it was later than he'd imagined—going on six. "It's Saturday. Aren't we supposed to have dinner together tonight? Where's Dad? And Mom?"

"Change in plans," said Beverly. "Your mother won't be able to make it. She'll drive out later tonight."

Hearing the sound of a motor roar to life, Booker stepped over to a window overlooking the lake. His dad was maneuvering the jet boat away from the dock. Fifteen feet out, he gunned the engine and took off in a straight line across the chop. "Where's he going?" asked Booker.

"You'd have to ask him," said Tommy, rising from his stool. "If anyone needs me, I'll be in the boathouse." Without another word, he left the room.

"Would you like a glass?" asked Archibald, holding up the wine bottle. "It's a wonderful Argentine Malbec. A high-altitude Mendoza."

"What the hell is going on?" demanded Booker.

"The new plan is to have the first family meeting tomorrow morning at ten," said Beverly.

Was this a reprieve, thought Booker, or simply putting off the inevitable? "I need to talk to my parents. So does Chloe."

"This has hit us all pretty hard," said Beverly, trying, as usual, to be the conciliatory one—the peacemaker. In the Deere family, it was a full-time position.

"What he wrote," said Booker. "In that book. Is it true?"

Beverly bit her fingernail.

"Was what he wrote about you true?" asked Archibald.

Booker shrugged. "None of it bothered me, if that's what you're asking. I deserved it. Deserved worse than what he said."

"The mutilated cat in your school locker?"

"I had nothing to do with that," he said, knowing he sounded defensive. "It was Shawn Odenkirk. He either found the cat like that or he did it himself. And then he tipped off the principal after he stuffed it in there."

"But you had a lock on your locker."

"A combination lock. His locker was right next to mine. I'm sure he saw me dial the numbers a bunch of times."

"So you brought a gun to school. You were going to shoot him."

Booker willed himself to stay calm. "That was never my intent. I just wanted to scare the shit out of him. In the book—Dad never said I tried to kill him."

Archibald swirled the wine around in his glass. "You see how problematic these things become when only part of the story gets told? I think it's a fait accompli that if Jordan somehow gets that novel published, people will trace it back to him. When a man is willingly blind, there's nothing you can say to change his mind, no way to get him to see reason." He pulled a pack of cigarettes out of his suit coat pocket and looked around for a book of matches. "I could strangle him for what he plans to do to Kit—and to you and Chloe. I could really do it. I'm not kidding."

Booker couldn't imagine Archibald, with his pale, intellectual softness, ever following through on a threat like that.

"Get in line," said Beverly, her chin quivering.

Booker's cell phone rumbled in the pocket of his robe. Pulling it out, he saw that it was a text from Chloe.

Come to my room NOW.

Offering Archibald and Beverly a hard look, he took off down the hall. Reaching Chloe's door, he knocked.

"It's open," she called.

He found her on her stomach, lying on the carpet next to the bed, chin resting on her balled-up fists. Unlike the baggy sweater she'd been wearing last night, the shimmery black workout suit she had on today allowed him to see how truly thin she'd become. The sight of her shook him. "You okay?"

"This is like water torture," she said, wiping more tears off her cheeks. "You read the manuscript last night, right?"

He nodded.

"Now you know."

He sat down on the bed. "What should we do?"

"What can we do?"

She twisted into a sitting position, drawing her legs up to her body. "There's something I haven't told you," she said, brushing her bangs off her forehead. "There's a guy."

"There's always a guy." If there was one thing his sister never lacked, it was male attention.

"This time it's serious."

"You're saying you love him?"

"More than anything on this earth."

"That's incredible news."

"I met him last year at a fund-raiser. His name is Hector Diaz. He's an ADA in L.A. He's so beautiful, Booker. He's funny and decent. And he's ambitious. He wants to spend a few more years in the district attorney's office, then move into politics."

It stunned him that he knew so little about Chloe's life.

"But Booker, there's more. I've always known that if something is terrible, it's also wonderful. You know?"

"Not really."

"I'm just beginning to see that the reverse is true. If something's wonderful, it's also terrible. Do you understand what I'm saying?"

"Umm—"

"I love Hector so much, but that love also means my life is no longer just about me. If I marry him and all this crap comes out, what happens then? If he's running for office and he's married to Jordan and Kit Deere's crazy daughter, with all the bad publicity it will generate, he might as well quit right now."

"How ambitious is he?"

"You mean, if it came down to it, would he chose me or his political career? I hope it would be me, but I can't say that for sure. And I can't risk losing him. I *can't*." With her eyes wide, wet, and brimming, she said, "I don't know what I'd do if he called it quits. That's why we've got to stop Dad from publishing that piece of trash. That's all I've been thinking about for days. We *have* to stop him."

Booker got up and walked over to the window to give himself a moment to think. Outside the summerhouse, the world looked serene as a purple dusk settled over the lake. Inside his head, Booker's thoughts were like sharp needles scribbling on his brain.

"Listen to me," he said, turning to face her. "Your copy of Dad's book. Did you burn the whole thing?"

"Every last page."

His copy was back in his room. "I need you to do something for me. Run out to the boathouse and tell Tommy to give you his copy. Then come and ask Archie and Beverly for theirs."

"And then what?"

"Build another bonfire."

She looked momentarily buoyed.

"Do you know how many people he sent it to?"

"The night I arrived, he gave me his word that nobody but family had seen it."

"So that's six copies, seven if we include his." Booker headed for the door.

"Where are you going?"

"Dad's study. I'll tear that room apart until I'm positive I've found every last manuscript and backup. And then I'm going to detonate his Dropbox account and his computer."

"There's always a way to retrieve computer data."

"Not if you remove the hard drive."

"And then what?" asked Chloe.

With his hand on the doorknob, Booker said, "Then we wait. When Dad gets home tonight, we need to be there to watch his reaction. We have to determine if he's got another manuscript stashed somewhere else. If he doesn't, then we're home free."

"If he does?"

"Then, between now and then, we better come up with an ironclad plan B."

11

Archibald arrived at the lake house the next morning just as two uniformed police officers and a chaplain were coming out the front door. He waited for them by his car, asked what was going on. One of the officers replied that Jordan Deere was dead.

Archibald backed up. "Dead?" Removing his glasses, he tried to swallow. "Was it . . . a heart attack?"

"A homicide," said the officer. "He was out jogging in Bayview Park. Someone shot him."

"Today? This morning?"

"That's right."

"Was it a robbery?"

"His wallet, rings, and watch were still on him. You a friend?"

He nodded. "Close friend."

"We've explained as much as we know to the family." The cop motioned toward the house.

Archibald called a thank-you over his shoulder as he rushed to the front door. He had to get to Kit. Inside, he found her half lying, half sitting on a couch in the living room. She looked deathly pale, her hands knotted together across her stomach. Beverly, thankfully, had gone to get the brandy. Booker, Chloe, and Tommy stood looking down at her, all grim faced, stunned into silence.

Archibald wanted more than anything to be a source of strength and support. "I talked to the police briefly on my way in," he said. "They told me."

Kit looked up at him, extended her hand. "I'm glad you're here."

"Are you okay?" It was a stupid question, one he regretted as soon as he'd said it. Of course she wasn't okay.

After handing Kit a small glass of brandy, Beverly sat down on the edge of the white leather couch next to her. "I'm so sorry," she said. "What can I do? Just tell me and I'll do it."

Kit sipped from the glass and stared straight ahead.

Chloe lowered herself to the edge of a chair across the room, covering her face with her hands, sobbing softly. Booker moved to the piano bench. Tommy couldn't seem to move at all. He remained absolutely still, arms at his side, eyes fixed on a painting of a sailboat above the mantel.

After a few tense, silent minutes, the brandy seemed to steady Kit and she sat up. "I can't believe . . . he's gone," she whispered, pressing her fingertips to her temple. "It's too much. How is it even possible?"

Chloe began to weep more loudly.

"Oh, honey," said Kit, her expression softening. "Come over here and sit by me."

Chloe gave her head a stiff shake.

Looking up at Archibald, Beverly said, "The detective who's been put in charge will be here any minute. He should have more information."

Kit's eyes widened.

"Don't try to stand," said Archibald, attempting to stop her from getting up.

"No," she said, forcing his hands away. "We don't have much time."

She moved unsteadily over to the French doors that led out to the terrace. "We have to talk about this. Please, all of you, listen to me." She paced back and forth across the carpet as Archibald sank down on the couch, watching a transformation occur. In a matter of moments she'd turned from a grieving widow and concerned mother into a general lining up her troops.

"We have to present a united front. *No* deviations allowed, do you hear me? We can't tell the police everything we know. Do I have to spell it out? You all understand why?"

Everyone nodded.

She ran through the story they would tell, hitting every major point several times, stressing that each of them, with the exception of Archibald, had been home all morning. Nobody should offer any information unless a direct question was put to them. "Beverly, go call Ray Lawless. Tell him what happened, that we need him here right away."

Beverly left the room.

"I have no idea if this investigator will want to question us when he gets here. If we are questioned, stay on point. And if you feel you're getting into trouble, Ray Lawless will be around to shut the questioning down." She met each person's eyes. "Jordan is dead. We all loved him and we will mourn him. But right now, *we're* fighting for our lives, you understand that, right? Our futures? In searching for the person who took Jordan's life, the police will, of necessity, seek answers from his family. We want to be seen as open and honest. We can't give them everything we know, but, in every way we can, we will help them. Are we clear?"

More nods.

"We have to manage this with great care. We can't afford to let matters get away from us."

When Beverly returned with a steno pad, Kit began issuing orders. "Call Morrison in Nashville. I want him to handle the press on his end. Tell him to figure out some way to divert all our landline calls from this house to his office. From now on, we use only our cell phones." She stopped, a tentative hand rising to her forehead. "We'll need to put out a statement. That should come first."

"But we don't really know much," said Beverly, her pen poised above the page.

Archibald assumed that, if the police got a search warrant for the house, one look at Jordan's shell of a laptop and they would smell a rat. From that point on, everyone in the family, and that included Archibald, Beverly, and Tommy, would be under suspicion. Kit could try to manage the situation all she wanted, but she had to know how easily it could spin out of control.

"Call Chuck Rios," continued Kit. "Have him write the statement. But tell him to run it past me before it's released. Call Buckminster at the record label. They'll want to put out a statement, too. Give them what we can. Someone needs to call the band members and his producer. Oh, and Garth Brooks and Alan Jackson. They should hear it from us, not CNN. And I want someone on the front gate twenty-four-seven. Is that clear? That gate will be locked at all times from here on out. Have Hughes come see me. We need to beef up our security."

"You mustn't be frightened," said Archibald, trying his best to sound reassuring. "Extra security is a good idea, but there's nobody out there who wants to hurt you or the kids."

"I'm not concerned about that," said Kit dismissively. "I'm concerned about paparazzi falling out of trees to take photos of us."

"What about . . . a funeral?" asked Chloe, biting at her trembling lower lip. "Seems like that should be our first priority."

"I better make more coffee," said Beverly, though she didn't move.

Everyone, with the exception of Kit, seemed shell-shocked.

People reacted in different ways to the death of a loved one, thought Archibald. Kit might not show her sadness the way Chloe did, especially when she thought she needed to take charge, to be the strong one for her children, but Archibald understood that when the spotlight was off, when the police had come and gone, when Kit was alone with her thoughts, the emotion she'd hidden out of necessity would all come rushing out. And once again, Archibald's deepest hope was that he could find a way to help. He would do anything and everything in his power to keep her safe.

Jane needed coffee. After her father, Cordelia, and Kit had left her restaurant last night, she'd stayed up late working in her office, not returning home until shortly before two.

Stumbling out of bed just after eight, she padded downstairs, her two dogs trailing after her. In a sleepy haze, she found fresh coffee beans and ground them, dumped them into the coffeemaker, poured in the water, then let the dogs outside. It was a beautiful, chilly autumn morning. She thought about going for a run with her lab, Mouse, but simply didn't have the energy. Gimlet, a curly-haired black poodle, didn't entirely understand the concept of proceeding in a straight line. She also happened to think sniffing was the point of every outing, which was why Jane left her home and only took Mouse when she ran. Jane adored Mouse. Mouse adored Gimlet. Gimlet adored everyone. They were an adoring family.

While the dogs roamed around in the backyard, she returned to the second floor to shower and dress. Sundays were her day off—if she took a day off, which was rare. The restaurant served a buffet brunch, straightforward service and rarely problematic.

She'd glanced through the reservation log last night and saw that they were full up from eleven until three.

Since she didn't have to dress in business drag today, she slipped into a pair of soft gray cords and found a black cotton turtleneck in her dresser drawer, which she tucked into her slacks. She piled her long chestnut hair, still wet from the shower, on top of her head and secured it with several bobby pins. Socks and boots came next.

As the dogs ate their morning kibble, Jane built a fire in the living room fireplace. While she enjoyed a fire at night, she loved sitting by a warm, quiet hearth in the morning. She supposed it was a leftover from curling up next to her grandmother's morning fires in her cottage on the southwestern coast of England. But mostly, she was a Minnesotan—suffering through increasingly stifling summers, yearning for the first crisp air of fall.

Sitting down on the oriental rug, her back against the couch, both dogs snuggled next to her, she sipped her coffee and watched the flames lick the bark off a birch log. She would have felt completely content if Avi had been with her, not hundreds of miles away in Chicago. Jane was old enough to remember when she wasn't constantly tethered to a cell phone. Because Avi's preferred form of communication when away was text message, and because business these days necessitated constant cell phone contact, Jane figured she might as well give up on her dream of being deliciously unreachable and go with the always-connected flow.

Pulling her cell from her pocket, she clicked it on and immediately felt the buzz that alerted her to messages. One was from a waiter—a guy who was angry with last night's manager and one of the runners. Jane would deal with that later. The message she was most interested in came from Avi last night at 3:14 A.M.

I think I'm drunk. Scratch that.

I know I'm drunk.

Chicago is a party town. Lucky me.

Dinner with Julia. We talked . . . about

you. It's weird that she knows you

better than I do. Did a couple

clubs. We danced. The music was

awesome. I hate the word awesome.

But some things ARE awesome.

Sorry. Didn't mean to yell.

I kept thinking you should be here.

Why aren't you here?

You're so sexy when you dance.

I let go tonight.

Shhh. Keep it under your hat.

To bed, to bed.

Stay tuned.

Jane put down the phone and gazed into the fire. She stayed like that, trying to decipher the meaning and intent of Avi's words, until Mouse raised his head and gave a deep growl.

"I heard it, too, babe." It sounded as if someone had knocked softly—almost timidly—on the front door. Why not ring the doorbell? she thought, scooping Gimlet into her arms and getting up. If she'd been in her study, or upstairs, she never would have known someone was outside.

She looked through the peephole before opening the door. "Dad," she said with a smile. "What are you doing here? Come in."

He was dressed casually in tan khakis, a light blue oxford cloth shirt and a navy-blue crewneck sweater. He looked almost as tired as she felt. "I know our dinner went kind of late last night," he said, bending down to give Mouse a scratch. "I didn't want to wake you if you were still in bed."

"Can I interest you in a cup of coffee? It's fresh. Or, hey. Why don't I make us breakfast?"

Patting the top of Gimlet's head, he said, "I'll take the coffee—if you've got a to-go cup. It sure smells good."

"You can't stay?"

"I got a call from Beverly Elliot, Kit Deere's assistant, about an hour ago. I'm afraid she had some terrible news. The police in Minnetonka got a 911 call around seven twenty this morning from a man who was doing his morning run along a jogging path through a remote part of Bayview Park. Seems he found a body just off the path in a deep section of brush. It was Jordan Deere."

Jane gave an involuntary gasp. "Is he—"

"He's dead. Shot at close range. That's all I know. Two uniformed officers and a chaplain had just left the lake house. An investigator's been assigned. He's apparently still at the scene, but intends to come by the house shortly. Kit asked if I'd drive out."

"Surely she's not a suspect."

"I doubt it. But with Jordan being such a public figure, all hell's going to break loose in the press when they get wind of it. She may need some help with that. While I was on the freeway, I got to thinking. I know this comes out of the blue, but maybe you'd like to come with me—if you have the free time."

"Me? Why?"

"Well, for starters, when we're done, we could have that breakfast together."

"Sure, I'd like that." There had to be more.

"The investigator my law firm has used for over twenty years retired a few months ago. So far, we haven't settled on a replacement. Now that you've got your license, I was wondering if you'd like to help me with this one. I'd pay you the same rate we always paid him. It's good money."

She was touched that he had such confidence in her abilities.

"If you want, we can include your partner in this, too. Maybe Nolan could stop by my office sometime next week so we could talk. You'll both need to sign confidentiality agreements."

"He's in St. Louis at the moment. His sister is having some kind of surgery. He wasn't too specific about it. He'll be gone at least ten days."

"That's fine. I'm happy to work with you on this one. What do you think? Are you interested?"

The last thing she needed was to take on something new, especially with Nolan unavailable for backup. The promise she'd made to herself—about spending the fall devoting the bulk of her time to her restaurant and to Avi—also weighed against it. Then again, remembering her conversation with Peter, her promise to take good care of their father, to spend extra time with him, made the decision easier. "Sure. Count me in."

"Wonderful, honey."

"Do you think someone in the Deere family might be responsible?"

"Anything's possible, of course. But for now, let's just say all is not well. I drove Kit out to their house on Lake Minnetonka last night after we finished dinner. She confided something to me, Janey. I'm trusting that you'll keep this to yourself, that I can give you certain information before you've signed the confidentiality papers. But you'll need to do it soon. Tomorrow, if possible."

"Of course."

"It seems that Jordan's manager—Tommy Prior—someone they all think of as family, also happens to be one of his oldest and closest friends. Prior apparently made several bad business decisions recently. Kit thinks it may be worse than what Jordan told her—that Prior may have actually embezzled money. Jordan was furious when he found out, but for some reason—Kit thinks it's misplaced loyalty—he refused to fire him. In fact, the guy has been staying at the house with Jordan, on and off, all summer."

"Sounds potentially explosive."

"The other point is, Jordan organized a family reunion for this weekend. Made sure everyone knew it was a command performance."

Jane had met Chloe and Booker a few years back at a party Cordelia had thrown for Kit's fifty-fifth birthday. "Did this family reunion have a specific agenda?"

"Kit said it was an effort on her husband's part to get everyone together in one place, at one time."

"For what reason?"

"She gave the impression that it was simply a social event."

"But it could be more."

He hesitated. "Jordan asked Kit for a divorce yesterday. That's why she needed to meet with me. I think it's also why he'd called everyone together. He wanted to tell them in person."

"So, do Booker and Chloe know about the divorce now?"

"I doubt it. Unless Kit told them, which doesn't seem likely." Her father jingled the change in his pocket. "What do you say? Can you scrap whatever plans you had for the day and come with me?"

"Just give me a minute," she said. She rushed upstairs to the bathroom, ran a comb through her hair and pinned it up into a bun. After applying some light makeup, she looked at herself in the mirror. She was getting older, for sure. Then again, she liked the way she looked—a face with more gravitas.

On the way back to her bedroom to grab her keys, she felt energized by the idea of working with her father. She could still make time for her restaurant. And then she remembered Avi.

For almost a year, Jane had been the personification of patience and support, doing everything she could to help Avi get her writing career on track, cutting her slack whenever she asked, putting up with her roommate, a woman who'd done her best to bed Avi, and in the process, split them up. Why did Avi have to live like that—almost committing, dropping the word "love," then backtracking, always with other women poised at the edges of her world, people and situations that she knew bothered Jane. And now Julia had entered the picture, a woman who relished playing with people, winding them up for the pure joy of watching them spin until they fell over.

A song had been playing in Jane's mind for days. She couldn't recall the name, but the words were a plea to a lover, "not to break her heart slow." If Avi wasn't interested, if Jane was just a diversion, a safe harbor for the times when she was feeling down, as she often was, with no real desire to make a life together, then Jane deserved to know. She wanted it quick. Like ripping off a bandage. It would hurt, but it couldn't hurt worse than the way she felt right now.

"I let go tonight," Avi had texted. What the hell did that mean?

12

"I need to see him," said Kit, kneading her hands together in her lap.

"I promise, Mrs. Deere," said Sergeant DePetro, standing in the living room of the summerhouse, hands crossed in front of him, back erect. "I'll make that happen. I also want to give you my word that I *will* put your husband's murderer behind bars. This is a priority case for us. For me personally."

Jane and her father had gathered with the rest of the Deere family to hear, for the first time, from the lead homicide detective assigned to the case. Because of Jordan's celebrity, this would undoubtedly be the highest profile case of DePetro's career. Not only would the country singer's death put the Deere family in the spotlight, it would place the detective center stage.

Jane had met Neil DePetro for the first time last fall, when she and Nolan had been working the case of a missing widower in Deep Haven. DePetro reminded Jane of an idealized cop in a Hollywood movie—tall, dark, and not so good-looking that he didn't seem plausible. His demeanor was brusk and efficient, lacking warmth, but projecting professionalism. This morning he looked badly wrinkled, as if he'd been roused out of bed at an early hour and had jumped into whatever clothes he could find.

The detective continued: "I wanted to meet with all of you like this because I need some quick answers. You've probably heard that the first forty-eight hours are the most important in any police investigation. I don't look at it that way. I believe the first minutes, the first hours are what's critical. That's why I asked for and received a search warrant to examine this property. Let's be clear. I'm not suggesting one of you is responsible. I'm simply saying that I wouldn't be doing my job if I didn't look hard at everything and everyone in Jordan's life."

Jane had picked a chair along the edge of the room, positioned so that she could see everyone's face. She figured that getting a sense of the Deere family dynamics was part of what DePetro was also after in meeting with them first as a group instead of individually. It might have been smarter to separate them and then try to tease out any differences in their stories. But this was DePetro's call and he would have to live with it.

"Let me begin," said DePetro, flipping open a notebook, "by giving you some details."

Archibald reached over and took Kit's hand. She offered him a grateful nod, squeezed his fingers warmly. Easing her hand away, she squared her shoulders and looked as if she was readying herself for a blow.

"Jordan Deere was found in a patch of tall brush off the running path that cuts through a densely wooded section of Bayview Park. A jogger found him at approximately seven twenty this morning. He immediately placed a 911 call, and EMTs were dispatched to the scene. Police secured the area and I arrived a few minutes later."

"Who was the man who found him?" asked Ray. He was seated on the couch, on the other side of Kit.

"Jacob Landauer," said DePetro, checking his notes. "A retired high school teacher. He jogs in in the park on occasion, said he'd never seen Jordan before. As you can imagine, he was pretty shaken."

"I understand that it was a gunshot," said Ray. "Did you find a weapon?"

"No. We did a grid search of the area and found nothing. We believe that the first round hit the victim in the temple. After he was down, the perpetrator put one more round into his chest. I'd say he wasn't taking any chances that the victim would survive. We're fairly certain a nine-millimeter handgun was used."

Kit raised a tissue to her swollen eyes.

"We'll have more details in a few hours, but from what I know about gunshot wounds, Mr. Deere probably died instantly. He didn't suffer. My team is still at the scene looking for evidence."

"Will there be an autopsy?" asked Booker. He sat on a love seat next to his sister.

"Absolutely not," said Kit. "There will be no such thing."

"I'm afraid that by law, autopsies must be performed on homicide victims." DePetro shifted his hands behind his back, spread his legs, a classic military "rest" position. Jane wondered if he'd been a soldier.

"I will not have my husband's perfect body hacked up by some medical examiner," cried Kit.

"Jesus, Mom," said Chloe, her eyes rising to the ceiling. "Dad's dead. Do you think maybe it's time to relax some of your beauty standards?"

Seated next to Jane, Tommy sat staring down into a mug of brown liquid, which from the smell of it, clearly wasn't coffee. Under his breath, he mumbled, "Die young, leave a beautiful corpse. What crap." He was the only one in the room wearing a suit. His hair, thick, wavy, and combed straight back, was almost entirely gray. Jane assumed he was older than Kit and Jordan, probably in his mid- to late-sixties.

"Let's move on," said DePetro, still standing in his at-ease position. "First question to all of you: Did Jordan Deere have any enemies?"

Kit was the first to speak up. "Everyone loved Jordan. Everyone. I can't think of a soul who'd want to hurt him."

Tommy grunted.

"You have something to add, Mr. Prior?" asked DePetro.

He cleared his throat. "Just that anybody who's been in the music business as long as he had makes his share of enemies."

"The country music business?"

"Yeah." He overenunciated each word, suggesting that, at this early hour, he was already wasted. "Artists have adversarial relationships with recording labels. With other artists. With band members. The list goes on from there."

"Are you thinking of someone specific?"

"What? No. I'm just saying it's wrong to say Jordan was universally adored."

Kit's gaze bore into him.

"What about girlfriends on the side? Boyfriends?"

"This may be difficult for some people to understand," said Kit, her eyes shifting from Tommy to DePetro, "but Jordan was completely faithful to me, as I was to him. You may think I'm being naïve. I'm not. I know my husband."

Ray turned to look at her.

"No marital problems?" asked DePetro.

"None. Our careers often separated us for months at a time, but we always stayed in touch. I won't say we never had issues. All couples do. But we worked them out."

So this was the way she was going to play it, thought Jane. Was it an impulse, or was she really that arrogant, thinking the police would never figure it out?

"Any money problems I should know about?" asked DePetro.

"None that I know of," said Kit. "Tommy was Jordan's manager. I'm sure he'd be more than willing to answer your questions."

As Kit continued to talk, Jane noticed that, with the exception of Archibald and her father, nobody in the room looked at Kit. They watched DePetro with near catatonic stares, but never focused any attention on her. Jane found it unusual—and perhaps telling—body language. Under normal circumstances, Jane would have expected the family to rally around the grieving matriarch. Instead, within the limits of a room in which they were all trapped, each individual was attempting to detach, to create as much psychic distance as possible. Or—perhaps they couldn't take their eyes off the detective because they were trying to determine if he was buying Kit's story. Jane wondered if DePetro had picked up on the strange group dynamics. She was sure her father had.

"I'd like you to tell me about Jordan's recent morning routine," said DePetro, folding his arms over his chest.

"Beverly and I have been in New Orleans for the last few months," said Kit, dabbing a tissue at the corner of her eye. "We didn't return until late last night."

"Chloe and I have only been here since Friday," said Booker. "We came for a family reunion."

DePetro arched an eyebrow. "Do you have them frequently?"

"Not as often as we'd like," said Kit. "We're busy people. It's why we decided to carve out some time to get together this fall."

"So nobody knows Mr. Deere's morning routine?"

Tommy raised a finger.

"Mr. Prior?"

He took a sip from the mug to steady himself. "I've been around, on and off, since the beginning of June."

"Did Jordan have regular habits?"

"He didn't used to, but for the last few months, yeah, you could say that."

"What was a typical Sunday morning for him?"

"Sundays were no different than any other day. I mean, he'd go to church when Kit was around, but normally he didn't. He was always up by six. He'd dress in sweats and head out the door between six thirty and seven for a morning jog."

"Always in Bayview Park?"

"I think so, yeah. He'd tried other places, but he liked Bayview because it was quieter, and the running path was well cared for but still rustic. He was usually home by eight thirty. Sometimes he'd take a swim, but most mornings he'd come back, shower and dress, and then make himself some breakfast. He'd sit out on the terrace and read the newspaper or check his e-mail."

"And then?"

"He worked in his office. In the afternoon, you could usually find him down in his music studio. Then, sometimes later in the day, he'd play golf, or he'd take one of the boats out."

"Dinner? Evenings?"

"He liked to have friends over to the house. He was a passable cook. Or he'd meet someone at a restaurant. At least once a week we'd go out to a movie or a concert. He liked a good time, but lately he was always in bed by eleven."

"Alone?"

Tommy's smile was cheerless. "My job obligations didn't include bed checks, Sergeant DePetro."

"You seem determined to tie my husband's death to some sort of sexual escapade," said Kit, her tone full of disgust.

"That's not my intent," said DePetro.

"Coulda fooled me," slurred Tommy.

One of the uniformed officers who'd arrived with DePetro and seemed to be in charge of the house search, appeared in the doorway and motioned to get DePetro's attention.

"One second," said the detective. He moved to the rear of the room to confer with the uniform. Listening closely as the woman filled him in on what appeared to be urgent information, he finally cracked a smile. "Good, good," he said, loud enough for Jane to hear. "Go go go," he said, waving the woman away.

Returning to the front, DePetro had a distinct swagger to his step, looking like a man who'd just won the jackpot. "So," he said, folding his hands together in front of him. "Did anyone notice anything strange about Jordan in the last few months? Did he seem upset? Worried? Anything out of the ordinary?"

Nobody moved.

"Nothing?"

"As I've already told you," said Kit, placing a hand lightly on top of Ray's. "Jordan was fine. Happy. Energetic. Working on new songs for his next album."

"Right. Did he ever use any illegal drugs?"

"Never," said Kit.

Everyone in the family nodded their agreement.

"Relationship with siblings?"

"He was an only child," said Kit. "Both parents are dead."

DePetro scratched the back of his head. "Well, I guess we're done for the moment. I'll need to talk to each one of you separately, but right now, let me thank you for your time. Oh, there is one more question I need to ask. You said that Jordan usually left the house around seven, Mr. Prior. Was that when he left this morning?"

"I was asleep," mumbled Tommy.

"Anybody?" When nobody answered, he said, "Surely someone knows what time he left the house."

"He didn't," said Booker, his gaze sliding to his hands.

"Didn't what?"

"Didn't leave."

"Of course he did."

"What he meant to say," said Chloe, examining the ring on her finger, "is that Dad didn't leave from here because he never came home last night."

DePetro blinked. "He . . . didn't come home? Where was he?"

"We don't know," said Booker. "He left in the speedboat around six thirty and never came back."

"Does he do that a lot? Not tell anyone where he's going? Not come home at night?"

"No," said Tommy.

If DePetro didn't see the handwriting on the wall before this, he did now. They were, as a group, stonewalling him.

"Nobody thought this was important information?" said De-Petro, trying to keep a lid on his anger. "Why didn't you tell me this right away?"

Thankfully, thought Jane, nobody had the guts to quip, "Because you never asked."

13

Before entering the Rhineland Grill later that afternoon, Booker paused by the reception desk to study his lunch date. Erin was seated across the room at a table by the windows, her arms wrapped tightly around her thin body. She held herself the same way she had yesterday, as if she were cold, in pain, or trying to hold something inside.

The more he saw of her, the more he realized how much less magical she was now—a faded version of the girl he'd once known. Somewhere along the way she'd figured out how to tame her wild curly hair, something he'd once thought impossible. It was shorter now. More trendy. Had the wildness in her soul been tamed, too? Because no matter how much he wanted to find the same fire in her eyes, it wasn't there. He wondered what had happened to those exciting, fierce, risky dreams she'd once talked about with such passion.

Her face had lost most of the fleshiness of youth, revealing an underlying bone structure he found even more appealing than the softness that had once driven him to distraction. More than anything, what struck him about her was her sadness. It didn't reveal itself in her expression, which she kept carefully neutral, but in the tight way she held her body. This assessment might be tinged with more than a hint of romanticism, though he didn't think he was wrong. He also figured that it might be something he wasn't supposed to notice. Something to do with her divorce.

On the drive up to King's Bay, Booker had begun to worry that she'd forgotten about their lunch date. Seeing her sitting at the table, patiently waiting for him, was what he needed to steady his nerves. Nowadays he wasn't used to being stood up, though around her, he sensed himself regressing. Remnants of the boy he'd once been were still clunking around inside him—the awkward, painfully self-conscious, depressed kid, raging at the flotilla of assholes who peopled his world, which included almost everyone he knew. The boy who was frightened to the point of inertia that he might never find a place to fit in and feel safe. A kid who hid behind bravado, but in reality had zero self-confidence, especially around the opposite sex. If you stirred all those elements together with a self-righteous, superior attitude, a reckless spirit, and a relentless libido, tossed in two bat wings and an eye of newt, you had the makings for an explosion of epic proportions. Were all boys ticking time bombs?

Booker had no desire to live in the past. He wasn't a kid anymore. Erin had once been the "unattainable." Now she was having lunch with him. He calmed himself with such thoughts, even though he knew they were probably lies.

The police had been amenable to interviewing him before the rest of the family. Booker had pleaded his case, explaining that he had an important afternoon meeting, one he simply couldn't miss. If that made him appear cold and insufficiently distressed by his father's death, he didn't care. As expected, the interview had been an empty exercise. He played the game his mother had mandated. His lack of candor had annoyed DePetro, who'd already figured out that the family wasn't the open book they'd initially appeared to be, but with so many others to talk to, Booker's interrogation had been mercifully short. Chloe hadn't wanted him to leave, in fact had begged him to stay. Watching Erin open the menu and begin to study it, he decided that he'd made the right decision.

Pulling out a chair, Booker sat down, smiling and saying, "I wasn't sure you'd be here."

She seemed puzzled by the comment. "Why wouldn't I be?"

Because I'm a sixteen-year-old pimply-faced jerk-off, he thought to himself. He'd taken more care with his clothes today. Gray Brooks Brothers wool suit over a black silk shirt, open at the collar. Erin was dressed more formally, too, in a slim navy-blue skirt and a kind of nautical-looking blouse—white, with navy-blue trim. He liked the retro look. It suited her.

"Anything sound good?" he asked.

"Soup, I think."

"And bread and butter?"

"Yes. Perfect."

He would have to tell her about his father, but not yet. Once the subject was brought up, it would become *the* focus of conversation. He was selfish. He wanted her all to himself for as long as possible. "You're different," he said.

She blinked a couple of times, looking unsure. "We both are. I called Chloe, in case you're interested. Left her a voice message. So far, she hasn't called me back. I assumed she's either pissed at me for something I have no memory of, or you've all been busy with your family reunion. How's that going?"

"Has your family ever had a reunion?"

"My oldest sister and her husband live in South Africa. It's not likely."

"You had a younger brother. A couple years younger than me."

94

"Henry. He's a pharmacist. He's also gay, lives in Colorado with his boyfriend."

"Your mom and dad still alive?"

"Both going strong. But we're not here to talk about our families, are we?"

"No? Why are we here?"

"Because you had this weird-ass crush on me in high school."

Booker held her eyes. "Did I?"

"Didn't you?"

"If I denied it, would you believe me?"

That elicited a smile.

The waitress arrived to take their order.

"The beef and barley soup," said Erin. "A bowl, not a cup."

"I'll have the same," said Booker. "And lots of bread and butter."

"We have a fresh baguette," said the waitress. "Or I can offer you our special: blueberry muffins."

"Both," they said, almost in unison.

"And coffee," said Booker. "Black."

"Same here," said Erin.

After the waitress left, the silence between them turned awkward.

"What do we talk about now?" asked Erin.

"I suppose we can take this any direction we want."

"And what do we want?"

He unfolded his napkin and placed it in his lap. "Let's start with something simple. Tell me all your secrets. Don't leave anything out."

She laughed at the absurdity.

A busboy walked up and set a bread basket between them. He placed the butter next to Booker.

Rubbing his hands together, Booker removed several slices of the baguette. While Erin helped herself to one of the blueberry muffins, he continued, "Look at it this way. If you can't tell your secrets to a man you haven't seen in fifteen years and probably will never see again, who *can* you tell?"

She sat across from him looking amused but remote.

He passed her the butter.

While DePetro questioned Beverly in the kitchen with the door closed, Kit asked Ray if he would mind stepping outside with her. He conferred with Jane briefly, then walked her out to the edge of the patio, where they sat down on a bench overlooking the dark, choppy water of Frenchman's Bay. Since this morning, the sky had turned cloudy and the temperature had fallen. The gloom of a late autumn chill settled into Kit, into her bones. She understood that Ray was upset. From the stony look on his face, he might even be ready to throw in the towel, tell her to find herself another lawyer. Kit hadn't gotten this far in life by sweeping problems away. She needed to face him, needed to know where he stood and, if possible, apply what pressure she could to make him stay.

"If you don't want to represent me and my family," she said, lifting her eyes to him, "I'll be deeply disappointed, but I do understand."

Ray stared off in the distance. He seemed to be mulling something over. "Why did you lie to the police? Or was it me you lied to?"

"I've never lied to you. If I didn't tell DePetro everything, it's because I consider it none of his business."

"There was money at stake in the divorce, Kit. People have been murdered for far, far less."

"I didn't murder my husband for his money. I can't believe you'd even suggest that."

"You asked to talk to me yesterday because you were worried

96

about the potential financial ramifications of a split. It was on your mind. You can't deny it. If Jordan contacted a lawyer, DePetro will find out. And then what? You lie about one thing, he'll wonder what else you're lying about. You already threw him that curveball by not mentioning the fact that Jordan left the house last night, that he never came home."

"First, with the exception of Beverly—and you—nobody knows that Jordan asked me for a divorce. I don't believe for a minute that he contacted a lawyer. As for his habits—where he goes, what he does—that's his business."

"You're not listening to me," said Ray. "This is a *murder* investigation. It changes everything."

"I won't allow my children to be hurt by this. They come before everything, even Jordan. Still, I can't win the battle and lose the war. Do you understand what I'm saying? Jordan's fans, the women, the religiously inclined, and that means the majority of the people who buy his CDs and come to his concerts, love him because they think he's a great guy. A hard-drinking, shotgun-carrying, horse-riding good old boy from Kentucky. And he was all of those things. But he was also a family man. A loving husband and father. His fans also understand that if he so much as crooked his little finger, he could have any woman he wanted. He did sleep around, but he was faithful to me in every way that counted. I may be an aging, not terribly well-known actress who is mere seconds from crumbling into old age—"

"That's not true and you know it."

"It is true."

"You're a beautiful, vibrant woman."

Her eyes widened ever so slightly. Again, she laid her hand on his. "You lie so sweetly I almost believe you mean it."

"Kit, look, I understand what you're saying. You're thinking about Jordan's legacy. But you have to weigh that against the hornet's nest of problems you could unleash on you and your family if you aren't straight with the police."

"I am *not* telling them Jordan wanted a divorce. No way on earth. I'm not telling them we had an open marriage. I assume that, since our conversation was privileged, you can't say anything either."

"I would never break a confidence."

He had no idea how deep her lies went. No one did, not even those in the family who, after reading Jordan's so-called novel, thought they knew everything. Armed with their partial knowledge, each person felt they understood what they were protecting by keeping to the story Kit had laid out for them. She was good at dancing around the truth. She'd had a lifetime of honing her skills. Some might say that she was living on a razor's edge, but for her, that razor not only produced a sense of exhilaration, it felt like home.

"So," she said, lifting her hand off Ray's. "Should I look for another lawyer?"

He followed her hand with his eyes as she rested it in her lap. "That won't be necessary."

"Good. I need you, Ray. I need someone I can rely on. Without Jordan—"

"You don't have to explain."

"He was the single most important person in my life and I loved him beyond measure." That *was* the truth. Tears welled in her eyes.

Ray put his arm around her, let her cry against his shoulder. Finally, leaning back and looking her square in the eyes, he said, "I shouldn't do this, shouldn't ask this question. I could defend you in a court of law without ever knowing, but this is important. To me. I have to hear it from you. I'll never ask again. If you lie to me—"

"I won't lie."

"Did you murder your husband?"

"No."

"Do you know who did?"

"Honestly, Ray. I don't."

"Do you think it could be a family member?"

She looked away. "Not my children. They had nothing to do with it."

"You know that for a fact?"

"They were both here all morning. With me. Yes, I know it for a fact."

"What about Beverly? Tommy? Or Archibald? You consider them family. Did they have any issues with Jordan?"

She hesitated.

"More secrets?" said Ray. He took both of her hands in his.

Her heart sped up, responding immediately to the animal warmth. She wished he would put his arm around her again and just hold her. "Oh, Ray, this is all so complicated."

Squeezing her hands, he said, "I suppose you've been through enough for one day."

"Thank you," she said softly.

"I should probably be with you when you talk to DePetro."

She nodded. She was a good actress. Then again, not all of her feelings, especially when it came to Raymond Lawless, were an act.

14

After lunch, Booker and Erin took a walk along the shore. As the wind buffeted them and waves crashed against the rocks, occasionally spraying them with a fine mist, they talked about anything and everything. It was stream of consciousness. Time passed without Booker even noticing. When he did look at his watch, he saw that it was going on six.

"I'm freezing," he said, shivering as he crossed his arms over his chest. "What do you say we find ourselves some hot chocolate?"

They climbed the graveled path up to the Hofbrau, a small chaletlike building perched at the edge of the King's Bay that served both alcohol and food. Finding a table near one of the three fireplaces, Booker spread the menu between them. "Or," he said, glancing down the row of drinks, "we could have Irish coffee."

"As long as it comes with whipped cream," said Erin, "it's fine with me."

Booker stepped up to the bar to place the order. While he was waiting for one of the bartenders to notice him, he saw an old drinking buddy of his, Clark Miller, come through the front door. Turning his back, he ordered the Irish coffees with extra whipped cream, and then slipped back to the table, keeping his face averted. But as soon as he pulled out his chair, Clark spotted him and began to head over. The look on his face, part sympathy, part eagerness, told Booker that he'd heard the news about his father.

"You know, Erin, there's something I need to tell you," Booker began, realizing how weird it would look if he didn't break it to her before Clark did.

She switched her attention from the menu to Booker. "Sounds serious."

"It is. It's about my dad. I didn't say anything before because—"

"Hey, Booker," said Clark, reaching the table and slapping him on the back. "Long time, man."

"Yeah, long time."

Smiling at Erin, Clark said, "Who's the lovely lady?"

"A friend," said Booker, introducing them.

Clark shook her hand. "Hey, man, I was so sorry to hear about your dad. It's all over the news. I mean, fuck. What the hell happened?"

"What about your father?" asked Erin.

"You haven't heard?" said Clark, glancing over his shoulder at the group he came in with, giving them a nod to tell them that he'd be right back. "He was out for a morning run and someone shot him. Unreal. Have the police found the guy who did it? Man, I am *so* sorry. Your family must be devastated."

"Your father . . . is *dead*?" said Erin, her eyes almost doing pinwheels. "Why didn't you tell me?"

"It's kind of . . . um . . . I didn't want to—"

"Jesus. What's wrong with you?"

Before he could come up with a reasonable answer, the believable excuse, Erin was up and on her way out of the bar. "Hey, wait," he called after her.

A waiter set the Irish coffees on the table in front of him, momentarily blocking his line of sight. "Shove off, okay?" he said to Clark.

"Sure, man. Again, sorry."

Booker wanted to go after her, but instinct told him to hang back. He watched her take out her cell phone and tap in a number. She stood in front of the reservation desk, speaking heatedly to the person on the other end of the line, so caught up in the conversation that she never even glanced Booker's way. Waiting for her to finish and hopefully return to the table, he began to form a question: Why had his father's death, a man Erin barely knew, caused such a huge reaction in her? Sure, she had a right to wonder about Booker's priorities because he hadn't said anything up front, but her pacing, the almost frightened look in her eyes . . . what the hell was that about?

3:14 A.M. With only a small table lamp burning, the therapist, Dr. James Stratton, sat on the leather couch in his home office. Having been awakened at such an early hour by a madman banging on his front door, he wore a bathrobe over his pajamas. His hair was rumpled, his eyes puffy, and gray stubble was visible on his fleshy cheeks.

Archibald sat in his usual chair across from the couch, shoes flat on the floor, hands resting in his lap. He'd been coming to see Stratton on and off for sixteen years. He stared straight ahead at nothing in particular. "Thank you for seeing me," he began. Not that he'd given the man much of a choice. "I'm here because I need to make a decision."

"All right," said Stratton. "Go on."

"I'm thinking about doing something I probably shouldn't. Something, for lack of a better word, that's wrong."

"And you want me to talk you out of it."

"No, not really."

Stratton seemed confused. "Perhaps you'd like to tell me a little more about this decision."

"I'm not sure I should. Or that I want to."

The therapist tapped a pen against his chin, trying, but failing, to hide his exasperation. "All right. Let's approach it another way. Can you tell me why you want to do it?"

That was an easy one. "Love." When Stratton merely nodded, Archibald felt like he should say something more. "For the people I love."

"Your family?"

"I can't let them down again. I have to protect them. The mess they're in, it's my fault. My failure."

"And why is that?"

His hand crawled up the front of his shirt. "Because, and I know this may sound somewhat grandiose, I see more clearly than they do. It's all moot now. Something terrible happened and I could have stopped it, but . . . I didn't. I'll have to live with that until the day I die. What I can't live with is . . . would be . . . if I allowed . . . there's someone . . . like I said, I have to be the one who helps them." This was harder than he thought it would be.

Shifting his position, Stratton said, "It's hard for me to comment when I don't have any specifics."

"Yes, okay. Okay." He touched the top of his head to make sure what was left of his hair was in its proper place. "I think the police may be about to target someone I care about."

"Target?"

"Arrest. Charge with murder."

The light dawned in Stratton's eyes. "Ah, so this is about your friend's death. Jordan Deere."

Archibald gave a tight nod.

"You think someone in his family may be responsible."

"Did I say that?" he snapped. "You'll *never* hear me say that."

"No, of course—"

"I try to understand myself, you know? What makes me tick? What makes others do what they do. The unexamined life—and all that."

"And I find that an admirable quality."

"I've always thought of myself as a good person. Helpful. Loyal. Giving."

Stratton nodded.

"So explain this to me," he continued, trying to drill down on why he'd come. "Are some people born evil and others born good? Is it physically impossible for some to be faithful to their partners? Do people vary in how deeply they feel? If so, are the ones who feel more deeply better human beings, or are they, by some odd twist of fate, cursed? Most importantly, does anybody ever really change?"

"I think," said Stratton, leaning forward, resting his elbows on his knees, "that those are hard questions. I also think we've moved into the realm of moral philosophy here. I can give you my opinion, but that's all it would be."

Archibald made a keep-talking gesture with his hand.

"Well, for one thing, I don't believe in fate, in the classical sense of predetermination. Some might say that temperament, our inborn gifts, shape who we become. I would agree with that—to the extent that we act on those gifts. I don't view the world as a conflict between good and evil, in the metaphysical sense. People aren't black and white. Marriage is always a negotiation. Humans make mistakes, and the reasons are complex. As for those who feel more deeply—and I do think that's a viable category—I think it can be both a gift and a curse. And finally, do humans ever really change? Archibald, if I didn't believe change was possible, I would never have devoted my life to psychotherapy. Of course we can change."

"For good or ill."

"Yes, either way I suppose."

Archibald reached into his pocket and removed a coat button, the one Beverly had placed in his hand before he left the lake house. He tried to recall the words from the first chapter of Genesis: *The woman . . . she did give me from the tree and I did eat.* Beverly had explained what needed to happen, and that he was the only one who could do it. Brushing his thumb across the smooth surface, he whispered to himself.

"I'm sorry," said Stratton. "I didn't catch that."

"I said, 'cleverness and stupidity.'"

"Ah, yes. Your two behavioral poles. While I'm not sure that's an entirely accurate assessment, let me make a guess. You think what you're about to do is . . . stupid. That it lacks moral intelligence."

"I guess we'll know tomorrow," said Archibald. He stood and reached for his coat.

"You're leaving?"

"You've helped me, Doctor. And now, I've got somewhere I need to be."

15

Late on Monday morning, Jane stopped by the theater to speak with Cordelia. Parking on the street, she entered under the marquee and took one of the elevators up to the second floor. Since her theatrical friend rarely watched or listened to the local news, there was a better than even chance she hadn't heard about Jordan Deere's murder. Jane wanted to break the news to her in person.

Nobody, it appeared, was manning the reception desk. Jane walked right through into Cordelia's office. The half-eaten Danish suggested that her friend was around somewhere. Feeling her cell phone rumble, she saw that she had a text from Avi. She sat down behind the desk, took a bite of the Danish, and read:

> More revisions from Elaine Ducasse
> this AM. Makes me wonder if I can
> put 2 sentences together without help.
> Think I should go back to bartending.
> Or stripping. What if this is another
> epic fail? What if she cancels my
> contract?

Like most writers, Avi struggled with self-doubt. But in her case, she also wrestled with what Jane thought was clinical depression. Jane hadn't realized it at first, but over the past year, she'd watched Avi sleep entire weeks away. At night, she drank. Since sleep and booze weren't good solutions, Jane had suggested that she see a doctor or find a therapist. Jane did her best to help Avi through her bouts of misery. She'd cook special meals, things she knew Avi loved. Avi's father had read bedtime stories to her as a child and often, crawling under the covers, listening to Jane read, was the only thing that could calm her down.

Another rumble—another message from Avi.

Are you pissed at me?

Looking up, Jane's first thought was . . . maybe. She hadn't texted Avi in a couple of days, which no doubt meant something. She slipped the phone back into her pocket. On her way out of the office, she found a workman in the hallway and asked if he'd seen Cordelia.

"She's in the main stairwell." He pointed to an arched doorway.

"Doing what?"

"Sitting on the steps."

"Just sitting?"

"Well, she's drinking from a juice box, if that's of any interest."

She thanked him. Halfway to the third floor, she found Cordelia, dressed all in black leather, eyes tightly shut, seated on the stairs. And she did indeed have a juice box in her hand.

"Who comes?" she intoned without opening her eyes.

"'Tis Jane, good madam."

"Ah, my lady. God's good greetings upon you."

"What are you doing?"

"Listening."

"To what?"

"Come sit thee next to me. Open your ears."

Jane hunkered down on the cold stone. After listening for nearly a minute and hearing nothing but the sound of hammers coming from inside the auditorium, she said, "Can we drop the Shakespearean English? You can maintain it forever. I've about reached my limit."

"Shhh," she said, raising a finger to her lips. "Don't you hear them?"

"Hear who?"

"Gilbert and Hilda. Granted, their voices are faint—kind of echoy and tinny. They're fighting. Something about a dress Hilda wants to wear to the opening."

"Seriously? *Your* opening?"

"It started in my office. One of them opened a window, then slammed it shut. Got my attention right away."

"That actually happened?"

"What's the worst one ghost can do to another? Murder is obviously off the table."

"Cordelia, you have to listen to me. I've got some bad news."

She opened one eye. "Want a sip of juice?"

"No thanks."

"It's full of nutrition."

"Only in the vaguest sense."

"What's the news?"

"It's about Jordan Deere."

The other eye opened. "What about him?"

Jane explained what she knew, trying to break it as gently as she could.

Through shocked tears, Cordelia demanded to know more.

108

"You should have called me right away. Hattie and I would have driven out to the lake house to hold Kit's hand."

"I doubt very much that the police would have let you in."

"I need details, Janey. Is Kit okay? Booker? Chloe?"

Jane unsnapped her old varsity jacket. "Everyone's taking it very hard, as you can imagine. As far as I know, the police didn't find anything useful at the scene. No footprints. No bullet casings. No weapon. They've got very little to go on. Except for one thing: they carted out Jordan's computer. Seemed to think they'd hit the jackpot."

"You were there?"

"Kit asked Dad to come out to the house." She took a few minutes to explain why she'd gone along with him.

Cordelia narrowed her eyes. "I hope your father realizes that *moi* has always been the deciding factor in your sleuthing successes. You're the brawn, I'm the brains."

Jane struggled not to roll her eyes, though they did tilt just a bit. "May I point out that I was the one who did all the work to become a licensed investigator?"

"True. But I'm the one who provided the psychic support. Lit the candles and burned the sage incense. And then I did that tarot reading for you and told you you'd pass."

There was no use arguing. In truth, Cordelia had been indispensable on more than one occasion.

"Tell me the truth: Do the police think someone in the family is responsible?"

"I can't answer that."

"But it's possible."

Jane nodded.

"So where do we start? You *have* to let me help. Those people are my friends."

Actually, Jane had already given that some thought. "Maybe

you could spend an evening with Kit—at the summerhouse. Talk to Chloe and Booker, too."

"You can't leave Beverly out of the equation. She's had a huge crush on Kit for years. And Tommy Prior, Jordan's manager. He's always been this buttoned-up, controlled, meticulous kind of man, but a couple of summers ago, I started to notice a change in him—and not for the better."

"Use all your wiles, okay," said Jane. "But be discreet. Don't hammer them with questions. Just be a willing ear. Maybe I shouldn't say this, but it feels like the whole lot of them are playing some sort of game."

"Explain."

Jane hesitated. "Since I'm working for my dad's law firm, I have to sign a confidentiality agreement. This is serious, Cordelia. It's not just you and me having ourselves an adventure anymore. I could be prosecuted if Kit finds out I've shared this information with you. Do you swear to keep it just between us?"

"Absolutely. Scout's honor."

"The day before Jordan died, he asked Kit for a divorce."

"Heavens!" Her hand flew to her chest.

"That's what she wanted to talk to my father about when she met with him at your house. But yesterday, when the detective in charge of the case—his name is Neil DePetro—asked her about her relationship with her husband, she said it was solid. No problems at all."

"She lied?"

"With perfect composure. She's quite an actress."

"One of the best. What else?"

"When DePetro called everyone together for an initial conversation, nobody in the room mentioned the rather significant fact that Jordan had left the house early Saturday evening—in a speedboat—and had never come back."

"Where did he go?"

"They claim they don't know."

"So let me get this straight," said Cordelia, leaning forward and folding her hands in a show of patience—or impatience. "Jordan spent Saturday night . . . somewhere. A place he could get to by boat. He left from that 'somewhere' to go running yesterday morning. Assuming he didn't leave his house on Saturday wearing running clothes or athletic shoes, he must have changed somewhere along the way. And if he left in a boat, how did he get to the park?"

"All good questions," said Jane.

Cordelia sat up straight. "Sounds like a job for Cordelia M. Thorn."

"It does, doesn't it."

Puffing out her chest, Cordelia continued, sotto voce, "You're not the only one with news. I got a call from a Minneapolis cold case detective right after I arrived this morning. Seems they caught a break. Major progress has been made on the skeleton we found behind the wall. Red Clemens tells me my staff and all the workmen were buzzing about it."

"I'll bet," said Jane.

"So," said Cordelia, leaning close. "Here's what I know."

Archibald carried a notebook with him as he moved in and out of the rooms in the theater basement. The place was a veritable treasure trove of old theater props and wardrobe memorabilia, some of it dating back to the early part of the last century. Cordelia needed to mine the wares on offer down here, he mused, lifting a ray gun off a pile of rope. Ray guns were popular in the fifties. He'd seen a few before, though none as elaborate as this one. He'd found one for sale on eBay a few years back. He shouldn't have been surprised. What wasn't for sale on eBay? "Love, integrity, friendship," he muttered to himself.

111

What Archibald needed was to be engaged in some sort of busywork this morning, something to take his mind off the fateful decision he'd made in the middle of the night. Sifting through a box of costume jewelry, he found a gold signet ring. When he moved it closer to the light, the top flipped up, revealing a space for a pill—or for poison. The ring had the look of real gold. "Can't be real," he mumbled. Then again. He dropped it into his pocket.

On a whim, he decided to check out the speakeasy. As he approached the door, he found strips of yellow and black crime scene tape stretched across it. The lower section had been ripped away. Ducking down, he came up on the other side and switched on the wrought-iron chandeliers. He was startled to find a man sitting alone at the bar. Because he was dressed in old jeans, a chambray shirt, and rough boots, Archibald pegged him as one of the workmen. "I'm sorry," he said, coming to a full stop. "I didn't realize anyone was in here." Odd that the guy had been sitting in the dark.

The man turned. "Mr. Van Arnam? My God, it's been years. Red Clemens," he said, moving off the stool. "Do you remember me?"

Archibald recalled the name, though he couldn't place the face. And then it dawned on him. "You're the maintenance man. You're . . . still here?"

"I asked Cordelia Thorn to hire me back."

He didn't remember much about the guy, except for one thing: Years ago, Archibald had caught him listening outside one of the dressing room doors.

"Got my old office back," continued Red. "Feels like old times."

"I'll bet."

"Never figured I'd run into you again, but hey, since I have, I should tell you how much I enjoyed your newest book. The one on Fort Snelling."

"You read that?" Oops, thought Archibald. Was that an elitist comment? Obviously the man could read. Archibald only meant that it didn't seem like the kind of book a janitor would be interested in.

"Are you working on something new?" asked Red.

"Actually, I am. A history of the micro cultures in Minnesota."

"Oh, sure. Like that book, *American Nations*. Loved his perspective. Did you read it? The author divides the U.S. into eleven different cultural groups."

"You read that, too?" As Archibald stepped up to the bar, his eyes drifted to a hole in the wall behind the bar. "What's that?"

Red eased back onto his seat. "Cordelia and that friend of hers. Lawless." He drummed his fingers on the counter. "Now what the heck is her first name?"

"Jane."

"Yeah, yeah. Jane. They noticed that someone had broken through part of the wall, then bricked it up. They asked me to break it down so they could see what was behind it. Turns out, it was a body. Or, more precisely, a skeleton."

Archibald pulled out one of the stools, brushed the dust off and sat down. "Tell me more."

"Well, the skull had a bullet hole smack in the center of the forehead."

"How grotesque."

"Yeah. Gave me the willies."

"Did you call the police?"

"Oh, sure. They came and looked it over, declared it a crime scene. That's why they put up the tape."

Eyeing the opening, Archibald gave himself a moment to process the situation. "Was it, I mean, did you know about the gangland murders that happened down here?"

"Yup. I heard."

"I wonder if it had something to do with that."

"Didn't," said Red. "I was up in Cordelia's office earlier this morning. She'd just got off the phone with a police detective. Seems the cops found a wallet and a ring in the debris under the skeleton. Belonged to the dead guy. His name was Chapman. William Edward Chapman. Disappeared in the summer of 1980."

"Chapman. Hmm. If they've got the dates correct, then it couldn't be connected."

"Cordelia mentioned that the cold case unit was able to track down the dead guy's sister. She told them that the family had never believed for a minute that he'd run off. They figured something terrible had happened to him."

"How incredibly sad," said Archibald. "And all that time, he's been buried behind that wall. Makes you wonder about human beings, doesn't it? Killing comes so easily to some of us."

"Not sure it's always easy," said Red. "But come it does."

As they sat in silence, Archibald began to feel as if he were at a real bar, that the guy next to him was the average sort of stranger he'd meet and talk to, the kind of man he might have a surprisingly intimate conversation with, thanks mostly to the alcoholic lubrication, but also to the anonymity—once they got up and left the bar, they'd never see each other again. "I wish I understood what makes people do what they do," he said, thinking about the last few days. "I don't mean just other people. I'm talking about myself, too. I try to plumb the depths, to understand my motivation, but then it occurs to me that my reasoning is much too facile. By 'facile,' I mean—"

"I'm familiar with the word," said Red, folding his hands, the edges of his lips curling into a smile.

"We all tell ourselves stories about how the world works. I think we lie to ourselves more than we care to admit. For instance, I've always prided myself on my ability to analyze data. But sometimes I wonder if, when it comes to my own life, my thoughts don't simply bang between two poles—cleverness and stupidity." Struck by how professorial he sounded, he stopped himself. "Listen, Red. I am curious about something. Why were you sitting in here in the dark before I came in?"

"I like quiet places. Don't much like crowds. It's why I always stayed away from the stage upstairs."

Archibald nodded. "Not a theater person."

"No, I love the plays, the actors—if I can slip in after the lights have been dimmed, when everyone is seated and quiet. I guess maybe it's a certain type of agoraphobia."

Glancing at the hole, Archibald pointed and said, "Don't you wonder what really happened there?"

"Not always smart to get too philosophical," he said, tracing a deep gouge in the bar top with his finger, "but what we've been talking about—it reminds me of one of Aesop's fables. The one about the scorpion and the frog."

Archibald had read the entire canon when he was a boy. "I don't recall that one."

"It's about this real nice, helpful frog. Lived on a riverbank. He gave rides on his back so that other critters could get across the river without drowning. Lots of bad currents running through it. One day this scorpion comes up to him and says, 'Hey there, Kermit, will you take me across?' Now the frog, he wasn't born yesterday. He says to the scorpion, 'I'd like to, man, but how do I know you won't sting me?' The scorpion says, 'I'm not suicidal. If I sting you, we'll both die.' So the frog let's the scorpion climb onto his back and get comfortable. Halfway across, the scorpion stings him. As they're sinking out of sight, the frog has just enough time to ask the scorpion why. Know what the scorpion says?"

"Don't remember," said Archibald.

"He says, *'It is my nature.'*" Red let the words hang in the air as he removed a pack of cigarettes from his pocket. "Yup," he said, tapping one out. "Figure that story just about says it all."

16

Jane's first official assignment for Raymond Lawless & Associates came that afternoon. Her father called and asked her to locate and interview as many of Jordan's local friends as she could find. He was concerned that Jordan might have contacted a lawyer before his death and thus left behind evidence of his intention to divorce. If so, and if DePetro found out about it, the fact that Kit had once again failed to inform him about something so potentially important to the case would push her to the top of the suspect list.

According to her father, no one in the family had any idea who Jordan might have contacted if he'd needed a local lawyer. With his computer gone, and no address book in evidence, her dad was left with a big question mark. In an effort to protect Kit from her own bad judgment, he wanted Jane to begin her search right away. Assuming that Jordan had confided his feelings to one or more of his friends, talking to them might be the best way to locate the divorce lawyer, if he or she existed.

Another key piece of the puzzle was the boat Jordan had sped off in late Saturday afternoon. Jane learned from her dad that it was blue and white, approximately fourteen feet long. He'd texted her a photo of the actual boat, so she had an idea what she was looking for. Once located, there was a good chance it would lead to the place where Jordan had spent his last night on earth. Finding it would be a priority for the police. At first light, two helicopters had been sent out to begin the search. Until the boat was found, Jane intended to keep her eyes open as she drove around the lake.

Her dad said he'd driven out to the lake house this morning and that it was a zoo, with friends and business staff descending from all parts of the country. Jane made a mental note to call her catering company and have half a dozen pastry trays sent over.

Before her dad had said good-bye, he'd asked her to go talk to Dahlia Grady, the woman who cleaned and restocked the Deeres' lake home twice a week each summer, and maintained the property for them during the winter months, when the family was mostly away. It wasn't much, but it was a start.

Jane parked her CR-V in front of a two-story Dutch Colonial and approached the front door. The wide front lawn had been raked, but the leaves from a giant maple had been swept into messy piles that, so far, had yet to be bagged. Ringing the bell, she waited on the front steps until the door was drawn back by a teenage girl wearing a red tank top, tight jeans, and a dazed look.

"Help you?" the girl asked.

"I'm looking for Dahlia Grady."

"Mom," the girl yelled, never taking her eyes off Jane. She fingered the gold stud in her ear, half leaning against door, taking in Jane's U of M varsity jacket. "Aren't you, like, kind of old to wear a letterman jacket?"

"Probably."

"Then why, like, do it?"

Jane had been cleaning out a bedroom closet a few nights ago, taking out her romantic frustrations by doing something useful, when she came across the maroon and gold jacket hanging way at the back. She hadn't seen it in years. When she tried it on and realized that it still fit, she stood in front of a mirror in her bedroom and decided she looked awesome—Avi's hated word. The dogs seemed to agree. "Maybe it's, like, my vain attempt to regain my lost youth."

The girl scowled.

Dahlia appeared behind her daughter. She was a small woman with short brown hair and wide, doll-like eyes partially hidden behind half-glasses. "Hi," she said. "Can I help you?"

Jane handed her a business card.

Adjusting the glasses, she looked it over. "You're a private investigator? Is this about Jordan Deere?"

"I'm working for the lawyer representing Kit and her family."

"How come they need a lawyer?"

"It's pretty standard in a murder investigation," said Jane.

"Uh-huh."

"I wonder if I could ask you a couple questions."

"Me? I don't know how I could help."

"I promise I won't take much of your time."

"Well," she said, sweeping a lock of hair off her forehead as her curiosity seemed to get the better of her reticence. "I just made a pot of tea. Come back to the kitchen."

As Jane followed her inside, the teenage girl returned to the couch, picked up the TV remote and changed the channel.

Dahlia poured tea into two cow-patterned mugs and nodded for Jane to sit at the table. "I'm still in shock about Jordan's death," she said. "You use honey or lemon?"

"Plain is fine," said Jane.

"I can't believe anyone would want to hurt that man," she began. "This is an awful world, you know that. When bad things can happen to such good people. It's why I don't watch the news anymore. All it does is depress me."

"How long have you known Jordan?" asked Jane.

"Eighteen—no, nineteen years. Poor Kit and the kids. They must be beside themselves with grief. I thought about calling over there, but I didn't want to bother them. I'll send flowers. This was supposed to be their special family time, you know. Jordan was so excited about the reunion."

"Have the police contacted you?"

The question stopped her. "Why would they contact me?"

"Sometimes people know things that might help but they don't realize the information they have is important."

She turned the mug of tea around in her hand. "I suppose. But . . . like what?"

Jane removed a notepad and pen from the inner pocket of her jacket. "For instance: Can you give me the names of any of Jordan's friends? Local people? The ones he invited over to the house? Or people he met for dinner. I understand he loved to play golf."

"Oh, that man. He was always reading golf magazines. Watching golf on TV. Have you ever watched a golf match?"

"Boring?" asked Jane.

"In the dictionary? Next to the word 'boring'? They have a golf club. Now, his friends. Okay. Let me think. There was Ann and Jerry Ott. They were over fairly frequently. I think Jerry sold him that new speedboat."

"Do you know where they live?"

"Wayzata, I think. Oh, and Virginia Austin. She was a good friend."

"Did they spend a lot of time together?"

"Oh, now. I know what you're thinking. No, it wasn't like that. Virginia was in her early seventies. Not sure where she lives, but I know she owned horses, stabled them on her property. Jordan would drive out and they'd ride together. That was another thing he loved. Horses."

Jane wrote the names down. Changing gears, she asked, "Can you tell me what a typical day would be like for Jordan?"

"Well, this summer in particular, his habits were pretty regular. Up early and out for a run. Home to shower and a light breakfast. Then he'd work in his office until at least one, sometimes later."

"Work on what?"

Lowering her eyes, she said, "That's something I wasn't supposed to know about."

"But you did?"

"I saw a few pages. Don't suppose it would hurt to talk about it now. Looked like a novel to me."

"He was writing a novel?"

"Think so."

"It wasn't, say, a memoir? You sure it was fiction?"

"There was lots of dialogue, so yeah, I'm almost positive. The scene I read was about this kid—his parents had this knock-down drag-out fight, which he overheard. Took place in Kentucky, back in the sixties. And then the kid goes out and rides his horse. He confides in the horse about his parents' fight, talks about how he feels. It was kind of sad and emotional. I felt sorry for the boy."

"Jordan grew up in Kentucky."

"Yeah, but it wasn't a biography. It was a story."

Jane wrote the word "novel" in her notes and underlined it. "So Jordan never said anything to you about it?"

"Not a word. That's why I figured it was a secret."

"What did he do the rest of the day?"

"Sometimes he worked down in his music studio, but most of the time I was there he'd be gone in the afternoons."

"Playing golf."

"I suppose."

"Did he stay out late? Was he a drinker? A partyer?"

"Sure, he drank, but I never saw him drunk in all the years I worked at the house. I have no idea about his evenings. I was always out of there by five."

"What about Booker and Chloe? What can you tell me about them?"

She sighed, took another sip of tea. "Booker was a quiet kid. We never said much to each other. Chloe was friendlier, but she had a lot of problems when she was in her early teens." She lowered her voice. "Food issues. Not sure you'd call it full-blown anorexia, but she sure did get thin there for a while. One year, she must have been fifteen, she never came to the summerhouse at all, not once. Kit told me she was in Europe, but for some reason, I never believed it. Jordan and Kit were always wonderfully generous to me. They were also very private. They really put in their time with those kids and their problems. But after their teens, they settled down. Booker went off to college on the East Coast, and Chloe went west."

Jane wrote Chloe's name and then the word "anorexic" with question marks next to them. All of this was interesting, though likely didn't have anything to do with Jordan's murder. "What about Beverly Elliot? What did you think of her?"

Dahlia laughed. "Badass Bev. That's what the kids called her. I think it was said affectionately. Beverly was great with them. So was Jordan's old friend, Tommy Prior. Those kids may not have had parents who were home every night of the year, but they were surrounded by people who loved them. Still, I don't imagine it was easy being the Deeres' kids, growing up in a fishbowl like they did. I think it's why Jordan and Kit tried to protect them, to keep their lives as private as possible."

"What about Archibald Van Arnam? Did you see him much?"

"Oh, sure. He was around all the time. He's Booker's godfather, you know. Ever since I can remember, he'd make sure Booker got some new electronic toy for his birthday, and Chloe would get a special stuffed animal. I overheard him once having this long conversation with Chloe about whether or not stuffed animals had souls. Chloe thought they did. Archie wasn't so sure. He can be such a curmudgeon. So intellectual and superior. It always surprised me when I'd see him with the kids. That's when the sweetness in him came out."

"I hear he doesn't like being called Archie."

"Chloe and Booker always called him that behind his back. They weren't being mean, just thought it was funny. I suppose I picked it up from them."

"And Jordan and Kit's relationship?" asked Jane.

"Solid as far as I know. Oh, they had their moments. Their tiffs. But it was never anything big. That is, with the exception of the children. Jordan thought Kit was too hard on Chloe. That she wanted her to live up an impossible standard. Kit felt Jordan never spent enough time with Booker, and that he was too lenient with him."

"What did you think?"

"That they were both right."

What parents didn't have child-rearing issues, thought Jane. Again, she wasn't sure if any of this was important to her investigation, though she wrote a few notes. "Did Jordan have any strange ideas, philosophies . . . anything that might have put him in contact with unsavory people?"

"No, he was just a regular guy. He was kind of superstitious. Always traveled with his oldest guitar—the one he was playing when he finally made it big. He told me once that on the night he started playing a new guitar, the concert didn't go well. So the next night he made sure the old guitar was sitting on the stage in a guitar stand. Seemed to work. He did that for the rest of his life. That old guitar was always on the stage somewhere."

"What else was he superstitious about?"

"Oh, lots of things. But the worst was crows."

"Crows?"

"He hated them—or was afraid of them. One time, when I was out sweeping the steps, I saw a crow land in the grass. It wasn't but a couple of seconds before Jordan came out of the house with a handgun and started shooting at the thing, all the while screaming for it to get out of his yard. It flew away before he hit it. Honestly, he really scared me."

"I'll bet."

"But that was the only time something like that ever happened. I need to make it clear, if I haven't already, that the Deeres have always been terrific to me. In fact, early on, when I was splitting from my husband, Jordan gave me the name of a family attorney he knew—a divorce lawyer. And then, when the divorce came through, he paid for all my legal fees. That was the kind of guy he was. He took care of his friends."

"This lawyer," said Jane, writing the word down and underlining it four times. "You say he was a friend of Jordan's?"

Dahlia nodded.

"Do you remember his name?"

She thought for a moment. "It was fifteen years ago. He was an American, but ethnically, probably Japanese or Korean. Wish I could remember his name. You know, I worry about my memory sometimes. Maybe I should start doing crossword puzzles to stimulate my brain cells."

"Do you think you could find it for me? I don't mean to push, but this could be important."

Setting her mug down, Dahlia said, "I'd have to look through my old files. I keep them in the basement. Might take a little time."

"You've got my card," said Jane. "If you want to help Kit and her family, this is the way to do it."

Dahlia removed the card from her pocket, read over it again, then placed it on the table. "I'm on it," she said. "I have a cleaning job this afternoon, but when I get home, I'll start looking. I'll call as soon as I find the name."

On her way back to the car, Jane took out her phone to check her messages. She had two voice mails.

The first was from Avi. "Jane, hi. It's me. Give me a call when you can."

Unusual, thought Jane sliding into the front seat of the Honda. A phone call instead of a text. Avi's voice sounded tentative, subdued, even a little nervous.

The second was from her dad: "Good news, Janey. Jordan's boat was found at the Heidelberg Club marina. The police aren't saying much. It's slip number 127. See what you can find out. Later, sweetheart."

The Heidelberg Country Club was one of the oldest private clubs on Lake Minnetonka. Though membership had once been restricted, it was now open to anyone who could afford the cost, which was, of course, another kind of restriction. Over the years, Jane had attended a couple of events in the banquet hall, one a wedding reception and the other a charity affair. She recalled lovely grounds with spectacular lake views, a pool, a couple of tennis courts, a marina and a nine-hole golf course. The club had been around since the early 1920s. The various outbuildings, all cream-colored stucco covered in geometric timbering, with dark cottage-style roofs, oozed a kind of picturesque Germanic charm. Approaching from the water or from the private drive that led to the front gate, Jane assumed that members were supposed to feel as if they were coming upon a small, prosperous, Alpine village. The main building, the Gasthaus on the northern edge of the property—on King's Bay—stood out from the other structures not only because it was bigger——four stories——but because it was made of stone. The interior had been preserved and looked exactly the same as it did in old photographs. In the last few years, the scuttlebutt around town was that the place was growing a little threadbare.

Lake Minnetonka was one of the ten biggest lakes in Minnesota——a state that advertised itself as having ten thousand lakes, though in reality, it was closer to twelve. Lake Minnetonka had some hundred and twenty-five miles of shoreline. Jordan's boat could have been anywhere along the shore. For the police to have found it so quickly was a major accomplishment, and would undoubtedly be celebrated on the evening news. It also suggested that Jordan hadn't tried to hide his destination on Saturday night. What that meant, in the larger scheme of things, was anybody's guess.

Deciding to call Avi right away and not stew about it, Jane tapped in her number. She waited through several rings until Avi picked up.

"Hey, Jane. You got my message."

"How come I merit an actual phone call?"

Avi laughed.

To Jane, it sounded less an expression of mirth than one of tension.

"Yeah, well. About that text I sent you the other night. I hope you aren't upset. I was pretty hammered. My first mistake was sending you a text when I was in such bad shape. My second mistake was sending it."

The subtext in that message, while cryptic, seemed clear enough to Jane. She'd read it over several times, always coming to the same conclusion.

"Not sure what you thought I meant," continued Avi. "Actually, I wrote it and *I'm* not even sure what I meant."

Getting into this can of worms over the phone wasn't smart. This was a conversation they needed to have face-to-face. "How are the revisions going?"

"Good. I'm pretty much done until I see see Elaine Ducasse again on Wednesday. I started thinking, hell, I've got a free day tomorrow. Why don't you fly down? From Minneapolis to Chicago is like, half an hour in the air. We could spend the entire day together. What do you say?"

"If it's such a short trip, why don't you fly back here? Just let me know when the plane arrives and I'll meet you at the airport."

"But, see, I promised I'd stay in Chicago until all the revisions are done."

"Are you suggesting you're trapped? That Elaine would drop the book if you weren't available the instant she asks to see you?"

Another nervous laugh. "No. Of course not."

"Where are you?"

"Me? Where am I?"

"Yes."

"I'm—"

"At the hotel?" asked Jane.

"Actually, I'm at a cabin on Lake Michigan. It's only about an hour away."

"Really? A cabin. Is it nice?"

"It's amazing. Right on the water."

"How'd you find out about the place?"

Silence. "It belongs to a friend of Julia's."

Ah, Julia. Jane assumed they'd get there eventually. "She with you?"

"No."

"So you're there all by yourself."

"Yeah. Right now I am."

Splitting hairs, thought Jane.

"She drove up yesterday around noon. I came up later in the day."

"And spent the night."

"Now, don't go making this into something it isn't. I slept in one bedroom, Julia slept in the other. She was just being nice to offer the cabin. I've been wound pretty tight with this book. She left to drive back to Chicago right after breakfast. I decided to stay on for a few more hours, do some thinking about the story arc for my next book. So, come on, what do you say? Can you fly down? I guarantee I'll show you a good time."

"I can't," said Jane, doing her best to ignore the obvious seduction in Avi's voice. "Too much going on here."

"Oh. Okay I understand. Well. Um. I, ah—"

"Let me know how everything goes with Elaine on Wednesday."

"Yeah, for sure. Maybe I'll stay up here another night. It's really beautiful. A great place to relax."

They talked for a few more minutes about nothing in particular, and finally said their good-byes. Jane sat for a moment with her hands on the steering wheel, staring out through the dirty windshield. So this was the way it was going to be. Half-truths mixed with outright lies. Had it always been like that with Avi, and she was just now seeing it?

Cut your losses, Lawless. Don't be a fool. Get out now.

Starting the motor, Jane sat for another moment, forcing her feelings away. She had to stay focused on the matter at hand. There would be time to think about Avi—to make decisions—later. Switching on the turn signal, she edged away from the curb. Next stop: the Heidelberg Club.

17

With throngs of business types, band members, and other assorted friends arriving at the summerhouse since early morning, Booker was slowly losing his mind. Chloe seemed to take comfort in the bedlam, spending part of her time in the family room helping brainstorm plans for the funeral and the rest of her time in the kitchen making sandwiches. She'd always loved to be around food. Loved to cook, even read cookbooks. What she didn't like, strange as it sounded, was eating. Booker had never seen her wolf down an entire package of cookies before. He figured it was the way she dealt with grief.

The ever inebriated Tommy crept around the edges of the activity, sipping surreptitiously from his mug of eighty-proof coffee, looking gloomy, and fearful that someone might actually say something to him that would require more than a one-word response. Beverly, playing her usual role as Ethel Mertz to his mother's top-banana Lucy Ricardo, busied herself by ferrying trays of Chloe's sandwiches between the rooms.

By eleven, Booker was up to his eyeballs in family solidarity, in soldiering bravely on, eyes fixed on the handsome visage of Jordan Emory Deere, the newly minted country music saint. When placed in the hands of their expensive public relations machine, his father's death seemed, for all its heartbreaking significance, to be simply one more excuse for an orgy of lavish promotion. Booker found the entire enterprise grotesque. He needed a bump, a joint, or failing that, some fresh air.

Grabbing his keys, he ducked out a back door, jumped in his rented Lincoln, and tore out of the compound, heading back up to King's Bay. Something had been bothering him ever since he'd watched Erin melt down after learning about his dad's murder. He'd formed a theory and, with nothing else on his plate, decided to take it for a test drive.

Yesterday afternoon, after returning to their table at the Hofbrau, Erin had stuck around long enough to be polite, to express her sorrow, though not long enough to finish her Irish coffee. For such a creative woman, she'd offered a pathetically standard excuse about not realizing how late it was and needing to get back to her room at the Gasthaus. Booker offered to walk her up the hill, but she made more excuses and eventually, after thanking him for lunch, left without so much as a backward glance. It would have been impossible not to notice that all the color had drained from her cheeks during that phone conversation out in the lobby. Again, an excessive reaction over the death of a man she hardly knew.

Booker stopped for gas in the town of King's Bay. As he sailed along the back road to the club's front gate, he mulled over his options. He could approach the situation any of several ways. By the time he was standing in front of the reception desk, he'd made his choice.

"Hi," he said, smiling at the young woman behind the counter. Since he had no perceptible charm and his looks never got him anywhere, he came straight to the point. "I'm Booker Deere, Jordan Deere's son."

"Oh. My." She seemed flustered. "I was so sorry to hear about your father. He was such a wonderful man."

"You knew him?"

"I didn't exactly *know* him, like as in friends, but we talked sometimes."

"That's nice." It was also odd. His parents maintained their family membership to the club, but as far as he knew, neither of them ever drove up here anymore. They preferred the newer clubs with better amenities, the ones closer to the summerhouse. Booker's dad loved the championship golf course at the Wayzata Country Club. The Heidelberg's course wasn't in the same league. "I'm tying up some loose ends," he said, drumming his fingers on the counter. "I understand my father made a room reservation for a friend— Erin O'Brian. I need to know if he paid for her stay. If not, I'll take care of it now."

The receptionist tapped the computer keyboard in front of her, checked the monitor. "It's all been handled. Looks like he put it on his credit card."

"He did? I mean, good. That's good."

"Anything else I can help you with?"

So Booker's theory had been correct. His dad was the "friend" who'd booked Erin's stay at the club. Had she called him or had he called her? That begged the question about why she was in town. She'd never really said. Was it possible that Erin and his father had stayed in touch all these years? Or had she called out of the blue to ask for the favor because she'd once been close to Chloe? Seemed like a stretch. It was even more of a stretch to think Erin's reaction to his father's death was simply because he'd paid for a room at the Heidelberg Club.

The receptionist's expression turned sad again. "It's such a shock. Your father, I mean."

"It's a shock, all right," said Booker. After reading his dad's manuscript, he'd gotten used to the idea that his old man had lied to him all of his life. The more he thought about those secrets, the more it all seemed kind of silly. But this? This was fascinating. You devious old goat, he thought, smiling to himself. What the hell were you up to?

Striding up the concrete jetty into the Heidelberg marina, Jane felt lost in an alternate universe—either that, or at a huge boat expo. She wasn't poor, by anyone's standards, but the people who docked their sport yachts, cruisers, and sailboats in this marina were in a different class altogether. Must be nice to own one of these monsters, she thought, knowing each cost more than most people's homes.

Finding slip 127 was easy enough. The crisscrossed yellow police tape had been visible from her car, even before she walked out to take a closer look. The boat itself was gone, as was any indication of police activity—except for the tape.

"They hauled it away about an hour ago," said a man sitting on a chair bolted to the aft portion of his yacht. He was attempting to untangle a fishing line on one of the dozen or so rods leaning against the rail.

Shading her eyes from the sun, Jane asked, "Did you know the man who docked his boat in that slip?"

"Deere? Not well. My wife has a bunch of his CDs, thought he was the sexiest man alive—well, except for me, of course." He winked. "Awful what happened to him."

"Did the police talk to you about it?"

"Nope. As I was heading in, they were leaving."

Jane stepped a few paces closer. "Deere left his boat here on Saturday evening. We're trying to figure out where he spent the night."

"*We?* You a cop?"

"I'm private, working for Kit Deere's lawyer."

"Ah." He yanked on the knotted fishing line, looking frustrated. "Deere was around quite a bit this summer. Most times I'd see him with his golf bag heading up to the clubhouse."

"Don't suppose you saw him on Saturday night."

"As a matter of fact, I did. No golf clubs that night. He tied off his boat, then waited in the parking lot until a car picked him up."

"Can you describe the car?"

He shrugged. "Black. Everything's either black or white these days. What happened to color? Yellow. Green. Blue. Anyway, don't quote me, but I think it was an Audi. Newer model."

"Did you get a look at the driver?"

"Sorry." He pointed to the top of a utility pole. "But I'll bet that thing did."

Jane turned to find a security camera. She wondered if the police had noticed it. It didn't seem like something DePetro would miss. "Did you ever see Deere with anyone? A friend. Man? Woman?"

"He ate at the Rhineland Grill on occasion. I'm afraid I never took much notice of who he was with." Instead of continuing to try to untangle the knot, the man took out a nail clipper and cut it off. After reattaching the hook, he secured it to the cork at the bottom of the pole and stood up. "Wish I could be more help."

"No, this is all good," said Jane. She handed over one of her cards. "If you think of anything else, give me a call."

"Will do," said the man, pocketing the card. "Somebody needs to fry for what happened to that poor guy. I hope you find the bastard. Or, you never know. I suppose it could be a woman."

"I wondered where you'd hidden that," said Kit, leaning her shoulder against the edge of the garage. "Since the police didn't find it, I figured you'd stashed it somewhere."

Beverly was down on all fours, a pile of dirt on either side of a

133

small, deep hole. She'd just removed a metal box and was brushing clumped soil off the top. "You shouldn't sneak up on people."

"Your secret is safe with me," said Kit.

Beverly gave a bitter grunt, sitting down cross-legged in the grass and pulling the box toward her. She did it the way she did everything, aggressively and impatiently. Opening the top, she removed a terry cloth towel wrapped around a 9mm Smith & Wesson.

"Why'd you bring that along?"

"Protection."

"Who from?"

Beverly shrugged. "Better safe than sorry."

"The police could come back. Maybe you should leave it buried."

"I need to get rid of it."

"Your father's gun? You said it meant the world to you when he gave it to you."

Beverly shook her head. "This is a nightmare."

Kit was learning firsthand about nightmares—the waking kind. She'd been imprisoned inside one ever since Jordan had asked for a divorce. Those few words had quite literally turned her life upside down. Her focus at the moment was simply hanging on. She had to stay strong, to protect her children and her husband's legacy. When she'd glanced at herself in the mirror this morning, an old woman had stared back at her. How could that be? Where had the time gone?

"Come sit down," said Beverly, holding out her hand. "Misery loves company."

Glad that she'd thought to change into a pair of jeans and a sweater for her walk down to the beach, Kit joined her on the dying grass.

"Did Archie finally leave?" asked Beverly.

"Poor man. All he wants to do is help."

"He's driving everyone crazy."

"I know."

"Including me."

Hands clasped around her knees, Kit said, "You know, years ago, I thought maybe the two of you—"

"No way," said Beverly. "Not my type."

"No." She knew that. Why had she said it? Maybe it was habit. But then, for Kit, pretending wasn't just habit, it was her life. "I need to say something."

"No. You don't."

Why did one moment of truth always necessitate another? "I don't know what I'd do without you. Ever since I can remember, you've been the rock at the center of my life."

Beverly wrapped the gun up and placed it back into the metal box.

"You know I love you."

"Sure."

Except, not the way you want, thought Kit. "Listen to me."

Beverly started to get up. "What should we have for dinner? I'll run up to the grocery store this afternoon. I could make a big pot of chili, or we could have—"

"Sit down. I don't want to talk about dinner. I want to talk about us."

"Nothing to say that hasn't been said."

Kit slipped her hand around Beverly's. "I know . . . you have . . . feelings for me. Feelings I've never been able to reciprocate. The only way I could deal with it and not lose you—and that was my greatest fear—was by pretending I didn't notice. By ignoring the elephant in the room. You have no idea how much I wish I could be the way you want me to be."

"Just stop, okay?"

"No. Now that it's out there on the table, you have to let me finish. I've taken from you and given very little in return."

"Not true. You've shared your life with me. Given me a job. A home. A family."

"But not what you really wanted."

Beverly closed the lid on the box. "Not everyone wants to jump your bones," she said, her voice full of bitterness. She seemed to regret the words the moment they left her mouth.

"It's just . . . I'm not attracted to women. I've thought about it, but it's not me."

"I get it, Kit. You don't need to draw me a picture."

"*Do* you get it? This has been hard for me, too. I owe you so much."

"Fine. You've acknowledged the elephant. Let's move on."

For years, Beverly had been a valued partner in crime. She'd known, and probably loathed, some of the men Kit had dated, and yet she'd helped her keep many of those assignations and long-term affairs a secret. How hard it must have been for her to watch Kit rushing off, in the flush of some silly new infatuation, leaving her behind to take care of business.

And that brought Kit back to the elephant. Had acknowledging Beverly's feelings been a mistake? Watching her brush dirt back into the hole and pack it down with her hands, she feared that the uninvited pachyderm wasn't merely some enormous unwanted visitor. It was a dangerous, mercurial, beast. Once acknowledged, given its due, but still shown the door, it could easily trample all Kit's delicately balanced plans on its way out.

As Cordelia was making a hasty exit from her theater office that afternoon, on her way to a meeting at the McKnight Foundation, she nearly trampled a woman who was coming into the main office from the hallway. "Oh, sorry," she said, noticing that the woman was teary eyed and unsteady on her feet. Helping her over to a chair, she asked, "Can I get you a glass of water?"

"I . . . I'm looking for Cordelia Thorn."

"That would be me."

The fifty-something woman had a strong, likable face, but seemed uncertain, disoriented, as if she were moving through a dream world.

"I was told you could show me . . . the hole in the wall. The man buried behind it, William Edward Chapman—he was my husband."

Now it was Cordelia's turn to need a chair. The police officer she'd spoken to never mentioned a wife. Just a sister.

"I'm Candice. Used to be Candice Chapman, but now it's Candice Johnson. I remarried. I've had a good life. Can't complain. Three wonderful children. For a long time I was angry at him. The rest of the family thought something terrible had happened, but me, I was sure he'd run off."

"That's—"

"I hated him for a long time. Everyone assumed we were happily married. Eddy—that's what I called him—was on the fast track as a banker, just like his dad. We lived in Bloomington. Nice house. Married six years. One morning he left for work and never came home."

"How did—"

"I guess his family was right all along. He didn't just take off on me—on his entire life. The thing is, I knew he wasn't happy. Not with his job, and not with me. I don't think we would have made it. I wanted children. He didn't."

"Not a—"

"No, not a good thing. It's silly, isn't it? That two people don't discuss something that important before they tie the knot. The police worked the case for months, but never did find out what happened. His parents hired a private investigator to continue the search. I thought it was a waste of time and money. At least on that one, I was right. The man's investigation never went anywhere."

The woman obviously needed to tell her story so badly that she barely took a breath. Cordelia decided to just sit back and listen. She couldn't seem to interject a thought or a question no matter how hard she tried.

"Back during the initial investigation, the police kept asking questions about Eddy's secrets—if he was into drugs, or gambling, or dating prostitutes. I mean, honestly. The man was pure Sammy Cream Cheese. He didn't drink. Didn't smoke. Was in a bowling league. He didn't even swear." She hesitated. "Then again—"

Cordelia lifted her eyebrows encouragingly.

"I could be wrong, but I think he was cheating on me. A few months before he disappeared, he started dressing nicer. Got his hair styled. Took off a few pounds. Not that he was fat. Eddy was a big, good-looking guy. He always could turn a woman's head. He promised me he'd be faithful, that he wouldn't be like his dad. But you know what men are like." She waited for Cordelia to nod. "Yeah, easy to promise, hard to follow through. The thing is, if we'd stayed together, we would have made each other miserable. Both of us would have eventually felt trapped. But when the police came by the house to give me the news, when I learned that Eddy's body had been found—" She took a breath, held it, then slowly let it out. "I could hardly believe what they were telling me. Eddy was murdered? My Eddy? His body stuffed behind a wall in the basement of some nameless, crumbling old building in downtown Minneapolis?"

"It's a theater. It's not crumbling."

"Who would want to hurt him? I kept asking myself that. And then I thought—"

"What? What?"

"Well, I mean, *you* think about it. What if the woman he was seeing was married? If her husband was the jealous type, if he owned a gun and was mad enough . . ." Her voice trailed off.

"Murdered by a jealous husband?"

"The oldest story in the book."

"But why bury him here? Was Eddy a theater lover?"

"We saw a few plays together before we were married. None after."

"Did he have ties to this building?"

"To the best of my knowledge, no."

"So why was he buried *here*?" asked Cordelia, musing out loud.

"I did love him," said Candice, sniffing into her tissue. "I never really mourned him because I was so angry. Now . . . everything's changed. I feel awful."

"You mustn't." Cordelia patted the woman's knee.

"To mourn properly, I need to see the hole. Will you take me?"

"Of course."

"You're very kind."

"I am," said Cordelia. She waited for the woman to pull herself together, then helped her up and led her to the elevators.

18

Jane was torn. She had a number of leads to pursue in order to locate Jordan's friends. On the other hand, stacks of work awaited her at the Lyme House. More critically, she'd put off an important meeting with her new sous chef.

Peer Valdimarsson was a Minnesotan who had spent the last ten years working his way through restaurants in Sweden, Denmark, Iceland, and Norway. His interest and knowledge of Nordic cuisine was why Jane had hired him. In less than two weeks, he'd presented her with dozens of new menu options that had taken her thinking about Scandinavian cuisine and turned it on its head. Since this was a new direction for the Lyme House, Jane had decided to offer an eight-course tasting menu and bring it out during the holiday season.

So far, they'd agreed on seven courses: a pork belly in a birchwood bouillon with roasted barley and watercress; duck eggs, wild garlic flowers, and sautéed radish; herring in red currant juice, elderflowers, beetroot, and wild mushrooms; bone marrow, chestnuts, warm chocolate, served with rye bread; and cardamom aebleskiver, roasted hazelnuts, and milk ice.

Jane needed no more than an hour of Peer's time to come to a decision on the final offering. She met with him before dinner that night and together they worked out the complete list, celebrating with an ice-cold shot of aquavit when they were done. They both wanted the Nordic cuisine tasting menu, if possible, to go up by the week before Thanksgiving. Some local sourcing still had to be worked out. This special tasting menu was something that customers would need to order a day in advance—also something new for the Lyme House.

Feeling buoyed and excited, Jane spent the next hour up in the main dining room, meeting and greeting customers. She stood briefly near the pass in the kitchen and watched the tickets fly in and the food, each plate a work of art, fly out. Business was good, even better than it had been before the recession. She felt a rush of gratitude mixed with a sense of pride as she walked back down to her office.

Her cell phone rang shortly after eight.

"Jane Lawless," she said, saving the computer page she'd been working on.

"Hello?" came a tentative voice. "This is Dahlia Grady—the Deeres' cleaning woman."

"Oh, hi." She'd been hoping she would hear from Dahlia tonight.

"Do you have a pen and a piece of paper? I've got the name of that lawyer who handled my divorce. The one Jordan recommended."

"Wow, great," said Jane. Pulling a notepad close, she said, "Shoot."

"Joji Mura. Really great guy." She repeated the number. "His office was in Hopkins. Not sure if it's still there."

"Wonderful," said Jane. "Much appreciated."

"I wish I could do more. I still can't believe anyone would want to hurt Jordan."

"This may help."

Dahlia seemed to want to talk, to process what had happened. "I don't believe I've ever known anyone who seemed more alive. It's just so hard to think he's gone, that I'll never see him again."

Jane sat back and mostly listened. They spoke for the next twenty minutes, until Dahlia said she had to go make sure her daughter had done her homework. Jane thanked her again and said good night.

The time had come for Cordelia to drive out to Frenchman's Bay and begin her due diligence at Chez Deere. Jane had asked her to insert herself into the investigation in her typically subtle manner, and that's just what she intended to do.

The first order of business, as always, was to decide what to wear to the occasion. Something subdued but hopeful. Something vibrant without being festive. Something soothing, but not maternal. Elegant, but not flamboyant. It occurred to Cordelia, as she pawed through her closet, that she could be describing her appearance as a fine wine. How appropriate.

Tossing a few frocks onto her bed, she concluded that red was perhaps too much. Yellow too hard on the eyes of the weeping. Black just *too* depressing. Green much too buoyant. Purple, the color of royalty was, like the Wee Bear's bed in the Goldilocks fairy tale, just right. A purple cape cardigan over tight black jeans and calf-high leather boots. Perfection itself.

The trip out to the lake was uneventful, except for an excited phone call from Hattie informing her that she'd finally received her first issue of *Sky and Telescope* magazine. It was hard for Cordelia to get worked up about these matters, so she simply let her little niece enthuse for a few minutes and then, as she approached the Deeres' lighted front gate, she said she had to go, that Bolger would give her a kiss good night from Cordelia and that they would have French toast—Hattie's favorite—for breakfast in the morning.

Cordelia sailed past the security guard with a simple wave of her driver's license. Kit had given the hired muscle a list of people who were allowed in. Cordelia had expected to see throngs of reporters and camera crews attempting to scale the walls. To her amazement, the road leading up to the gate was dark and quiet.

Chloe met Cordelia at the front door.

"Mom said you were coming," she said, giving her a welcoming hug.

Since she had on a coat, Cordelia asked her if she was going out.

"Booker's pulling his car around. We're off to see a movie. I hope that doesn't sound cold."

"Depends on the movie," said Cordelia.

"Funny." She didn't laugh. "I've cried so much in the last two days I'm not sure I've got any tears left in me."

"Everyone grieves in their own way. Don't let anyone make you feel bad or wrong about your process. When I lost my mother, my feelings of loss came in waves. I could go for days without any sadness at all, and then I'd be driving home from a store and I'd have to pull over because my eyes had turned into water faucets."

Chloe gave Cordelia another hug.

"You know how sorry I am about what happened. Any time you need to talk, just give me a call. That goes for Booker, too."

Booker honked. Chloe thanked her and left.

Cordelia spent the next few minutes wandering through the first floor. Most of the rooms were abuzz with activity of one form or another, filled with men wearing ties and dress slacks and women in business drag. She asked a burly young man in a western-style shirt stuffing the last bite of a sandwich into his mouth if he knew where Kit was.

"In the kitchen," he said.

Cordelia knew the house well. In a way, the reality of Jordan's death hadn't really hit until this moment. She was used to seeing him bustling from room to room, offering refills on drinks, encouraging guests to get something to eat, talking animatedly, laughing. He'd been a beautiful man. Vigorous. Charismatic. Perhaps a little too fixated on his career, but then most successful people were. His music, especially the lyrics to some of his ballads, reflected a sensitive side that wasn't always apparent in normal conversation.

Unable to find Kit in the kitchen, Cordelia walked into the breakfast room. It was her favorite place in the entire house, with its long row of small-paned windows facing east toward the bay. In the morning, it was filled with sunlight. Tonight, however, the room felt shrouded in gloom.

Kit sat at a table made out of old, weathered wood planks, a bottle of wine and a half-filled glass in front of her. A weak wedge of light from the kitchen fell across the far end of the room. "I wondered if you were still coming," she said. She didn't look up.

Cordelia pulled out one of the captain's chairs and sat down. "Tell me how you're doing—and don't give me the same bullshit you give everyone else."

The comment caused a brief smile. "I've been better. Let's leave it at that."

"Anything new from the police?"

"They were here again a couple of hours ago. Did more searching."

"And? Did they find anything?"

"Booker said he saw one of the uniformed officers put a plastic bag in the trunk of a squad car. I have no idea what was in it."

"Have you talked to the lead detective? Can't remember his name."

"DePetro. No. Not today. The less I see of him, the better." She pressed her hands to her eyes. "God, but I miss him. It's crazy, you know? Days would go by and I wouldn't even think about him. His presence in my life was such a given—like beautiful background music. Now—"

"This is different."

"You think?"

"How are the kids handling it? I saw Chloe when I came in. She looked pretty rough."

"Chloe wears her heart on her sleeve. Always has. She's been gutted by everything that's happened. I'm *so* worried about her. We've gone on several walks together. She's eating erratically, and you know what that means. I'm terrified this is going to kick off another episode. I tried to broach the subject, but she cut me off. Said she was okay. Of course she's not okay. Cordelia—" She hesitated. "This is hard to admit, but I'm scared. I'm her mother. I should know what to do, how to reach her. But I don't. Maybe Jordan was right. Maybe I did insist on impossible standards when she was growing up. I know I haven't always been the best mother, the best example—"

"Does she seem depressed?"

"She's always a little depressed, but she's on medication. She sees a therapist regularly. I guess, as long as she's still talking, as long as she comes out of her room to be with the family, then we're okay. It's just . . . it's all so hard." She took several swallows of wine. "Booker, he's another story entirely. It's like his dad's death hasn't even fazed him. I don't understand it."

"He's always been a stoic."

"Yeah, you're right, but I'm his mother. Why can't he let his guard down with me? I've been trying to spend private time with both of my children, to be open with them about my feelings. At the same time I've been trying my best to hold it together because there's so much to do. Statements to the press. Funeral arrangements. Papers to be executed and signed. Business decisions. And

Tommy, he's been in a bourbon haze ever since Sunday morning. We need him to help us make decisions. He should be the one talking to Jordan's recording label. Get this: The company wants to put out a memorial CD. Pisses me off, you know? They can't even give us five minutes to grieve before they move in and start figuring out a way to make money off the situation. I've had half a dozen freelance writers contact me wanting to get my permission, and my help, to write Jordan's authorized biography. One guy is already working on a true crime angle. You shake a tree in this land of opportunity and flocks of slimy, money-hungry hustlers fall out. I'm not against making a living, but this is way beyond the pale."

Cordelia's gaze drifted toward the windows, to the distant lights across the bay. "It's hard to take this all in, to believe it's happening."

Kit released a quick, resigned breath. "I'm glad you're here. It helps to talk."

"Did Jordan leave a will?"

"Everything's in trust. The money is primarily divided between me and the kids. There are a few substantial personal bequests. One to Tommy. A few charities. I inherit the house in Nashville. Chloe gets this one. Booker inherits the horse ranch."

"What on earth is Booker going to do with a horse ranch?"

Kit glanced over. "Jordan's last little joke. I find it hilarious."

Hilarious or nasty, thought Cordelia. "And how's Beverly doing?"

"She's——" She shrugged. "Beverly."

"The good-hearted grump. Is that a cliché? Like the hooker with a heart of gold?"

"Might be. But it's who she is."

"I can't remember. How long have you known her?"

Kit sighed. "Since we were kids. And then, during Beverly's first year at the U—the same year I was crowned Princess Kay of the Milky Way—I used to crash at her apartment when I couldn't get home. Eventually, I moved in with her and her roommate. It was fun. We were young. We knew a lot of the same people. She quit school to get a job her junior year. Just couldn't stand all the studying. I didn't blame her. It wasn't for me, either. By that time, I was doing local theater, starting to make a name for myself."

"Did someone mention my name?" asked Beverly, coming through the door carrying a tray of dessert pastries. "Anybody hungry? I've got a few left."

"This is crazy," said Kit. "I'm hiring a caterer first thing tomorrow morning. You're going to run yourself ragged cooking for all these people."

"I didn't make any of this," said Beverly, setting the tray down on the table. "Jane Lawless sent half a dozen boxes of the stuff over from her restaurant, along with four of their signature cheesecakes."

"That was incredibly kind," said Kit.

"I have great taste in friends," said Cordelia.

Kit held up the wine bottle. "I'm happy to share."

"I'm fine," said Cordelia. She hadn't seen Beverly in several years, and wasn't surprised to find that she looked much the same as always—a walking, talking advertisement for Cabela's. Cordelia freely admitted that she was a snob when it came to clothing. Not that she was against the "Cabela's look," just not 24-7. Tonight, Beverly was swathed in her usual construction-worker chic: olive-green canvas pants and heavy-duty plaid flannel shirt. With her blunt-cut gray hair, and deeply tanned skin, she gave the impression of a handsome older butch, someone who didn't care what others thought of her as long as she was comfortable. Cordelia generally took the same position. She'd always been on the side of people who'd figured out what was right for them and strode off proudly into the world in their black Dracula capes or hunting-gear drag.

"Sit with us," said Kit, nodding to an empty chair. "I thought that since Cordelia was here, she might take our minds off our problems. Why don't you tell us what's happening with you? Your new theater?"

"Ah, yes, the Thorn Lester Playhouse."

"The new love of your life?" asked Kit.

"Yes, I believe that's true, although my new love seems to have a few warts."

"Nothing too terrible, I hope," said Beverly.

Both women gazed at her expectantly, waiting to be entertained.

"Actually——" What she was about to say had ghoulish aspects to it. Nevertheless, she knew it would become one of her favorite anecdotes. "Jane and I were in the basement of the theater a couple of days ago looking at a section that had once been used as a speakeasy back in the late twenties and early thirties. Archibald Van Arnam's doing some research for me on the history of the building. As I understand it, the two people who owned the place at the time were in some sort of financial trouble that caused a gangland shoot-out. They were, shall we say, rubbed out. You can still see the bullet holes in the old mahogany bar in the basement."

"Leave it to you to buy a theater with a history," said Beverly.

"There's more," said Cordelia. "While we were looking around, we found this bricked-up section behind the bar. When we broke through it, which we had to do because . . . you know . . . inquiring minds . . . we found a skeleton. The skull had a bullet hole clean through the forehead."

"Part of the gangland shooting?" asked Kit.

"At first, we weren't sure. The police came out and bagged the evidence. A ring, a billfold, the bones—and the skull. I found out this morning that the skeleton belonged to a man."

"The plot thickens," said Kit, giving Beverly an amused look.

"The guy's name was Chapman. Seems he went missing in the summer of 1980."

"Chapman?" repeated Kit, eyes narrowing, more interested now than amused. "Do you know his first name?"

"William Edward. Apparently, he went by Eddy."

"Eddy Chapman?" said Kit, sitting up straight.

"You knew him?"

"He was a banker? Early thirties?"

"That's the guy." Switching her gaze to Beverly, Cordelia noted a similar change in expression.

"He was a regular at your theater back then," said Beverly.

"I even dated him," said Kit, looking more than a little flustered.

With all the stolen glances ricocheting between the two women, Cordelia felt like she was watching a ping-pong match. "You must have known he disappeared."

"I thought . . . I mean, I assumed, when he stopped calling, that he'd lost interest."

"He was married."

"He was? Are you kidding me? He never said a word about it."

Beverly reacted by folding her hands on the table and staring at them.

"I can't believe it," said Kit. "And to think, all these years, he was buried there in the basement of that theater." She shivered.

"A homicide," said Cordelia. "His wife said he left for work one morning and never came home." She waited for a reaction. When there was none, she said, segueing flawlessly into her sleuthing idiom, "If you knew him, maybe you've got some idea who might have wanted to hurt him."

"No. No idea at all," said Kit.

"You?" asked Cordelia, turning to Beverly.

"I only talked to the guy a couple of times. I can't even remember what he looked like."

All three women were startled by the sound of a knock. "Excuse me," said the burly young man in the western shirt. "The police are here and need to talk to you, Mrs. Deere."

"Now what?" said Kit, pushing away from the table and following him out, with Beverly hot on her heels.

Cordelia hurried after them, skidding to a stop in the front hall. A tall, dark, reasonably attractive plain-clothes officer flanked by two uniforms, one a man and the other a woman, held up a piece of paper.

"Sergeant DePetro," said Kit. "What's going on?"

"I have a warrant here for the arrest of Thomas Prior."

"Tommy?" said Kit, looking startled.

The young man in the western shirt pointed to a hallway. "He's in the media room. I think he's asleep."

"Show me," ordered DePetro.

Everyone gathered in the doorway to watch DePetro and the officers surround a man slumped over a table, snoring.

"Mr. Prior?" said DePetro, shaking his shoulder. "Wake up." When Tommy didn't move, DePetro nodded to one of the uniforms and said, "Wake him."

Grabbing the back of Tommy's hair, the male patrolman yanked his head up.

"Hey, stop it," said Tommy, pushing the man's hand away.

"Thomas Prior, I am arresting you for the murder of Jordan Deere."

"Huh?" he said, looking around for a few upside down seconds. "What—"

As DePetro read him his rights, Tommy tried to stand. The

male officer pulled his hands behind his back and handcuffed them.

"Why . . . why are you doing this?" demanded Tommy, swaying on his feet, his eyes frozen wide. "I never . . . you think I murdered Jordan? That's crazy."

Kit leaned over to Cordelia and said, "Go call Ray Lawless. Tell him about the arrest. That it's an emergency."

Backing out of the doorway, Cordelia returned to the kitchen. Grabbing a cordless off the island, she tapped in Ray's home number. "Come on, Perry Mason," she whispered, drumming her red nails against the granite counter. "Answer the goddamned phone."

19

It was going on midnight when Jane pulled into her driveway. As thoughts of Jordan Deere and his family tumbled around inside her mind, she did a double take. Backing up a few feet, she saw that Avi's car was parked in front of the house. She hadn't expected this and was hardly prepared for the conversation their problems demanded.

Entering through the back door, Jane heard the usual patter of dog paws as Mouse and Gimlet raced into the kitchen to greet her. She crouched down and pulled them into her arms. Gimlet did her happy dance, balancing on her two back feet. Mouse nosed Jane's hand, asking for a scratch. Finally, the welcome complete, Jane rose and grabbed a bottle of single malt off the counter, poured herself a drink, downed it in one neat gulp, and then walked out of the kitchen, through the dining room, into the living room.

She was still struggling with how best to handle things, when, instead of Avi, Julia stood up and turned toward her. She'd been sitting on the couch.

"What are you doing here?" demanded Jane.

"What a wonderfully warm welcome. It's nice to see you, too."

"Where's Avi?"

Julia gave Jane a quizzical look. "She's in Chicago."

"Then why is her car outside?"

"Ah," said Julia. "I get it. You thought she'd come back to spend the night. No, sorry. It's just me. Avi left her car in the airport lot. I asked for her keys before I left, since I didn't want to take a cab when I got back to town. Poor Janey. You're disappointed."

"How did you get in here?"

"Your neighbor, Evelyn Bratrude. She came over to let the dogs out about eight. Saw me sitting on the front steps. We're old friends, you know—from the years you and I were together. She let me in. Don't blame her. She didn't think she was doing anything wrong. She's always been such a help to you with your various varmints. I see you have a new dog. The curly little black one. Never thought of you as the poodle type."

"She was a stray. Needed a home."

"Sure," said Julia, moving around the end of the couch to face Jane without any furniture between them. "You're good with strays."

"You shouldn't be so hard on yourself, Julia. I didn't think of you that way when we first met."

"You're getting better at sparing with me. I like that." She stepped closer, sniffed Jane's breath. "I see. I could be wrong, but I'd say that's scotch. Aren't you going to offer me one?"

"You're here for a reason. What is it?"

"Can't I merely stop by to say hi? See how you're doing? I thought we agreed to be friends. Lesbians are supposed to be good at that—not kicking the ex out the door forever just because the relationship fizzled."

"That hardly covers what happened to us. Lies don't really qualify as communication."

Julia smiled as she stepped around Jane and sauntered toward the kitchen.

Jane figured she'd have to play her game if she wanted to find out why she'd come. She also figured that Julia had hauled her usual fire bomb with her. Like Robert Duvall in *Apocalypse Now,* she loved the smell of napalm in the morning.

Standing in the kitchen doorway, Jane watched Julia pour herself a drink. She was still a beautiful woman. Golden hair. Slim and elegant in her gray pinstriped business suit and high heels.

Julia held up the bottle, nodding to the empty glass on the counter. "Another?"

"Why not?"

They took chairs on either side of the kitchen table. Jane was tired, but the booze had centered her. As the alcohol moved through her system, she felt her muscles loosen, her senses sharpen. She'd drunk enough scotch in her time to know that the last sensation was pure fiction.

"So," said Jane, trying to move the conversation along. "Are you sleeping with Avi?"

"Whoa. Where did that come from?"

"If you don't want to start there, where do you want to start?"

Tipping the glass back and taking a sip, Julia said, "How about this: Our girl's doing really well."

"Girl?"

"Oh, don't be such a tight-assed feminista."

"*Our* girl?"

"We both have an interest in her. She's quite a find. I'm glad Ducasse & Ducasse got to her before the book was shopped around New York."

"There's no way you're going to do for her what a major press would."

"That's where you're wrong. We're going to make her a huge name. Just wait and see."

154

"You act like it has nothing to do with her writing ability and everything to do with your promotional efforts."

"No," said Julia, fingering her silver necklace. "It's like any good relationship. Both sides have to do their part."

Jane tossed back her second scotch. "Have we done enough foreplay now? Can we get to the point? Are you sleeping with her?"

Julia's smile was filled with amusement. "Get your mind out of the gutter."

"Answer the question."

"You tell me. *Am* I sleeping with her?"

"Yes."

"She's not who you think she is."

"Meaning?"

"She's damaged goods. I don't know who did what to her. She told me some of the details, but I'm sure there's more. She hides who she really is—and she's good at it."

"And what do you think you know?"

"For starters, she's full of rage. She holds it in most of the time, but if you know where to look, you can see it and, let me tell you, it's scary. She's unstable, Jane. Up and down. She's sexually promiscuous. I saw her come on to a waitress the other night. It was so blatant it was embarrassing. You're going to have a hard time living with that, trust me. She . . . disappears. I mean, right in front of you. She just goes away. She drinks too much. Maybe she's an alcoholic, I don't know. She's brilliant, sure. She can be funny as hell, and she's incredibly perceptive. But she's also a depressive, thinks the world has wronged her in some fundamental way."

"And you love her."

Leaning forward, resting her arms on the table, Julia said, "I don't love her, dummy. I love you."

"And you're expressing your love for me by sleeping with my girlfriend."

"I know this may seem difficult to fathom, but yes."

Jane winced. Took a couple of ragged breaths. This was Julia at the top of her game, twisting a situation to fit her needs. It was as if she were a modern-day alchemist, turning leaden lies into golden truths. "Do me a favor. Love me a little less."

"Not possible."

"I want you to leave."

"Okay, but don't say I didn't warn you." Finishing her drink, she pushed away from the table. "I do love you. Nothing, and I mean *nothing,* in my world is ever simple—except that."

20

Jane held her landline between her shoulder and ear as she pawed through the refrigerator looking for something to eat. After tossing and turning all night, at one point dreaming that Avi and Julia were beating each other bloody during a roller derby match at the foot of her bed, she felt a dull fatigue settle behind her eyes. It was going to be a long day.

"I was in high-sleuthing dudgeon when I arrived at Chez Deere last night," said Cordelia, bubbling with energy on the other end of the line. "Only problem was, the single piece of info I ferreted out had to do with the body we found behind the wall at the theater."

Jane wasn't sure she'd heard her correctly.

"Before the cops arrived to apprehend poor Tommy Prior, I'd been telling Kit and Beverly about the skeleton we found behind the wall. Turns out—and this has to be the Bermuda Triangle of coincidences—they both knew the guy. Is that wild or what? What are the odds?"

"A billion to one," mumbled Jane. "Two billion."

"Are you actually listening to me?"

"I think so."

"What's wrong with you?"

"Nothing a little sleep wouldn't cure."

"Jane," she said, drawing the word out. "I know there's trouble in paradise with you and Avi."

"Meaning what?"

"When you stop talking to me about your various girlfriends, there's always trouble."

"Nice to know I'm so predictable."

"Does your lack of sleep mean something significant? Have you moved on? Is there someone new on the horizon?"

"There's nobody else." She was a restaurateur, for Pete's sake. She should have more to eat in her refrigerator than week-old tuna salad, pickles, capers, prepared horseradish, and a slice of moldy Jarlsberg. Sure, there was a pint of Ben & Jerry's Chunky Monkey in the freezer, but for breakfast? That way lies madness, she thought, closing the refrigerator door. Grabbing an apple from a bowl on the kitchen counter, she drifted into the living room, the dogs trotting along beside her, hoping for their usual piece of apple core.

"So you're not going to tell me what's going on in your love life?"

"When I figure it out, you'll be the first to know."

"Have you heard from your dad this morning?" asked Cordelia. "I was the one who called him last night, you know. Kit wanted to stay with Tommy until they dragged him out to the squad car, so she asked me to phone."

In fact, Jane had heard from her father. It was the only reason she was up and basically though barely functioning. His call had awakened her after nine. Not exactly early. She felt like a slug for still being in bed. "Tommy's arraignment is set for this morning. Dad's representing him."

"Any idea what this incontrovertible evidence is that the police say they have on him?" asked Cordelia.

"Not yet. We'll probably hear something later today."

"I hate to say it, but after Tommy was carted off, both Kit and Beverly seemed relieved. I'm not saying they were happy—"

"I get it," said Jane, dropping down on the couch. "Who wouldn't want to be off the hook in a murder investigation?"

"When Booker and Chloe got home, I detected some relief in their eyes, too. I like Booker, but boy that kid keeps such a tight rein on his feelings. First thing he does when he finds out about Tommy is head to the kitchen and make himself a chocolate sundae."

When Jane was tired, she became highly suggestible about food. All of a sudden, ice cream sounded like the perfect breakfast.

"Anyway, I've got to take off," said Cordelia. "Much ado today."

"Yeah, me, too. Are you at the theater?"

"About to walk into a meeting. Later, Janey."

"Later," repeated Jane, already on her way to that carton of Chunky Monkey in the freezer.

Joji Mura's secretary, a Margaret Thatcher look-alike, led Jane back to a conference room at the far end of a carpeted hallway. She invited Jane to sit down, said that Mr. Mura would be with her shortly, and then asked if she could get Jane a cup of coffee.

Since she was already flying on caffeine and sugar, Jane declined the offer. She stood by the windows for a few minutes looking up at the heavy, gray morning sky. She turned around when the door opened, finding Dahlia Grady's divorce lawyer a much older man than she'd expected. With his straight silver hair, heavy dark glasses, plump face, and easy smile, he looked like an aging Asian cherub. He nodded to a chair, then sat down across from her. "So," he said, folding his hands. "How can I help you?"

She briefly explained about Dahlia and that she was a private investigator working on a homicide investigation. Taking out one of her cards, she pushed it across the table.

"Sure, I remember Mrs. Grady. She was a friend of a friend."

"Jordan Deere."

The mention of his name caused Mura obvious pain. "Is that the homicide you're working on?"

"For Kit Deere's attorney, Raymond Lawless."

"You're related to Mr. Lawless? You have the same last name."

"He's my father. I wonder if we could start with a few comments about your friendship with Jordan?"

He leaned back in his chair. "Well, we met at a charity auction, must be twenty years ago."

"You knew him well?"

"He was a dear friend, the kind of man who genuinely liked other people. That's rare, in my opinion. It was hard not to like him in return."

"I understand he'd talked to you recently about divorcing his wife." It was a stab in the dark. She hoped it would pay off.

"Yes," he said, a little hesitantly. "More as a friend than as a lawyer. His attorney in Nashville will handle it for him. It's an unfortunate business. But then, it was inevitable, I suppose. Under the circumstances."

"Could you elaborate on that a little?"

"Well, of course, because Jordan is—was—gay. I'm sure everyone in the family knows about that by now. The novel, and all. I'm hardly telling tales out of school."

"No, of course not," said Jane, nodding, keeping her expression neutral.

"The marriage was never meant to be anything more than a, shall we say . . . arrangement. Over the years, Jordan and Kit came to care deeply about each other. Frankly, I think that's the only reason the . . . arrangement . . . lasted as long as it did— that and the children, and of course, Jordan's need for, again, for want of a better term . . . his privacy." He leaned back, made a bridge of his fingers. "But people change. Situations change. Jordan felt it was time to move beyond his old way of thinking. He's a huge name in his field. Sold something like forty million records worldwide. Twelve studio albums. A couple greatest hits albums. He has a Grammy, a dozen CMA awards, and he penned at least twenty-five number-one hits. So, yes, there would have been career issues to deal with, but I believe he was ready for them. He felt it would be different coming out now, though country music isn't exactly welcoming to gay talent. It would still have been a struggle. But he just kept saying, 'What's the worst that can happen?' He was already a millionaire many times over, happy with his life. He felt coming out would be a positive action. A breath of fresh air in a section of the music industry he felt needed a reality check. I have to say I encouraged him. Now I wonder if that was a mistake."

"Meaning you think he might have been murdered to prevent that information from becoming public knowledge?"

His lips tightened. "I have no idea why Jordan was murdered, Ms. Lawless."

"Can you tell me when you talked to him last?"

"Last Thursday. Before he left, we scheduled a meeting for yesterday morning. Obviously, that never happened."

"Do you know if he was planning to change his will? Or if he already had?"

"His estate was in a trust," said Mura. "So, no changes. Except for one new bequest. That's what we were going to talk about."

"Can you tell me about that?"

"I'm sorry. You understand." He pushed his glasses, which had slid down his nose, back up. "I understand Tommy Prior has been arrested for Jordan's murder. I know he's been struggling with alcohol addiction for several years. And then there was that business about the hundred thousand he, well, shall we say, borrowed."

Jane tried to downplay her eagerness as she made notes. "Do you have any specific information about that?"

"No, I'm afraid I don't." He glanced at his watch. "I hope I've been of some help to you. I'm afraid I have another appointment."

"I understand," said Jane, feeling her cell phone buzz inside her pocket. When she took it out, she saw that it was a text from her father.

Mura rose from the table. "It was good meeting you. Just so you know, I plan to contact the police later today, tell them what I can. It's a sad business. I'd like to see whoever murdered Jordan put in prison."

She thanked him for his time, shaking his hand.

"If you need to stay in the conference room to take that call, please feel free."

Once he'd left, Jane clicked on the message.

Strange developments. Call ASAP.

She tapped in his number.

"That was quick," her father said, sounding out of breath.

"Just met with Jordan's lawyer friend. Boy did I get an earful."

"Give me the highlights."

"Jordan was gay. Kit knew about it from the very beginning."

After several seconds of silence, her father said, "I see. That does change things."

"Jordan wrote a novel. From what I can piece together, it may have been somewhat autobiographical."

"Anything else?"

She explained about Tommy embezzling money.

"Look, honey, I want to hear all the details, but right now, I need you to do something for me. Tommy is being released."

"You got the judge to post bail?"

"The arraignment was canceled. All charges have been dropped."

Jane clicked her pen shut and slid it into her pocket. "I thought they had his coffin ready to nail shut."

"Apparently not. I don't have all the particulars, but I will shortly. I need you to drive to the jail and pick Tommy up and then take him back to Frenchman's Bay. Can you do that for me?"

"Sure."

"Talk to him, Janey. See if you can get him to open up. Maybe he knows something about what you just learned."

"I'll do my best."

"DePetro agreed to meet with me, so I'm heading over to his office right now."

"Good luck."

"Thanks. You know, I have to say that I think this goes much deeper than I originally thought. We forget the first rule of criminology at our peril."

"And that is?"

Another few seconds of silence. "Everybody lies, Janey. *Everybody*."

21

Jane found Tommy sitting on a bench outside the police station, eyes closed, head tilted back against a brick wall. He looked every inch the man who'd spent his night in an interrogation room.

When she approached, he sat up. As the bright light penetrated, he closed his eyes again and grimaced. "You here to take me back to the house?" He moved like an arthritic old man.

"You doing okay?" she asked.

"I'll live."

As they walked back to her car, Tommy began coughing and couldn't seem to stop. Jane popped open the glove compartment once they were seated and pointed to a box of tissues.

"Look," he said, wiping his mouth, "I'm starving. Can't even remember the last time I ate. Could we stop somewhere?"

"Fast food okay?" she said, nodding to a Burger King on the other side of the street.

"No, it's not. What about the Red Lion? It's close. I'll direct you."

Jane had her answer. She'd suggested the Burger King because she wanted to know if he was truly hungry—or thirsty. His need for a drink rolled off him like a fever.

"You'll have to pay," he said, turning to look out the side window as they moved out into traffic. He said nothing more until they were seated in the main dining room and he'd ordered a bourbon. Glancing at the menu with little interest, he muttered, more to himself than to her, "I can't believe they let me go."

"Do you know why?" she asked, checking out the burger options. Even if he wasn't hungry, she was. Ice cream for breakfast hadn't been her smartest move.

Tommy ran both hands through his hair. Now that the alcohol he'd been craving was just moments away, his mood seemed to brighten, although only marginally. "They said they found a button from my coat at the crime scene. Proof positive that I'd been there and murdered Jordan." He raked his knuckles against the stubble on his cheeks. "They kept hammering at me to tell them how it all went down. I kept telling them that the button had either been planted, or someone had borrowed my coat on Sunday morning without asking. Either way, I did *not* murder my best friend. End of the story. But, of course, it wasn't. They had their proof and no matter what I said, evidence is evidence."

"So, if they had proof that you're guilty, why'd they let you go?"

"No freakin' idea." When the bourbon was placed in front of him, he immediately put his hand on it, almost as if he were afraid it might crawl away. He took a long, slow sip, smiled slightly, then let out a sigh. "You a Bruce Springsteen fan?" he asked.

The sudden change in subject threw her. "Sure."

"I've never liked country music." Lowering his voice and looking over his shoulder, he added, "Believe me, you don't want to say that out loud in Nashville."

"Are you telling me you didn't like Jordan's music?"

"Never. Give me a rock song any day. Besides, today's country music is just pop by another name."

"Okay," said Jane, not terribly interested in this bend in the conversational stream. "All pretty heterosexual, too, I guess you could say."

"You got something against heterosexual?"

"No. But it does suck up all the air in the room, given half a chance. At least it feels that way if you don't share the . . . vibe."

"You're gay?"

She nodded. "Just like Jordan."

He looked up at her sharply. "Where did you get that idea?"

"You saying it's not true?"

"I'm saying——" He took another swallow. "Jordan was as straight as I am."

"In case you're interested, his friend Joji Mura told me."

"Jesus." He downed the last of the bourbon, seemingly annoyed that it had disappeared so quickly.

"Are you saying he got it wrong?" asked Jane.

He held up the glass, motioned for the waitress to bring him another. As he waited, shredding a napkin for something to do, he muttered, "That's private information, Ms. Lawless. Not for public consumption."

"Jordan was in the closet."

He flicked his eyes to her, then away.

"Do you know anything about a novel Jordan had been writing?" asked Jane. "Something about his childhood?"

His eyes rising to the ceiling, he said, "Joji told you about that, too? Look, let me make this clear. You and your father work for Kit Deere. That means you keep whatever Joji told you to yourself."

"Even if I do, it won't matter. He plans to tell the police what he knows."

"Jesus H——" He squeezed the back of his neck.

"Is that why Jordan was murdered? Someone wanted to make

sure he stayed in the closet." It was a stab in the dark, but she figured it was an educated stab.

He refused to comment until the second bourbon was set in front of him.

Jane hoped the booze would make him more talkative. She decided to take a more gentle tack, give the alcohol some time to work its way into his system. "Tell me, Tommy. How did you and Jordan meet?"

He rolled the glass between his palms, shook his head.

"Not a pleasant memory?"

"Hell."

"Maybe you don't remember."

"Oh, I remember."

When the waitress stepped up to the table, Jane ordered a cheeseburger and an iced tea. Tommy finished the second bourbon in two quick gulps and asked her to bring him another, this time a double.

Settling in, oiled by the alcohol lubricating all his synapses, his voice grew more intimate. "I guess it wouldn't hurt to tell the story." He appeared to debate for a moment, then continued. "I'd just turned thirty. I'd been a lawyer for six years, working for an arts law firm in Saint Paul. On weekends, I occasionally helped my dad at his jewelry store in downtown Minneapolis. I'd been working there on and off since high school. I'd taken over the books because my old man wasn't, shall we say, very detail oriented. One day, this hunky young guy with black hair, dark shades, and a crazy sexy smile saunters in looking for an engagement ring. My uncle was about to step over to help him, but I got there first." Tommy looked down into his empty glass, smiled at the memory.

"Did you sell him a ring?"

"Not that day. He was a talkative sort of person, had a southern twang, so I asked him what he was doing in town. He explained that he was a country singer, that his uncle owned a bar and he was playing there on weekends. He told me I should come."

"But you don't like country music."

Raising an eyebrow, he said, "No, but Jordan impressed me, especially his looks."

"And why would his looks be important to a straight man?"

He squirmed in his seat, then shifted backward, away from her. He forced a laugh. "I know this is going to feel like it's coming out of left field, but, as it happens, I'm gay. Now, that surprises you, doesn't it. I can tell you didn't expect it."

If that was what he needed to think, it was fine with her.

"People, the few friends who knew about us, always told me I didn't look gay. Neither did Jordan."

"What do you mean 'look' gay?"

"You know. Limp wristed. Swishy."

That comment reflected the kind of internalized homophobia Jane would have expected from someone who'd spent his life in the closet. And it struck her as not only sad, but tragic.

"This may sound ridiculous," he continued, "but it was love at first sight—for both of us. Not just lust, although that was part of it. From that day on, we were together."

"A committed couple?"

"Yes."

"What about the engagement ring he'd come to your father's store to buy?"

"Right," he said, looking up as the waitress set the double bourbon in front of him. "I understand why that would be your next question." He forced another laugh. "That's the next part of the story."

·   ·   ·

"The empress surveying her kingdom," called Red Clemens.

Cordelia had been scrutinizing the stage from the balcony and was annoyed by her maintenance chief's sudden appearance. The last thing she wanted was to be interrupted, mid-swoon. The construction was almost complete. All the ceiling details had been re-gilded, the chandeliers refurbished and gleaming, and the sweeping carved plaster ornamentation on each side of the stage had been repainted with the lovely pastel colors of its former glory. The final part of the scene, the new theater curtain, would be delivered and installed on Thursday, two days from now. The theater, once covered in avant-garde black paint, decades of dust, and moldy carpet was beginning to emerge as the turn-of-the-century jewel it had once been. Even Gilbert and Hilda had quieted down, perhaps awed by the transformation.

"Cordelia, you need to come down," insisted Red. "I have to show you something."

"Can't it wait?"

He moved up the aisle to get a better look at her. "I suppose, technically, it could. But I think you should see this sooner rather than later."

"Oh, horse hocky," she said with a groan. Sailing down the side stairs, she met him at the bottom uttering one impatient word. *"What?"*

"It's easier for me to show rather than explain." He led the way up to the stage, then through the curtains that led to the backstage area. "It's good that the dressing rooms haven't been repaired yet." He stopped at the last door. Turning to Cordelia, he said, "I thought, after discovering the body behind the wall downstairs, that I should look around, see what else I could find."

"Meaning what?" She jutted out her hip. "You think we have more dead bodies stuffed behind our walls?"

"It seemed like, since I know this place better than anyone else, that I should at least look." He entered a dressing room and flipped on the light.

As had been the case with the rest of the theater, the individual rooms were dusty and dilapidated, with scuffed wood floors and black walls. This particular dressing room had a single table and chair against one wall, a battered built-in shelf along another.

Red stepped up to the shelf. "Watch this." He twisted a small, round knob and the shelf opened inward.

Cordelia's mouth dropped open.

"There's a hidden stairway and two small rooms on this end of the building. The original architect must have designed it that way."

She approached the opening. "Why? Used for what?"

"That's anybody's guess. But I know what it was used for in the late sixties through the midnineties." He cleared his throat, then whispered, "Assignations."

"No," said Cordelia, suppressing a grin. "You know that for a fact?"

"There are two access points. This one on the third floor and one in the janitor's closet on the second. Each access point allows you to connect to the stairway that hugs this end of the building, with one room, approximately six feet wide by ten feet long, on the second and third. And yes, I've seen actors, directors and all manner of theater staff and their friends go in and out. I even sat in the stairway once—I was pretty young—and watched a director, a real letch, entice an actress into one of the rooms. She held the candle while he carried the bottle of champagne and two glasses."

"Who were they?" asked Cordelia.

"I shouldn't—"

"Tell me."

"Jonathan Klaxon and Lana Webb."

"Those sluts." Cordelia had worked with both of them. "Will this theater never stop surprising me?"

"Like I said, I need to show you something." Removing a flashlight from his back pocket, Red threaded his way sideways into the opening and waited for Cordelia to follow.

"This is like something out of a horror movie," she said, wiping away cobwebs that seemed to attack from all sides. The stairs were built of dark, stained wood planks that creaked ominously under their weight as they moved slowly downward. The light from the flashlight cast long shadows along the brick wall. Cordelia looked down once, saw the outline of the stairs thrown against the wall, and decided to keep her eyes resolutely level. "Boy, you'd really have to be in the throes of passion to brave this."

Coming to a stop in front of a door-sized opening, Red turned to Cordelia and said, "I thought I should check out the rooms. You know, see what was what."

She didn't like the sound of that.

He pointed the beam inside.

Cordelia had fully expected a fantasy bedroom, an opulent four-poster bed—or at the very least, a Victorian couch—complete with silks and satins, pillows and comforters, candlesticks with tappers dripping wax. Instead, she found a bare space—more closet than room—pure Midwest Gothic, covered in the same rough wood as the stairway. A large, ancient-looking trunk had been shoved into the far corner.

"Not exactly the Ritz," she mumbled.

Stepping over to the trunk, Red opened the top and held the flashlight so that Cordelia could see inside. "This is what I found."

Peering inside, she felt a wave of nausea roll through her stomach. "Lord in heaven." The gaping eyes and leering, chipped grin of a skeleton stared back at her.

"I thought you should see it right away," said Red, almost apologetically. "You'll want to call the police."

"Give me that," she said, whipping the flashlight out of his hand.

Pointing the beam at the skeleton's forehead, she flinched when she found what she expected—and feared—would be there.

A small round hole.

"Name me three gay country music singers," said Tommy, now on his second double bourbon. This time, he'd ordered a plate of French fries to go with it. "Or, let me rephrase that. Name me three *out* gay country music singers. There are plenty of closet cases."

"I think I read about one just recently," said Jane, finishing up her cheeseburger. She'd been happy enough to let Tommy talk. In his alcohol-infused condition, he was proving to be a wealth of information. It seemed to her that he'd been holding so much inside for so long, that he couldn't help himself. Thoughts just tumbled out. "It was a man. Can't remember his name."

"Okay, one guy. Also, there's a show on TV right now called *Nashville.* On that show is a gay country singer storyline. And guess what? The man is deep in the closet because, if he wasn't, it would tank his career. Maybe by the end of the series, he'll be a successful out gay country singer. I wouldn't bet on it, but let's say it's the way it plays out. But this is 2014. It wasn't like that thirty years ago when Jordan was just starting out."

"You're saying he needed a beard."

He shrugged, dragged a French fry through a pool of ketchup.

"And Kit became that beard. But I don't get it. He was nobody back then. Why take a chance like that, give up the hope of finding someone she could really love and make a life with?"

"You'd have to ask her."

"You don't know?"

Chewing the French fry thoughtfully, he considered it. "Well, first: If you heard Jordan sing back then, you knew. He had it—whatever 'it' is. Star quality, I suppose. The songs he was writing, even way back, were outstanding—I could see it, and remember, I don't even like country songs. This guy was going places. It was just a matter of time before he caught a break and hit it big. And then, beyond that, Jordan did sleep with the occasional woman back then. I think Kit simply fell in love with him. It was easy to do. Later on, after they had kids and he was a big name, she decided to stay with him, even though, by then, she knew the truth. I mean, why not stay? He didn't care who she slept with. She had complete freedom, plenty of money, was making a success of her own acting career by then. And being connected to a big name like Jordan didn't hurt her career, let me tell you."

"Are Chloe and Booker his kids?"

"Oh, absolutely. Never any doubt about that."

"Did Jordan ask for paternity tests?"

"Sure. He wasn't stupid."

"So, did Kit know about your relationship with Jordan?"

"Not the first few years, of course, but later, yeah. Back when Jordan was first starting out, it occurred to me that he could use a manager. My interest and experience dovetailed perfectly with his needs. Well, I mean, there were things I had to learn, but I was free and dedicated. You can't beat that. I started calling around, trying to find him gigs. I suggested we produce a few songs, make multiple tapes, also take some promotional photographs. The gigs I found for him got him started professionally and it all took off from there. For two years, we were like this big, crazy family. Jordan and Kit, little Chloe, and then me, Kit's best friend, Beverly, and their friend, Archibald. Archibald had responsibilities in Minnesota, so he couldn't travel with us all the time. But he was around. The rest of us did everything together. Traveled together. Ate together. Laughed and cried together. Looking back, I'd say it was the happiest time of my life. Jordan loved me and I loved him. We were building something together. But I could also see how much he loved Kit and Chloe. I never minded. I loved them, too. I wasn't even surprised when Booker came along. It just seemed right, you know?"

"So they were still sleeping together?"

"No, but Jordan told me they wanted another kid, so they started trying."

"That bother you?"

"Not in the slightest."

"And you and Jordan were together through it all, the entire time."

He stared down at the half-eaten plate of fries, folded his hand around his drink. "Until recently, yeah. People always say what a great guy Jordan was. I don't deny that. But he had a lot of bitterness in him, too. And he could be cruel. It was all there, under the surface. Not what he showed to the world. But to me, yeah, and to some extent, to Kit, although I have to say I bore the brunt of it because he was often angry about some contract detail, or a tour, or what the label was, or more often, wasn't doing. I knew he slept around some, but a few years ago, he started cutting me out of his life—never any time for Tommy anymore. His excuse was that he didn't like my drinking. But, hell, I drank because I was unhappy. *He* made me unhappy. It snowballed from there. I made a few business mistakes, at which point he withdrew even more. And then, this summer, I started to wonder if there wasn't another man— someone he was serious about."

"Was there?"

"I'm not positive, but I think so, yes. He was never gone at night, but he was often away in the late afternoons. I didn't pay much attention at first. Eventually, it began to occur to me that he'd leave wearing, say, jeans and a polo shirt, and come home in shorts and a T-shirt. So I asked him about it. He told me, in no uncertain terms, that it was none of my goddamn business."

"Did Kit know about this new man?"

"I doubt it. I mean, maybe I'm wrong. Maybe something else had captured his attention, but if so, I have no idea what it could be."

"That could explain where he went the night before he died."

Tommy finished his drink, then set the glass down hard on the table. He was clearly angry. He may not have realized he'd given up a compelling motive for murder, but Jane did. Just because the police had released him, didn't mean she was having lunch with an innocent man.

"I think I've said enough," said Tommy, eyes rising to hers.

If Jane had been his lawyer, she would have stopped the conversation before it ever began.

175

22

That afternoon, Booker found his sister's door open. Pausing at the threshold, he watched her pack up three suitcases spread across her bed. Since she had on jeans, an oversized sweatshirt, and a baseball cap with her hair pulled into a stubby ponytail and threaded through the back, she didn't look like she was leaving imminently. "Going somewhere?"

She turned and frowned. "The family love fest is officially over."

"You mean, now that Tommy's been arrested, we can all get the hell out of Dodge."

"Couldn't have put it better myself." She stepped over a chest of drawers and began to clean it out.

"You don't exactly travel light."

"Shut up."

"Mind if I come in?"

"You already are in."

He stepped over to a window and gazed down at the driveway. "Archie's here."

"When is he not here? Mom asked him to give one of the eulogies at Dad's funeral."

"Has she set a date yet?"

"Mid-November in Nashville. That's all I know."

Booker flopped down on a chair. Next to it was Chloe's journal—always a bad sign. She only journaled when she was depressed. "When does your flight leave?"

"Haven't booked one yet. That's the next thing on my list."

Scratching his chest through his shirt, he said, "You don't find it weird, and perhaps worthy of comment, that Tommy—of all people—apparently murdered our father?"

"You think it's weird?"

"What was his motive?"

"He stole money."

"So? That was more than a year ago. And what did our father do about it? He sent him to rehab."

"Then it's something else—more secrets."

"I've been thinking about Dad's novel. Do you suppose Tommy might be 'Nathan' in the story—the gay country singer's long-time and long-suffering lover?"

"Not good-looking enough."

"He was when he was younger. And remember, real life is different than fiction."

"Nah. No way."

"I'm just saying, none of this makes any sense to me."

"Murder isn't supposed to make sense."

He hated it when she got all smart-assed and flip. Since she wasn't in a reflective mood, he opted to switch subjects. "Listen," he said, watching her fold up a sweater and tuck it neatly into the suitcase. "You remember Erin O'Brian, right?"

"Erin from high school? Jesus, what made you think of her?"

"Have you heard from her recently?"

"Why would I?"

Erin had said she'd called Chloe, left her a message. "You two were pretty close."

She stopped and stared at him. "Where's this going?"

"She's in town. I thought maybe you'd want to invite her over to the house."

"Um, no, not really."

"Did she and Dad . . . I mean, were they especially friendly?"

"*Friendly?*"

"No, I don't mean it like that. Can you think of any reason why they'd be in contact?"

"When?"

"Recently."

"Were they?"

He nodded.

"Guess you'd better ask her."

"I was hoping you'd do it for me."

Glancing over at him, she said, "I'm leaving, Booker. You're not fifteen anymore. Be a man and do it yourself."

He went back to scratching his chest. "She's changed."

"You saw her?"

"I ran into her at Cordelia's theater. We ended up going to lunch."

"My God, you've still got a crush on her, don't you." She hooted.

"Don't be ridiculous."

She sat down on the edge of the bed, crossed her legs, gave him one of her most serious, sisterly looks. "You've really got to grow up, Book. I'm telling you this because I love you, and because . . . well, nobody else is gonna do it. You think you're the strong, silent type, that you mask your emotions so well that nobody can guess what's going on inside you. That's bullshit, babe. Maybe, for those who don't take the time to actually look, for people who are too caught up in their own lives to give it some basic thought—"

"You mean our parental units."

"I read you just fine, Book. And since we're on the subject, this act you've perfected, the one about being a deeply conflicted, complicated badass, dark and mysterious and tortured, always dropping broad hints about the horrible creature living inside you that's just aching to explode, a monster you're barely keeping under control, and on and on and on. It's utter crap, bro. Total daytime TV melodrama. You're one of the nicest guys I know."

"A nice guy wouldn't have done what I did."

"In *high school,* Booker. I did stupid things, too."

"So we're both sick and twisted."

"We're human." She got up and stepped over to the closet, turned her back to him. "I'm still mad."

"Mad about what?"

"That our dad couldn't let sleeping dogs lie. I can't believe he put everything that happened in that goddamn book of his."

All subjects, for his sister, led back to the manuscript. "Chloe, listen to me. I already told you. We don't have to worry about that. We burned all the hard copies, and the hard drive is gone. It's been handled. End of story."

"I wish."

"You worry too much."

"What if we forgot something?"

"We didn't."

"Nothing is ever that simple."

He began to fidget in his chair. Not feeling like he wanted to stick around and have his sister analyze his every twitch, he rose to leave. As he moved past the window, he caught sight of a man walking purposefully toward the house. "Like a lamb to the slaughter," he said under his breath.

"What?" said Chloe. "Who's out there?"

"Didn't you always wonder why Mom was so interested in the opposite sex? There was Dad, and then there was the guy she had on the side. I suppose she thought, since we were kids, that we never noticed. At least we know now that it wasn't all her fault."

"Meaning what?" She joined him at the window. "Oh."

"Lover Boy's back."

"You think he's after Mom? How tacky is that."

"Other way around, Chloe. Mom's got her sights locked on poor Ray Lawless. One day he'll look back and realize he never knew what hit him."

As soon as Ray walked into the living room, Kit could tell by the hard set to his jaw that something was wrong. Her first instinct was to ask Archibald and Beverly to leave the room, though before she could get the words out, Ray announced that Tommy had been released.

"That's . . . wonderful news," said Kit, sensing that her smile was too bright. "What was the bail set at?"

"You misunderstand," said Ray. "He's not being charged. The arraignment was canceled. He was let go."

"But . . . I thought—" She lowered herself onto the couch.

Ray took a seat on the opposite end of the room, on the piano bench. "I just left DePetro's office. Here's the story, as I understand it."

Archibald sat on the couch next to Kit. His eyes rose to Beverly, who remained standing by the fireplace.

"DePetro spent several hours yesterday morning personally going back over the crime scene at Bayview Park. As he was nosing around, he discovered a button on the side of the running path. He assumed that, since it was brown and blended in with the leaves and dry grass, it had been overlooked. He asked for and received a second search warrant for this house. When one of the patrolmen found Tommy's coat and saw that it was missing the button in question, they arrested him."

"So why let him go?" asked Beverly.

"DePetro's team finally looked at the photos taken at the scene on Sunday morning. In those photos, no button was present. That means, in case I need to spell it out for you, that the button De-Petro found yesterday morning was planted. Planted by someone who had access to Tommy's coat. Who had access? You did. All of you, including Chloe and Booker. The conclusion DePetro reached was inescapable: In trying to point the finger of guilt away from the people in this house, the exact opposite reaction was achieved. If he's able to pull a print off that button, one of you is headed for jail."

When Ray's gaze landed on Kit, it felt like a blow. She fought to keep her eyes level with his.

"It was a craven act in and of itself," continued Ray. "But in the larger scheme of things, you've all moved to the top of DePetro's suspect list. My congratulations."

"Feel free to lose the sarcasm," muttered Beverly.

"I don't suppose you'd like to tell me who planted it? Doesn't matter if you did it to protect yourself or someone else. I'm here to tell you that it was an insanely stupid move."

Kit nodded for Archibald to get up and close the French doors that led to the hallway. When he'd resumed his seat, she said, "All right. You've made your point. I have no idea who did it and fur-thermore, I don't want to know because there's nothing we can do about it. Tell us what happens next."

"One of you will be arrested," he said.

The coldness in his voice made her shudder.

Waiting a beat, Ray said, "Why didn't anyone tell me Jordan was gay?"

"Where did you hear that?" demanded Archibald, placing his arm protectively around Kit's shoulders.

"Are you saying I've got it wrong?"

"Of course it's wrong. Jordan was—"

"Stop it," said Kit, shaking off his arm and getting up.

181

Ray's expression hardened. "If I was blindsided by that kind of information in court, it could easily mean the difference between an acquittal and life in prison. Do I make myself clear? Do you *get* it?"

"Don't talk to her like that," said Archibald. "You have no idea what she's been through."

"The police will want to question all of you again," said Ray. "If you thought the questioning was harsh last time, just wait."

"You're angry," said Kit. "You have every right to be and I'm sorry. Don't blame the others. It was my decision. After so many years, it's a knee-jerk reaction. The children didn't even know about Jordan until a few days ago. You remember what I said to you about winning the battle but losing the war? The war is that secret."

"I understand, but to the police, it will look like just another lie."

"If you don't tell them, how would they find out?" demanded Beverly.

"Joji Mura, the lawyer my daughter spoke with this morning. He plans to phone DePetro later today. He's an old friend of Jordan's. Sounds like he knows pretty much everything. Face it, Kit. It's inevitable. It's going to come out."

Kit's mind began to spin. There had to be a way to maneuver through this minefield. She simply had to find it.

"What I need you to understand," continued Ray, aiming the comment directly at her, "is that when the police learn about the divorce and about Jordan's sexuality, *you* will become, from that moment on, their prime suspect. You had the most to lose."

"I did not murder my husband," she all but screamed.

"Sweetheart," said Archibald, rising and taking her hand. "Calm down. *Please.* The stress isn't good for you. No one will believe you had anything to do with Jordan's death."

This was the horror she'd worried about for years. The secret she and Jordan had spent a lifetime protecting would be out in the open, dissected in the tabloids, chewed over on the evening news, and spread in lurid, fabricated detail from one end of the Internet to the other. Then again, nobody had mentioned that wretched novel. She hoped everyone in the room understood that, at all costs, it needed to remain a secret. Meeting Ray's eyes, she asked, "Does this mean you're done as my lawyer?"

"This is what I do, Kit. I'm a defense attorney. Of course I'm still on board."

"You're saying it's your job to defend the guilty."

"I defend *people,* guilty or innocent, in order to keep the wheels from coming off the justice system."

"But you think I'm guilty."

"I told you. It doesn't matter what I think."

"It *does.* I lied to you, okay, but not about that. You can't believe I would ever murder my husband."

"You want my advice," said Beverly, her voice overflowing with disgust. "Get rid of Lawless. He obviously doesn't trust you. You need someone on your side. Someone who believes you're innocent."

"I couldn't agree more," said Archibald. "Why use some local yokel when you could hire yourself a nationally known defense attorney."

Ray stood. "It's your decision, Kit. Say the word and I'm gone."

"No." Reaching out her hands, she said, "I want you. I need you."

His voice softened. "Good, then, we've got work to do."

23

"What *is* this place?" said Jane, feeling the stairway creak under her weight.

"Like I said on the phone," said Cordelia, pointing her flashlight ahead of them, "you need to see this for yourself."

As they descended the steps, Jane saw that the police had set up lights to illuminate the long, narrow room. "When did they get here?"

"About an hour ago."

Jane had just dropped Tommy back at the summerhouse when the SOS call came in from Cordelia. "I don't want to put too fine a point on this," said Jane, watching a mouse scurry along the edge of the stairway, "but perhaps the cold case team should do a systematic search of the entire theater."

"Already on their agenda. They need a warrant to make it official. I can't believe Octavia is out of the country and I have to deal with this on my own."

Jane wasn't sure what Cordelia thought her sister would bring to the table, unless it was even more melodramatic foreboding.

"We can't go in," whispered Cordelia, blocking Jane from

moving closer than a few yards from the entrance to the room. "The cold case team is doing their official examination. But, I mean, isn't this just too creepy? Not only is the building haunted, it seems to attract skeletons."

Jane offered a friendly nod to an officer who was stretching yellow crime-scene tape across the top of the door. To Cordelia, she said, "Did you find out anything about skeleton number two?" She figured they might as well start numbering them.

Cordelia pressed a finger to her lips. "Follow me," she whispered, heading back up the stairs. Once they'd returned to her office, she sat down behind her desk, motioning for Jane to sit across from her. Tapping her head, she said, "This time, I kept my wits about me and, before I called the cops, I did a little bit of digging myself, taking great care not to mess too much with the crime scene."

Jane wasn't sure that had been a good idea, though since it was a fait accompli, she wanted to know what her friend had learned. "And?"

"I found a billfold, opened it ever so carefully with the tip of a pen." Looking like she was about to burst with excitement, she blurted out, "I saw the driver's license. I know the name of our latest dead body."

Jane mentally cringed. This was a real human being they were talking about, someone who'd been shot, assassin style, and then stuffed in a trunk inside a secret room behind the walls of an old building.

"Stanislaw Melcer!"

"Stanislaw Melcer? That was his name?"

"Yes!"

"Other than the fact that he's the second homicide victim you've uncovered, does the name mean anything to you?"

"No!"

"Then why are you so excited?"

"I don't know!" Her elation evaporated as she slumped in her chair.

"The only thing that connects them," offered Jane, pushing her hands into the pockets of her jacket, "is the men's manner of death and the fact that they were both hidden in the theater."

"I think they're connected by more than that."

"Like what?"

"No idea."

"Just intuition."

"Nothing is ever 'just' intuition, Janey. Gut feelings are powerful."

"Did you learn anything else from his driver's license?"

"The month, date, and year it needed to be renewed." Closing her eyes to search her memory banks, she repeated, "June 16, 1986."

"So, since a driver's license is good for four years, that puts the year of his death anywhere from 1982 to 1986. What was happening at the theater here during those years?"

"Exquisite question," said Cordelia, whipping open one of her lower desk drawers and pawing through the contents. "Thanks to Archibald, I have the answer at my fingertips." She dropped a file folder on her desk and opened the cover. Placing her finger at the top of a column, she drew it down until she found the information she needed. "Oh, sure, Piccolo. I know the two people who ran it."

"Call them," said Jane. She needed to bring Cordelia up to speed about all the revelations she'd learned from JoJi Mura and Tommy Prior, but for the moment, that could wait.

Cordelia pressed a button on her phone and said, with deep solemnity, "Mitford, bring me the bible."

Jane had seen this immense tome more than once. It looked

like something Dickens would have written about—a tattered, patched, and frayed, possibly even decaying, antique address book that Cordelia had likely been given at birth, one in which she'd entered every name, address, and phone number from every human being she'd ever encountered that might have some bearing on her life in the theater.

Mitford, her longtime secretary, a woman she'd poached from her old job at the Allen Grimby Repertory Theater, came through the door holding the book carefully in both hands, as if she were afraid it might disintegrate into a pile of dust before her eyes.

"Thank you, Mitford. That will be all. Now, let me see." She wet a finger and began flipping through the crumbling pages.

"Why don't you have Mitford transfer the information in that book to a computer file?"

Cordelia gave Jane a half-lidded look. "*Please,* dearheart. One does not trample on tradition." A few more flipped pages and she had it. "Daria Marsh. Here we go." She tapped in the number. "People move a lot, so often as not, the phone numbers don't—" She blinked. "Daria? Is that you?" Smiling she said, "Cordelia Thorn here. How are you? Long time, yes."

Jane scrolled through her cell phone messages while Cordelia made her initial pleasantries. She had a text from her father asking her to call him ASAP. Two voice mails from her restaurant manager. Nothing from Avi.

"Yes, that's the name," said Cordelia. "Stanislaw Melcer. Ah, you say he was an actor?" She listened, making notes on the front of the file folder. "Missing? Heavens. When? I mean, can you remember the production he was in? The year?" She wrote the answers down, underlining them. "Yes, this is a huge help. I can't tell you what I'm working on, but rest assured, you'll read about it in the newspapers." She listened a moment more. "Sure, let's get together for

187

lunch one day soon. I'll have my secretary call you and set up a date. You, too, darling. Ta." Tossing her pen down, she wiggled her eyebrows at Jane.

"So?"

"He went missing during rehearsals for the 1986 production of *Happy Birthday, Wanda June*. He'd been cast in the part of Dr. Norbert Woodley. Great play. I remember seeing it. Actually, I—" Her voice trailed off.

"What?" asked Jane.

Pulling out of her trance, Cordelia cleared her throat and tittered. "I must be remembering this wrong. It's just too . . . coincidental."

"What is?"

"I think . . . no, can't be."

"Cordelia."

"I believe Kit starred in that production. I'm not absolutely positive, but it seems to me she played the part of Penelope Ryan. Even if I'm right, it can't mean anything. She worked at this theater a lot back then. It was the heyday of her career in Minnesota, before she started acting nationally." Locking eyes with Jane, she said, "I'm right, aren't I? It doesn't mean anything?"

"Let's look at the facts," said Jane, still clicking through her phone. "She knew the first man who died—the one who was buried in the basement."

"Right."

"And she might have known the second man who died, the one found today."

"Possibly."

"Both were killed with a bullet to the forehead."

"Well—"

Jane stuffed her phone back in her jacket pocket. "And her husband was murdered on Sunday morning by a shot to the forehead."

Without moving a muscle, Cordelia said, "There's got to be a flaw in that reasoning."

"Name it," said Jane, knowing full well that the logic was sound.

"I feel like I'm going to throw up."

"I'll find you a wastebasket."

"That's kind of you."

24

As usual, Booker and his sister stood outside the closed door to the living room and listened as Ray Lawless delivered the news that Tommy had been released from custody because the button the police had found, the one that placed Tommy at the scene of the crime, had been planted. What had begun as Ray's attempt to deliver that news had turned into a heated argument. Before it was over, Booker and Chloe were back in her bedroom. All the lies and family secrets appeared to be coming apart, which was fine by Booker. Chloe, he feared, was also coming apart. He watched her pace and mutter, frustrated that none of his soothing words seemed to penetrate. Since he had no particular belief that the world would be a dandy place after the Jordan and Kit Deere informational apocalypse, he decided to get out while he still could.

He arrived at the Heidelberg Club and sat in his car listening to music, trying to unwind. He kept his gaze firmly fastened to the front door of the main building, willing Erin to come out. She did just that half an hour later. She emerged wearing shades and a nondescript tan raincoat. She looked like she was dressing for the role of the female spy in an espionage movie. Because he didn't know what sort of clothing she normally wore, he assumed it meant nothing more than a poor fashion choice.

He waited in his car, watching her get into a white Ford Focus, undoubtedly a rental, arrange the seat belt, and then drive off. He followed at a judicious distance as she pulled out onto the main road and headed straight for the freeway.

Forty minutes later, as the sun was swallowed by a thick bank of clouds, she pulled into another parking lot, this one at a church on Lyndale Avenue in south Minneapolis. Booker parked across the street and waited to see if she would go inside. It took a few minutes, but she eventually left the car and walked slowly, almost hesitantly, up to a tall chain-link fence. Behind the fence was a playground where several dozen children were playing on slides, swings, jungle gyms, and other assorted equipment. Erin hadn't said anything about having friends in town with young children. Scanning the side of the building, Booker noticed a sign that said, PLAY-DAY DAY CARE.

Curious.

Erin scanned the playground until she spotted a little girl sitting alone in a sandbox. The girl had curly brown hair and wore over-sized clumsy black rain boots and a coat that looked like it was made from a patchwork quilt. As soon as Erin found her, she grasped a section of the chain link, almost as if she wanted to reach out and touch her. Even after the children had gone inside, Erin continued to stand by the fence, a small lonely figure buffeted by a raw autumn wind. Booker found her behavior puzzling. When she turned to walk back to her car, the pinched expression on her face suggested a woman in pain. There was a story behind this visit and he needed to know what it was.

Following Erin back to the Heidelberg Club, they arrived as daylight was beginning to fade. This time, after parking his car, he made no effort to hide himself. As she worked her way against the stiff breeze toward the front door, he called, "Erin, hey. Wait up."

Maybe he was kidding himself, but when she turned around, he thought he saw the tiniest hint of pleasure in her eyes.

"What are you doing here?" she called.

"Oh, I don't know. I was in the neighborhood."

"Sure." She smiled.

"Let me take you to dinner."

"Not tonight, Booker. I don't think I'd be very good company."

"But you're leaving soon, right? We won't have that many more chances." He bet himself that he could make her cave. "Come on. We can either eat here, or we can drive into King's Bay."

She turned to the door, then back to him. "Let's eat here."

He offered her his arm. It was a dweeb move, but by the time he'd analyzed it, she'd already taken it and they were sailing through the front door. God help them both if she continued to bring out the dweeb in him.

Dinner that night was nothing short of amazing. He could tell she needed cheering up, so that's what he did. He hadn't realized he possessed any charm at all until he heard the words coming out of his mouth. He got her laughing and kept at it. The wine helped, as did the hokey accordion player, a fat guy wearing lederhosen and kneesocks. The food seemed unusually good. Or maybe it was just the company. Whatever the case, they didn't stop laughing, didn't really move into a more intimate space until their final cup of coffee—until the restaurant had almost cleared of guests and the soft, romantic glow from the candles began to penetrate.

Booker wasn't sure how to approach the questions tumbling around inside him, the ones about her connection to his father, and the newest enigma—the little brown-haired girl at the day care center. He wanted to understand her. He wanted it all at once, fast, easy, like taking a pill. He needed answers, but wanted them without doing any hard work. Mostly, he was afraid that if he pushed, she'd run away. And yet didn't he have to trust that they'd connected tonight? That it meant something. Wires had touched and sparked, bright enough for an entire dining room to see.

"So," he said, wiping his lips with a napkin, "how much longer do I have you for?"

"You mean, when am I leaving?"

"You know, Erin, Minnesota is beautiful in the fall."

"The fall's almost over."

"November can be nice."

She played with her wineglass. "I wish you'd take that job at Cordelia's new theater."

"Because?"

"I'll be back in February, when she starts work on my play. Would be nice to think you'd be here."

"Do you have other friends in town?"

"Not really."

This was harder than he'd imagined. He couldn't exactly admit that he'd followed her to the day care center. "What about your marriage?"

"What about it? It's been over for a long time."

"You never mentioned if you had any children."

She looked up as if somewhere inside a stitch had come undone. "No. I have no children."

He found the sentence oddly constructed. "Did you ever want one?"

"Why all the questions about kids?"

"I never wanted children. Until recently."

"Really? What changed your mind?"

He shrugged. "Not sure."

Glancing at her watch, she began to push away from the table.

"You're not leaving."

"I'm afraid I have to. An early appointment in the morning."

"Please, just a little while longer. We were having such a great time." Until the conversation had turned to children. Placing his hand on top of hers, he said, "Have dinner with me just one more time. Tomorrow night. We can go anywhere you want."

She seemed torn.

"Erin, I like you. I think you like me. I don't know where this will go. Probably nowhere. But it can't hurt to have one last dinner."

Finally, relenting, she said, "I'd like that."

"Great. Where?"

"Here. Seven o'clock."

He wanted to kiss her, even if it was only a peck on the cheek. He got up, but before he had the chance, she was already on her way to the door. Sitting back down, he motioned to the waiter for the check. As he waited, taking a last sip of coffee, he thought back to a comment a friend had once made to him. If you've got important questions, the man had said, make sure you have at least one of the answers. That way, you'll know if you're being lied to.

Seattle, he thought to himself. Who did he know in Seattle? It occurred to him that a buddy from college, Griffin Turner, another theater major, had been hired a couple years back by the Seattle Repertory Theatre. With a well known playwright in their midst, surely his friend would know something about Erin O'Brian—or could find out. Tomorrow night, when they met for dinner, Booker would be armed with facts. If he only had one more chance with her, he intended to make it count.

25

At her father's home in Saint Paul that evening, over a dinner of take-out Chinese, Jane went through the notes she'd taken on her conversations with Joji Mura and Tommy Prior. She'd already given him the high points over the phone, but he was equally interested in the details.

"Let me get this straight," said Ray, fingers interweaving over his stomach. "Jordan comes to town and meets Kit."

"At that point, according to Tommy, he was more bisexual than exclusively gay. But he was also actively looking for a beard. He didn't lie to Kit. She knew from the beginning."

"How did they meet?"

"Never thought to ask that question. I'm sure Kit would tell you."

"But will she tell me the truth," he said, musing out loud. "Seems to me, the most important question is, what did she get out of it? Unless she was actually in love with him."

"Again, Tommy did say she was attracted to Jordan, and she could see he was going places."

"The attraction I understand," said Ray. "But not the marriage part. Why saddle yourself with a sham marriage on the off chance that the guy hits it big in the music business? Kind of a long shot if you ask me. She participated for thirty years in helping him create this house of cards. That couldn't have been easy."

Jane sipped her Coke. "Do you think Jordan was murdered by someone in his family?"

"Family or family intimates. That's where DePetro is headed. He'll nail one of them. My fear is, it will be Kit."

"Because you think she's innocent?"

He laced his fingers behind his head. "She had the most to lose if the divorce went through. And if the world found out she and Jordan had been lying about their marriage all these years—the fallout would be hellish."

"There's no way to keep that secret anymore."

"No," he said, leaning forward to grab his beer bottle.

She watched him take a sip, wondering what he was thinking. "You like her, don't you."

"Like who?"

"Kit."

His smile was wistful "Yes, I do. I've always been attracted to her. I think a lot of men are. She has a quality—hard to put your finger on. She's fun. Unpredictable. And she was incredibly beautiful as a young woman. Still is, in my opinion."

Jane wondered if his attraction to her might cloud his judgment, though she didn't say it out loud. Hearing the doorbell, Jane asked, "Are you expecting someone?"

"Not that I know of." He rose quickly and left the kitchen.

Jane began to clear the table. She was putting the leftovers in the refrigerator when he came back holding an envelope.

"Someone left this," he said. "They stuck the letter in the door, rang the bell and took off." He sat back down at the table and ripped the top open with his finger. "Huh," he said, opening up a single folded piece of white typing paper.

"What is it?"

"I got one almost like this in the mailbox this morning. Except that one said, 'R.A.Y.M.O.' And now this one says, 'R.A.Y.M.' What am I supposed to make of that?"

Jane took the note and studied it. There were no other marks on the page. "Let me see the envelope."

He handed it to her. "There's nothing on it."

"Strange," said Jane, flipping it from back to front.

"A lot of strange people in this world doing a lot of strange things. And I've represented most of them." He grimaced, then grinned. "Let's not talk about business all evening. Tell me how you are."

"Me? Good."

"And how's everything with Avi?"

"She's in Chicago at the moment."

"I suppose you miss her."

"I do."

He studied her over the top of his beer bottle. "Can't say she makes you very happy. Just something I've noticed."

"That's not true."

"Isn't it?"

"We have some things to work out."

"Okay."

"You don't like her?"

He rubbed his jaw thoughtfully. "It's not a matter of liking or not liking her. I'm not sure she knows what she wants. I've seen her high and low—all over the place emotionally. She doesn't seem like a terribly good candidate for a stable, long-term relationship. Again, just a father's observation."

Before Jane could figure out how to respond, her dad's landline rang.

"Better get that," he said. He reached behind him and snatched the cordless off the counter. "Raymond Lawless. Oh, Kit, hi." He listened. "I expected as much. I think our best course of action is for me to contact DePetro and tell him that you're done talking, that there will be no more interrogations with you or anyone in your family." He listened again, pinching the bridge of his nose. "Kit, that's not smart. You hired me for my expertise in matters like this. It's my opinion . . . Kit . . . Kit wait." He looked over at Jane. "Yes, I understand that, but at this point, redeeming yourself with him isn't possible." He bent his head and didn't speak for almost a minute. "If that's your decision I can't stop you. Yes, I can drive out and we can go through some of the questions he's likely to ask. As long as you understand that you're doing this against my advice. All right. I'll be there shortly."

As he set the phone back on the kitchen counter, Jane raised her eyebrows.

"DePetro's office called. He's scheduled a meeting with Kit tomorrow at nine A.M."

"You think he's planning to arrest her?"

"I don't know," he said, getting up, patting his pockets for his wallet and keys. "What I do know is that she shouldn't be talking to him. I honestly think she's planning a charm offensive. It's ludicrous. She thinks she can present herself as cooperative, that by using her wiles she can help herself in some way. We're long past that point."

"But she insists."

"She does. Which means I have to go, Janey. She's my client."

And you'd do this for any client who asked, she thought. Accused thieves, rapists, murderers. Sure. Goes without saying.

"I'm sorry I have to cut our evening short," he said, slipping on his navy cardigan, "but you understand."

She did understand. Perhaps more clearly than he did.

26

DePetro pressed a button and started the digital recorder. "It's Wednesday, October twenty-eighth, nine seventeen A.M., and I'm beginning my second interview with Katherine Deere. Also in the room is Mrs. Deere's attorney, Raymond Lawless." He looked up, opened a folder and took a pen out of his inner coat pocket.

Kit nodded to him pleasantly, folded her hands. She refused to look at Ray, who'd made his opinion clear: She shouldn't be here. She knew the questions would be tough and tricky. She would simply have to get through it. She'd instructed Ray to let the conversation play out, not to object or shut it down. This was her last chance to spin the situation to her advantage.

"Mrs. Deere," said DePetro. "I'd like you to walk me through last Sunday. You said you were home all morning, as were your children, Booker and Chloe."

"That's right," she said, her voice creamy and soft.

"You've also said that Tommy Prior was home, as was your assistant, Beverly Elliot. And that Archibald Van Arnam arrived later. Shortly after ten. Is that correct?"

She nodded.

"Please respond with a yes or no."

"Yes."

"When was the last time you talked to your husband?"

"Saturday morning. Beverly and I had just flown up from New Orleans, where I'd been starring in a play. He came on board right after we landed to welcome us home."

"And it was during that welcome home that he asked you for a divorce."

Knowing that DePetro had talked with Joji Mura yesterday, Kit felt there was no use keeping up her act. "Yes, that's correct."

DePetro clicked the top of his pen. "Your husband was gay, is that correct?"

"May I assume this is information you won't release to the press?"

He paused. "No, I won't release it. For the moment."

"And that you'll let me or Ray know before you do release this information?"

"Agreed."

Kit felt she'd won an important concession. "Then, yes. My husband was gay."

"You knew he was gay when you married him?"

"Yes."

"Then why did you marry?"

"I loved him." By the expression on DePetro's face, Kit could tell it wasn't the answer he'd expected.

"He and Tommy Prior were . . . together for many years."

"Yes."

"Tommy spent time at your house."

"He did."

"And you knew he and Jordan were . . . lovers."

"Not right away, but eventually. Within the first year."

"Did your children know their father was a gay man?"

"Not then."

"But they do now?"

200

"Yes."

"Was it a recent revelation?"

"It was."

"How recent?"

"Last week."

"Why, Mrs. Deere? Why tell them now?"

"My husband said he thought it was time."

"And you agreed?"

"I didn't have a choice in the matter."

"Did that make you angry?"

She tugged at one of her earrings. "No, of course not. It was always his decision."

"It must have come as quite a shock to your kids."

"I'm sure it did."

"How did they feel about Jordan coming out of the closet? About the world knowing that the two of you had lived a lie all these years?"

"Our love for each other was never a lie. As for how the children feel, it's not my place to speak for them."

"All right. Back to Sunday morning. You said you hadn't talked to Jordan since he asked you for the divorce on Saturday. I'm in possession of cell phone records that show Jordan placed a call to you at six twenty-seven on Sunday morning. You talked for approximately four minutes. Do you deny that?"

Kit glanced over at Ray, unable to escape the shock in his eyes. "No, I don't deny it."

"You lied when you said you hadn't talked to him since Saturday."

"I, ah . . . yes, I did."

"Why?"

"Habit."

"Excuse me?"

"I lie about my relationship with Jordan out of habit. Surely you can understand."

"What did you and Jordan talk about on Sunday morning?"

"He wanted to know if I was okay. He knew he'd dropped a bomb on me about the divorce and said he was sorry, that he would always love me, but that he stood by his decision. He apologized for leaving the way he did on Saturday night, not being there when I returned home."

"Did he tell you where he went?"

"No. And I didn't ask."

DePetro slipped his pen back into his shirt pocket. "Go on."

"I told him we needed to talk, and he said we would. Later that day. He'd called a family meeting for ten o'clock. He asked if everyone was still planning to be there. I said they were."

"By *family* meeting, who do you mean?"

"Myself, Chloe and Booker, my oldest friend Beverly, Tommy, and Archibald."

"That's your family?"

"It is."

"And at this family meeting, Jordan was going to break the news about the divorce."

"I imagine."

"Your children would have been pretty upset by all this."

"They're adults. They would have coped."

"But you had the most to lose."

"*Jordan* had the most to lose," said Kit.

Leaning back in his chair, DePetro studied her for a few seconds. "We were able to track your cell phone on Sunday morning. Assuming you had it with you, you left the house around seven and didn't return until close to nine. Is that true?"

"I—"

"You don't have to answer that," said Ray.

"I'm happy to answer. I have nothing to hide." She rearranged her sweater, retied the belt. "I did leave. I thought I'd spend some quiet time in the sanctuary at my church before mass began at nine. But when I got there, I saw that there must have been an early mass scheduled, so I left and drove around."

"You drove to Bayview Park."

"No, I did not."

"We have records of your cell phone pinging off a cell phone tower not two miles from there."

"Our house isn't more than four miles from the park. I wanted to be alone, to have some time to think, so I drove out to Bay Point Ridge, high above the park, and sat watching the waves."

"At the very least, you cannot state unequivocally that nobody in your family left your house that morning if you weren't even home."

"I *can* state that," she said, raising her voice for the first time. "I know because nobody in my family murdered Jordan. It's not possible."

"It's not possible because *you* murdered him."

The words felt like darts hitting her skin. "I didn't."

DePetro allowed himself a small smile. Paging through the papers in front of him, he stopped when he found the one he was looking for. "Mrs. Deere, I wonder if you could tell me if you know any of these people. First, Dr. Daniel Woodson."

"Never heard of him. Who is he?"

"Charles A. Nash."

Kit was momentarily thrown. "Yes," she said carefully. "I know him."

"In what capacity."

"He was a friend. Many years ago."

"A lover?"

"That's right. Jordan and I, for obvious reasons, didn't have an exclusive relationship."

DePetro returned to the page. "Samuel L. Burke?"

"Another friend."

"And lover?"

"Yes," she said.

"Donald P. Greer. Arturo Young. John D. Flemming. William Timothy Hudson. Alvin Bates. Kyle Todd." He looked up. "All men you slept with?"

The smug look on his face caused her throat to tighten. "Yes."

"Shall I go on?"

"What's your point?" asked Ray, his tone a mixture of disgust and impatience. "As Kit just said, she wasn't in a monogamous relationship with Jordan Deere. Nor was Jordan with her."

"Tell me who Myron Oliver is," said DePetro, his voice uncharacteristically mild.

Kit bristled. "Another man I slept with."

"Where did you meet?"

"New Orleans."

"So this man was a recent . . . admirer."

"I suppose. Yes."

"What did you two talk about?"

"Could you be more specific?" asked Ray.

"Mrs. Deere, did you ever tell Mr. Oliver that you were so angry at your husband that the only solution left to you was murder?"

"Absolutely not," said Kit, sitting up straight. "I never said that."

"What did you say?"

"That I was angry, sure. Maybe I said something like, 'I'm so furious I could kill him.'"

"And the difference between those two statements is?"

"You have to understand the context. I was at Myron's house. It was late and we'd been drinking. I was confiding my feelings to him, telling him about my frustrations with Jordan. It's just . . . something people say when they're angry, when they've had too much to drink. I didn't mean that I was planning to murder Jordan. That's just crazy."

"And Myron never said to you that he could help. All you had to do was say the word."

Kit blinked. "He didn't mean that, any more than I meant what I said."

"You didn't tell him that you'd think about it?"

"No. Absolutely not."

"And you never lie, Mrs. Deere, so we can rely on your word."

The room began to tilt.

"During our search of your house on Sunday afternoon," continued DePetro, abruptly changing topics, "we found your husband's laptop. We took it with us and had some of our technicians examine it. It seems the laptop is missing its hard drive. Care to comment on why that is?"

Her eyes jittered into focus. "I have no idea. You'd have to ask my husband about that."

"Which we obviously can't do."

"No," she agreed.

"Was there something on that laptop that you, or someone in your family, didn't want us to know about?"

"Now you're fishing," interjected Ray. "Kit, don't answer that."

"You lie so easily and so often that you wouldn't know the truth if it bit you in the ass," said DePetro.

"That's it," said Ray. "Unless you're arresting my client—"

DePetro closed his file folder.

Kit held her breath.

"No, I'm not arresting her. Not yet. But cooperation goes a long way," he said, directing the comment to Kit. "Sometimes lawyers don't help you, they hurt you."

"Kit," said Ray, rising from his chair. "We're done."

27

"Just the woman I wanted to see," said Archibald as Cordelia sauntered into one of the conference rooms on the second floor of the theater's east building late Wednesday morning. "You're never going to guess what I found." He'd been itching to show her.

"I'm not sure I can take any more surprises," she said, groaning.

"Don't be silly. You're going to love this." He swiveled his chair around and flipped through several badly framed oil paintings. Selecting the smallest first, he held it up. "Know who that is?"

She leaned forward to get a better look. "Someone historic. The painting looks old."

"It's Elijah Samuelson, the man who built the main theater building."

"Ah," said Cordelia. "Love the bowler. Might have to get one of those myself."

"And this," said Archibald, setting another, larger painting on his knees. "Guess who."

"No idea."

"Gilbert and Hilda King."

Cordelia squinted. "You've got to be kidding."

"Why?"

"Gilbert looks like Elton John during his straw-hat period. And Hilda is the spitting image of Eleanor Roosevelt." She leaned halfway across the table. "Hmm. That's quite a dress. And I've never seen a turban like that before. Black sequins, with that silver star on the forehead and a single feather erupting from the top. Hilda was a real fashion plate. I think I know what I'm going to wear to our grand opening."

The idea failed to impress Archibald, but then clothes had never been his thing. "There's one more," he said, lifting up the largest canvas. "This is Albert Manly Parker, the architect of the building. He was quite famous in his day. I think you should redo all of these oil paintings in elaborate gilt frames and hang them in the lobby. A way to honor the history of the theater."

"This isn't a theater, it's a charnel house."

"Pardon me?"

She pulled out a chair and sat down. "You haven't heard the latest. The cold case detective who came out yesterday afternoon to examine the skeleton Red found in that hidden room—"

"Wait, wait," he said, holding up a hand. "I don't know what you're talking about."

He listened closely as she explained, in mind-numbing detail, what had happened yesterday. "I had no idea," he said when she finally stopped talking.

"And then," she said, revving up for part two of her rant, "they asked if I'd allow them to bring in a team to look through the entire building. *For freakin' dead bodies!* They arrived around five and worked all night. I mean, I didn't want any more surprises, so it was all good, but *heavens.* As soon as I walked in this morning, I was met with the search report." Her eyes nearly bugged out of their sockets. "They found *another* skeleton. That makes three. And that doesn't even count the gangland hits, Gilbert and Hilda. Five dead bodies in the Thorn Lester Ossuary. Think I should change the name of the theater? Has a certain dramatic ring, don't you think? Especially if we end up doing a lot of Shakespeare."

"You mustn't hyperventilate."

"If there ever was a time to hyperventilate, it's now. The cops think there's a serial killer out there using my theater as his own personal mausoleum."

"Serial killer? That's a little strong."

"Look up the definition. A serial killer is generally a man who has killed at least three people over an extended period of time, someone who does the killing within a defined geographical area—a comfort zone, otherwise known as *this freakin' theater*—and generally uses the same method." She drew her arms wide. "Check, check, check, and check."

"Will you let me make a comment longer than two words?"

"What? Oh. Go ahead. Happy to have you put this into perspective for me."

"Don't be snide."

"My sister certainly isn't around to do it. I hate her, sometimes, you know? She's off in Europe having herself a grand old time while I'm back here dealing with Jack the Ripper."

Archibald wasn't in the mood to make any more attempts to calm her down. He wasn't particularly calm himself. He decided to ask a few leading questions and then shovel her out the door. "Have the police been able to find out anything on the last two skeletons?"

"Not much." She unwrapped a lump of bubble gum and popped it into her mouth. Chewing like a madwoman, she said, "What amazed me is that Kit knew the first guy, the one Jane and I found in the speakeasy buried behind the wall."

"Kit . . . knew him? You spoke to her about it?"

"Sure. Why not? She dated the guy. Even Beverly remembered him. They said he just disappeared one day. Poof. Gone."

"Cordelia, you have to listen to me."

She unwrapped another lump of gum. "What?"

"This is important. Leave Kit out of your theater problems."

"Why?"

"She already has so much on her plate that she's nearly drowning. Cut her some slack. Do you realize she was interrogated again this morning? She thinks she's about to be arrested. She's so stressed that I fear for her health. Her sanity. FYI, I don't think Ray Lawless is providing her with the best counsel. If it were up to me, I'd dump him and hire Mark Geragos. Or Gloria Allred. But back to the subject at hand. Weighing Kit down with your problems at a time like this is unconscionable."

Cordelia slowed her chewing. "I never thought about it that way. I just saw it as a fascinating coincidence."

"Fine. That's what it was. And now, if you love Kit as much as you say you do, you'll leave it at that." When she stopped chewing he could tell his words had finally penetrated.

"The Old Deep and Dark," she said, blowing a thoughtful bubble. Sucking it back in, she added, "When you think about it, it may be the theater's nickname, but it's also a good description of the human heart."

Jane had been wondering about Red Clemens since the day she'd first met him. He always seemed to be around, popping up when you least expected, a kind of human jack-in-the-box with his carrot-red hair and the gap in his front tooth. Because he'd worked at the theater on and off for over thirty years, she also figured he would be a source of information. She found him puttering around a room in the basement of the theater—part office, complete with battered oak desk, lamp, and file cabinets, and part workshop, with a heavy worktable along the back wall, an assortment of shop shelving and a pressboard grid full of tools. In the corner, a CD player was blasting out an old Long John Baldry album. "So this is your lair," called Jane, standing in the doorway and smiling.

Turning down the music, Red smiled back. "Can I interest you in a cup of coffee?"

The smell was tantalizing.

He lifted a stack of old seventy-eight records off a chair. "Cream? Sugar?"

"Black." She saw that he had a mini-refrigerator behind the desk. "All the comforts of home."

"Everything I need," he said, removing two mugs from a cupboard and filling them about two-thirds full. He handed one to Jane, then sat down behind his desk. The wooden chair creaked agreeably under his weight.

"I met your father once," he said, blowing on his coffee. "Didn't realize he had a daughter."

"And a son."

"He's a very successful lawyer. He defended the man who raped my niece."

She flinched. "I'm sorry. What he does is a necessary part of the justice system." She knew the comment was true, but it was also too easy.

"Pays well, too."

"Yes, I suppose it does. Sounds like you're angry at him."

"Yup. Sure am."

"You think the man he represented was guilty?"

"He raped three other women, but of course, the judge wouldn't allow that information to be made available to the jury."

"So he got off?"

"Your father did an admirable job."

She tried to let his anger slide past her. "Again, I don't know what else to say except I'm sorry."

"So I guess that means Kit's found herself a real crackerjack attorney."

"Do you know Kit well?"

"We're friends. Not close."

Glancing around, Jane saw that the walls were almost entirely covered in yellowed theater posters. A pile of books, all thin, narrow volumes, were stacked at the edge of the desk. Interesting, she thought. Poetry. Attempting to move the subject to something less fraught, she asked, "Do you enjoy poetry?"

"Yes, ma'am, I do. Always have."

"When I was in college, I read a lot of T. S. Eliot, Mary Oliver, Billy Collins. And for years after I kept finding new poets to love. But lately, I don't seem to ever pick up a poetry book."

"You should go back to it," he said, wrapping his fingers around the mug. "We make the mistake, as we live our lives, of moving away from—instead of toward—our inner selves."

"I suppose." She noticed a couple of scrapbooks propped against the wall.

Red followed her eyes. "Would you like to see some of the people I've met?" He pulled one free and opened it, pushing it across the table to her.

She scanned the snapshots. "These were all taken here at the theater?"

"They were. Some upstairs. Some down here in my office."

"I didn't realize this place was such a mecca for famous people. Is that Garrison Keillor?"

"It is."

There was a photo of one of the best-loved governors of the state, Elmer L. Anderson, and another of the one-time owner of the Minnesota Twins, Carl Pohlad, both standing next to Red wearing big smiles. "Lord, is that Brad Pitt?" She could hardly believe her eyes. Pitt had his arm around Red, like they were old buddies. She flipped through the pages more quickly. Most of the people in the snapshots were strangers, but occasionally she did recognize a well-known face. Dan Rather. Demi Moore. Sting. "Quite a scrapbook," she said.

"Yup, I'm pretty proud of it. Represents a lot of years of hard work."

"You've been here how long?"

"On and off since I was fifteen years old. My parents' house wasn't far from here, as the crow flies. My family was always hurting for money, so the kids were expected to find jobs and bring in whatever we could. Since I loved the theater, I stopped in one afternoon to see if I could find something here. I kept coming back until they hired me."

Jane continued to page through the scrapbook. "A lot of pictures of Kit Deere in various costumes."

"She was always my favorite," he said. "Early on, I had what you might call a schoolboy crush on her. In some ways, I guess I still do. Believe me, I'm not alone. She has that effect on men."

Jane sipped her coffee, finally approaching her main question. "How did you learn about the secret staircase and those two rooms?"

"Well, now, that's kind of an interesting story. Like I said, I had this crush on Kit—I knew her as Kit Haralson back then—when I was young. One summer, when she was appearing in a play at the theater, I decided I was going to meet her or die trying. I went backstage during intermission one night, intent on introducing myself. I found her dressing room by looking through the keyholes. Wasn't hard. The door wasn't even locked. I could see her inside, sitting at this dressing table with a bouquet of red roses, but by the time I got up the nerve to knock and push my way inside, she was gone. I was completely flummoxed. There was no way out of the room except for the door I'd just come in, and yet she'd disappeared. I had to figure out how it happened."

"When the curtain rose on the next act, was she missing?"

"Oh, no, she was up onstage, beautiful as ever. So I had to ask myself, what the heck was going on? One afternoon a few days later, when the theater was pretty much empty, I went into that dressing room and began searching for a secret exit. Felt like the only explanation to me. I finally discovered the round knob on the edge of the bookcase. If you twist it, the bookcase opens inward. Thankfully, I'd thought to bring a flashlight, so I followed the stairs down and found the rooms. It became pretty clear to me what those rooms were used for, at least during my youth. I have no idea why they were built in the first place. You'd have to ask the architect. Actually, I hadn't thought about those rooms for years, not until we discovered that skeleton in the speakeasy. That got me to thinking. Figured I should check them out, so I went down yesterday and found that trunk with the second skeleton inside." He drained the coffee in his mug. "And now I hear the cops found another body."

"A third one?" This was news to Jane.

"It isn't a *him* this time. It's a her."

Jane's first thought was that she needed to rush upstairs to talk to Cordelia, though she knew the skeleton wasn't going anywhere, and she wasn't quite done with Red yet. There were so many old theater props scattered around the room that she got up to examine them more closely.

"Take a good look," said Red, propping his feet up on an orange crate. "I've got a stellar memory, if I do say so myself. I can probably tell you what production each of those is from."

In the corner of one of the open metal shelves, she found a box of playbills organized by year.

"Cordelia's friend, Archibald Van Arnam, wanted to take that box, but I wouldn't let him. He's doing research on the theater

213

and he thinks it entitles him to everything in it. I collected those myself, so as far as I'm concerned, they're mine."

Jane paged through the stack back to 1986. It only took a moment to find the playbill for *Happy Birthday, Wanda June*. "The skeleton you found downstairs," she said, opening the cover to find the cast list. "His name was Melcer."

"Stan Melcer?" said Red, frowning. "Sure, I remember him. He was in quite a few productions. Come to think of it, he did go missing during one of them."

"Happy Birthday, Wanda June."

"I think that's right," he said, pressing his fingers to his forehead. "He played a doctor."

"Dr. Norbert Woodley." She read down the list. "And . . ." Her voice trailed off.

"And?" he repeated.

Cordelia had been right. "Kit Deere was in the same production. She played the part of Penelope Ryan."

"I remember now. The two of them——" He looked up at Jane. "Yes?"

"Well, I don't like to tell tales out of school. I mean, she was a married woman at the time."

Jane returned the playbill to the box and then pulled up a chair directly in front of him. "Tell me. Please. It could be important."

"Well, see, Kit had, shall we say, a reputation. Every now and then she liked to engage in these little private romantic interludes." Gazing down into his mug, he added, "If I'm going to be completely honest, I'd have to say that I always hoped her eyes would alight on me one day."

"She was sleeping with Melcer?"

"Yes, I think so. But something happened. She cut it off and it upset him. I remember hearing them argue one night after the final curtain."

"Do you remember what was said?"

"He told her she'd be sorry if she turned her back on him."

"Was it a threat?"

"Oh, I don't think so. Just hurt feelings."

"Did you ever see them argue again?"

"No, not Melcer and Kit. But I did walk in on a heated conversation he was having with that friend of Kit's. The woman who took care of her kids."

"Beverly Elliot?"

"Yeah, that's the one. I'd never seen her so red-faced and furious before."

"Do you remember any of the specifics?"

"Sorry. I'm not the kind of guy who listens at doors."

"How long after that conversation with Beverly did he go missing?"

"Let me think." He ran a hand down the front of his shirt. "Maybe two weeks."

"Did anybody report the fact that he was missing?"

"Sure. He wasn't married, but he had a brother. I remember him coming to the theater to see if anyone could shed any light on what had happened to Stan. No one could. It became a police matter, and then I guess I forgot about it. I think we all figured he'd show up sooner or later."

But he hadn't. Now that Jane had proven that Kit and Beverly had both known two of the three people who'd been murdered and buried inside the theater, the idea that they were coincidences no longer seemed possible. If what her gut was telling her turned out to be true, a multiple murderer had been hovering around the edges—or perhaps had actually been inside—the Deere family for over three decades. Jordan had been his most recent victim. The most important question seemed to be, would there be more?

28

"I disgust him," said Kit, head in her hands, sitting at the island in the kitchen, still trying to process what had happened in that interrogation room. "I think he's done with me."

Beverly, who was standing in the doorway, gave a contemptuous grunt. "Ray Lawless isn't the only one around here who's disgusted by your behavior."

"Meaning what?" Kit could feel Beverly's penetrating stare even without looking up.

"Meaning I am, too."

"I would think the number of men I've slept with could hardly come as news to you," said Kit.

"No, but this does." She yanked back a stool and sat down. "You're about to be arrested for murder and all you can think about is that you've disappointed your latest boyfriend."

"He's not my boyfriend."

"No, but you want him to be. You have an addiction, Kit. Admit it."

"There's been a spark between us for years."

"So what? Who cares?"

"I care."

"Are you *that* afraid of being alone?"

"Don't be silly. I won't even dignify that with a response."

"What then? Are you lining up boyfriends to visit you in prison?"

Kit shut her eyes. "You can be so hateful."

"Sexual drama is what you live for. Without it, you must not feel like you're alive. Well it's high noon at the O.K. Corral, Katherine. It's time to stop thinking about men and start thinking about how we're going to survive this."

"That's all I *have* been thinking about."

"That and Ray Lawless."

"Maybe we should use your gun. Shoot our way out."

Beverly's smile was mirthless. "Can't. Took out the pontoon this morning and dumped it in the lake."

Kit put her head down on the cold granite countertop. "I'm tired, Beverly. This fight—and that's what my life has felt like all these years—has just about done me in."

"Yeah, well. You'll land on your feet. You always do."

"Not this time. Everyone thinks I'm a slut, or will once the tabloids get hold of the story. *You* think I'm a slut. So do my children. The point is, juries acquit decent, God-fearing women, but sluts, they get what's coming to them."

"Kit, look, I . . . I made a mistake. Came down too hard on you."

"It's all right. I deserve it. I have a lot to think about. If you don't mind, I'd like a few minutes alone."

"I'm sorry."

"Me, too."

"No," said Beverly. "I can't leave it like this. Look at me." She waited until she had Kit's full attention. "I'd do anything for you."

"Good to know."

"I mean it."

"I know you would," said Kit, squeezing Beverly's hand. "And I appreciate it. It's just . . . there's nothing to be done. The writing's on the wall, to quote an old saying. All that's left is for DePetro to come and arrest me."

Jane waited in her father's outer office, making a futile stab at talking football with his paralegal, Norm Toscalia. "So, how about those Vikings, huh?" She glanced through her e-mails, tossing most of them in the trash.

"Yeah, how about them," he muttered, sitting behind his desk and tapping the keys on his laptop. "I've pretty much given up."

"On what?"

"The team. The season. The quarterback. The coach. The offensive and defensive lines. The organization. The hot dogs."

"That doesn't sound good."

He looked over his shoulder. "You're not a football fan, are you?"

"Well, actually, no." She saw that she had a text from Avi, one that had been sent less than an hour ago:

> I'm home. Stop by my apartment
> when you can.

The door to Jane's father's office opened and a woman in a pink and white raincoat emerged. She nodded to Jane on her way out.

"You can go in now," said Norm, continuing to tap away at his laptop.

"Hope the Vikings improve," said Jane.

"Oh, yeah. I'm really gonna hold my breath on that one."

"Hey, honey," said her father. He got up and walked around his desk to give her a hug. "I'm so glad to see you. If I haven't said it before, I like our new arrangement. Gives me an excuse to see you more often."

Before she took a seat, she handed him the signed contract he'd had his secretary send over to her house. Noticing a piece of paper on his desktop with the word 'R.A.M.' typed in the center, she said, "Did you get that today?"

"Yeah. I'll probably have another one tonight. 'R.A.' It feels like someone is erasing me, letter by letter. Stupid."

She wasn't sure how seriously to take it. "Look, Dad, maybe this is some sort of warning. Or even a threat."

"Even if it is, what am I supposed to do about it?"

"Maybe you should come stay at my house."

"You're going to protect me?"

"Sure. Why not? Mouse has great ears—and big teeth. I've got a security system, you don't."

"It's a joke, Jane. Just someone trying to rattle me. It's not the first time some idiot's tried that. You can't let things like this get inside your head."

"Okay, okay." She knew enough to back away before she got a lecture on boundaries. "So, how did Kit's charm offensive go?"

As he sat back down, he loosened his tie. "It was a disaster. De-Petro's caught that woman in so many lies, it's no wonder he thinks she's guilty." He explained about Jordan calling Kit the morning he was murdered, about Kit leaving the house and driving to the ridge above Bayview Park, putting her less than half a mile from the crime scene.

"You think he'll arrest her?"

"I do," said her dad, leaning back, making a bridge of his fingers. "His problem is that he doesn't have any hard evidence. No weapon. No witnesses. No forensics. If Kit hadn't given him that gift of mass fabrications, he'd have nothing at all."

"So you're saying what he has is circumstantial."

He nodded.

"But can't prosecutors win circumstantial cases?"

Sighing, he replied, "Yeah, they can."

"Look, I may have some information that will complicate De-Petro's investigation. Ours, too, unfortunately."

He turned his full attention on her.

She reminded him of the skeleton that she and Cordelia had found behind a wall in the basement of the theater, and then continued on from there. Kit's personal connection to the first two. The names of the men and one woman, and when they went missing. The manner of all three deaths—a gunshot to the forehead. She didn't have to connect the final dot. Her father saw it immediately.

"Jordan was murdered in exactly the same way. Do you have any other information on the third victim? The one the police found last night."

"Nothing beyond what I just told you."

He looked away, digesting the information. "What are we dealing with? A thirty-year-old vendetta? A psychopath? Jealousy? Twisted justice? Listen, find out everything you can on that third victim and get back to me. It's not the break in the case I was hoping for, but if nothing else, you're right. It will throw a major spanner into the case DePetro is building."

"If it does turn out that it's all connected, it lets Booker and Chloe off the hook. At least that's something." She figured with everything that had landed on the Deere kids recently, they could use a break.

Her father grabbed his phone and punched in a number. "De-Petro needs to gather ballistics on all the gunshots. If it turns out—" He stopped, listened. "Hi. This is Raymond Lawless. I need to speak with Neil DePetro. Tell him it's urgent."

Jane had already come to the same conclusion. If the gun used to kill the three victims in the theater matched the one used on Jordan, DePetro's case had just metastasized into a full-blown search for a serial killer.

29

The *mystery* of Erin O'Brian had come to take precedence over Booker's infatuation—if that's what it was—with her. In the last day, he'd discovered some facts about her personal life that had left him with even more questions. Why was she in town on his father's dime? Why had she stood outside a day care playground, all her attention focused on one little girl?

At seven P.M. that night, Booker entered the Rhineland Grill and waited in the bar until Erin joined him. "You look astonishing," he said, taking in her sleek black dress and sexy makeup. He wondered how she thought the evening would end. Probably the same way he did, though he doubted it would ever come to pass because of the questions he intended to ask.

Over dinner, he kept the conversation light. It might be the last time they sat like this, enjoying each other's company, feeling the electricity of their attraction clear to the soles of their feet. When she reached across the table and touched his hand right after they'd ordered a dessert to share, he knew if he didn't approach the subject soon, he never would.

"I got a call last night from a friend. We roomed together when we were in college. Griffin Turner? He's been working at the

Seattle Repertory Theatre for the last few years." He already knew the answer to his first question.

"Sure, I know Griffin," said Erin, her gaze roaming the room. "Not well, but we've been at a few cast parties together."

"Griffin mentioned that you had a child. A little boy."

Her unblinking eyes held his.

"You never mentioned him. Actually, you told me you didn't have any children."

Her lips drew together as she examined her wineglass.

"What's his name?"

"Damian."

"How old is he? What's he like? I think it's really cool that you have a kid."

Looking away, she said, "He died. Two years ago. A year later my marriage came apart."

"Oh, God." He'd had no idea. Griffin had either conveniently left that part out or he didn't know. "I should never have brought it up. It's none of my business. God, I'm an asshole. I'm *such* an asshole."

"It's not your fault," said Erin, draining the wine from her glass. "It was an accident. He was seven years, four months and nine days old. My amazing, beautiful boy." Her breath caught in her throat. "You . . . you had to know him to understand how special he was."

"Erin," he said, leaning toward her. Did he really want to push this, knowing what he now knew? "I saw you yesterday. At that day care center."

Her eyes widened. "What?"

"You were watching a little girl."

"You followed me?"

"I needed answers. I know you talked to my father recently, more than once. That he paid for you to stay here. Why did he do that? What were you talking to him about? I'm sorry about your

222

boy, truly I am, but my father is gone, too, and, I mean, I know you had nothing to do with that—" The words stopped him. He did know that, didn't he? Forging on, he continued, "What I don't get is what was going on between you two." He was making a mess of things, not expressing himself well at all.

Erin watched him steadily, her fingers kneading her napkin. "I can't believe you followed me."

He lowered his head. "I suppose you hate me now. I'm an untrustworthy SOB. An obnoxiously intrusive creep. A controlling scumbag."

"You sure love to criticize yourself," she said softly.

"Might as well use my extensive vocabulary of abuse on myself."

Silence followed his comment, brief, but undeniably charged.

"If you really want to know, I'll tell you. But it's not easy for me to talk about, so I'll make it short."

He nodded as he pushed his half-full glass of wine across to her.

"My husband wanted something good to come from Damian's death. I didn't really think that was possible, but I went along with his wishes. We signed an agreement to donate our son's organs. We knew his heart would go to a child who was desperately in need of a heart transplant. We buried Damian and eleven months later, Tony filed for divorce. I was having a very hard time of it back then. Couldn't write. Couldn't sleep. Couldn't eat." She reached out with a shaky hand and pulled Booker's wineglass closer. "I don't blame Tony for leaving me. We weren't going to make it, not after what had happened. But it was just one more blow, you know?"

"You don't need to do this," said Booker.

"No, I want to tell you. Maybe it explains why I am the way I am. What happened to the girl you once knew. Last June, I began to wonder about the child who'd been given Damian's heart. I

223

needed to find him—or, as it turns out, her. I had to see her, be near her. It didn't take long for it to turn into an obsession. The problem is, you can't just call up your doctors and demand to know what became of your child's donated heart. It's not something you're ever supposed to find out. Even so, I began to wonder if there wasn't some way. That's when I first contacted your father. He was the only man I knew who had virtually unlimited financial resources and who might take pity on me and offer his help.

"Booker, your dad was the most incredible man. He'd always been warm and kind back in Nashville, when I was friends with Chloe, but when I explained what had happened, what I needed, he understood instantly. He said he couldn't imagine what he would have done if he'd lost you or Chloe. He promised he'd see what he could do.

"I thought, when I didn't hear back from him within the first month, that he'd forgotten. I didn't blame him. There was no reason he needed to indulge the whims of an old friend of his daughter's. I kept searching, on my end, to find out as much as I could, but at every turn, doors refused to open. And then, three weeks ago, your father called to say his investigator had found the child. What was so odd was that the girl lived in Minneapolis. When she'd received the heart transplant, two years ago, the parents had been living in Houston. The surgery was done at the Mayo Clinic in Rochester. While they were in Minnesota—I guess it was several months—the father was offered a job. It meant the family would have to move to the Twin Cities. He eventually took the position and the family relocated.

"Your father and I talked on the phone several times after that. He eventually sent me a plane ticket and made reservations for me at the Heidelberg Club. He said he was here all the time, so it would be easy for us to meet."

"Did you," asked Booker, "meet?"

"We had two long lunches and one dinner. For the first time since I'd lost my son, I really let all my feelings come out. He was a wonderful listener. Since I've been here, I've driven into Minneapolis four times. Each time I've been able to stand near the little girl for at least half an hour."

"Do you want to meet her?"

She shook her head. "Just seeing her play with the other children, watching her smile, seeing the delight in her eyes when a bird lands on the ground near her . . . it's enough. I don't claim to understand it, but she's so much like Damian. She even looks like him. To think that a part of my boy is still alive, that his heart is still beating in the here and now . . . it means the world to me. It feels . . . like maybe the worst is over and I'm beginning to heal." Looking up at Booker she said, "You can see why I took the news of your father's death so hard. I'd really come to love that man. His loss, it was huge."

Ironically, Booker's urge to comfort her for her loss threw his own barely felt sense of loss into stark relief, and that disconnect brought him up cold. His first thought was that he truly was a rotten son. That also happened to be his second and third thought. The weird thing was, he was learning more—and thinking more—about his dad now that he was gone than he ever had while he was alive. For the first time, he was beginning to sense a void opening up inside of him, an urge to go to his father and hash things out, ask questions, make amends. The fact that that was no longer possible nearly dissolved him. "I'm so sorry," he said. "For all of it."

"Booker," said Erin. "You have to listen to me. I thought, when it came to being hard on myself, to personal vilification, I was world class. But you're even better at it than I am."

"How can you be hard on yourself?" he said earnestly. "You're incredible."

In spite of the bleak conversation they'd been engaged in, Erin couldn't seem to help herself. She smiled. "We're a real pair, aren't we. I think I'm a waste of space and you think I'm wonderful. You think you're worthless, and I think you're——"

"What?"

"One of the nicest guys I've ever met."

Nice, he thought. The same thing his sister had called him. It wasn't wicked cool, edgy, or sexy bad, but he could work with it. "So what do we do now?"

"Eat our dessert."

"And after that?"

"You need an outline?"

"Just a thumbnail sketch."

"Well," she said, finishing off the wine, "I think we'll start by taking the elevator up to the third floor. And then we'll walk down the hall to my room, where you'll kiss me good night."

"And then?"

"That's as far as my working draft goes."

"So, once we're on our own, it's okay to improvise?"

She grinned. "I would expect nothing less from the man who's going to help stage my play next spring."

"Am I?"

"I live in Seattle. You live in New York. Getting together in February in the middle of the country seems like a good compromise."

"If you think I'm waiting until next February to see you again——"

The waiter arrived with the crème brûlée and set it in the center of the table. After producing two spoons, he said, "Can I get you anything else?"

"The check," said Booker.

30

Ducking under the overhang, Jane stood outside Avi's building and buzzed her apartment. The rain had begun less than an hour ago, but was already starting to come down as sleet. A miserable night was in store for anyone who had to be out. Checking her watch, she turned back to her car and saw that Mouse had hopped into the backseat. He was staring out the side window, nose pressed to the glass.

"Yes?" came Avi's voice.

"It's me," said Jane.

The lock clicked open and Jane flew inside. Once up on second, she was about to knock on Avi's door when it opened and the most wonderful aroma wafted out.

"Wow, what do you have in the oven?" asked Jane.

Avi stepped back and allowed Jane to enter. No hug. No kiss. Not even a welcoming smile. "On my way back from the airport, I figured I better stop off and buy some food. I didn't have anything here. I also didn't have much energy, so I bought a pot roast, some onions and carrots and potatoes and shoved it in the oven when I got home."

Even without the hug and kiss, Jane was glad to be somewhere warm and dry, and even more glad that Avi was back home. "You got your hair cut." It was shorter than normal—parted on the right side. Avi pushed the androgynous boy look about as far as it could go. She was tall and thin, and liked to wear boy clothes with clunky, colorful athletic shoes. When she wasn't bartending, she wore heavy horn-rimmed glasses. Earrings and sultry makeup cast against type and made the look work.

"The flight was crap," she said, stepping over to the couch and fluffing a throw pillow. "I hate flying, if I haven't said that before. Let me take your coat."

"Mouse is out in the car," said Jane, hesitating by the doorway. "I dropped Gimlet at the groomer. I have to pick her up by nine."

"Go bring Mouse in," said Avi. "The more the merrier. Besides, with him in the room, maybe you won't yell quite as loud."

"I wasn't planning on yelling."

"Well, whatever pain you intend to inflict, I deserve it."

Avi's eyes seemed glazed. Jane wondered how much she'd had to drink. She went back out to the car, clipped Mouse's leash to his collar, then walked him back inside, fearing that the evening might not end well.

"Hey, boy," said Avi, crouching down and giving him an extravagant rub. In return, Mouse licked her face and hands, finally sitting down and lifting a paw. "You're my man," she said, eyes glistening. "Jane, look, I can't wait around for the other shoe to drop. You know what happened between Julia and me. I could say I was sorry, but what does that accomplish?"

"I guess, if nothing else, it would make me think you're sorry."

"Ha. Funny." She got up, and without looking at Jane, disappeared into the kitchen. "It didn't mean anything," she called. "Just sex. I don't have any feelings for her, other than gratitude. And maybe I feel a little sorry for her. She's lonely."

"So this was a mercy fuck?" said Jane, standing in the doorway, watching Avi remove the roasting pan from the oven.

"You don't usually use that kind of language."

"I'm not usually this angry."

"Okay. I knew it," said Avi, cursing after she burned her hand pulling off the roaster cover. She rushed to the sink and turned on the water. "Stupid to think you can cook a meal for a professional chef."

"Stop spinning," said Jane, moving up to her and turning her around.

"Are we over?" asked Avi.

"Only if you want us to be."

"I thought . . . I mean, I came back early because . . . because I was thinking . . . God, I'm a writer and I can't even manage a coherent sentence."

"I wish I understood you better," said Jane. "I'm not sure we've ever had a conversation about being exclusive, not dating other people. It's possible that I just assumed it because it's what I wanted. I've never hidden the fact that I love you, though I've never been entirely sure how you feel."

Avi pulled away and began to dish up the plates of food. "I don't like drama, Jane. Confrontations. You know that."

"You'd rather we forget what happened and just move on."

"Yes," she said, trying to look brisk and purposeful as she carried the filled plates out to the dining room table. "If you forgive me, I would. Wine?" she asked, holding up a bottle of Pinot Noir.

"No thanks."

They sat down and began to eat in silence.

How pleasant, thought Jane. The idea of being anywhere but there suddenly appealed. "This is good," she said, making a stab at conversation.

Avi nodded. And then she burst into tears, covering her face with a napkin. "This is such a friggin' mess," she said, her voice a rasp. "I'm not a coldhearted bitch. I'm not. I am sorry. I don't know what to do, how to make you see that I do care about you."

"Why don't you ever use the word 'love'?"

"What?"

"Well, I mean you've used it—in reference to me—but rarely."

Her lips parted, though she said nothing. Finally, after taking a sip of wine, she said, "I don't trust the word."

"Or the emotion."

"I've loved more than a few women in my time, or thought I had. One, I was totally head over heels for."

"Sarah."

"I moved us across the country, at my own expense, to make it work with her. I took care of her baby while she started that new job. And when Gracie was old enough to go to school, when Sarah no longer needed my services, she showed me the door."

Avi had ended up in Minneapolis, working at a bar downtown. That's when she and Jane had first met.

"She never loved me. But boy, she sure could toss out the word when necessary to keep me happy."

Jane's eyes rose to the water-stained ceiling. She'd heard all this before, more than once, and it was starting to feel old.

"Look, Jane, you need to understand something about me. I create people for my stories. It's what I love most about writing. But I also do it in my life. I meet someone and right away I start spinning a tale about who they are. It may have nothing to do with reality. That's a problem. I told you once, I fall in love too easily. It's because I construct the person I want to be with. Doesn't matter who they really are. Except, it eventually does matter, when my fiction stops working."

"Did you do that with me?"

"I'm trying not to."

"I'm not Sarah," said Jane.

"You don't know how happy that makes me."

At least they could agree on that.

"Since we're having a serious conversation, maybe this is a good time to tell you about an idea I've been kicking around for a while. You're going to be surprised, or possibly even a little bewildered at first. I'm hoping you'll climb on board, because it will affect our relationship in an important—and I believe—an amazing way."

Jane had little hope that the minimal amount of food she'd eaten would digest any time during the next century. Avi might as well pile it on. "Okay."

"You know how strongly I bonded with Gracie, how devastated I was to be cut out of her life. Well, here's my idea. I want a baby. I believe that's what's been missing in my life. What do you say? Will you raise a child with me?"

Jane was rarely at a loss for words, but this was one of those times.

"I know, I know," said Avi. "It's not what you were expecting."

"No," was all Jane could squeak out.

"Will you think about it?"

"Now? You want to have a baby right away?"

"More than anything."

Folding her napkin with great care in an effort to stave off the volcanic eruption gathering steam inside her, Jane said, "Let's think about this. Your first book will be published sometime next spring. Correct me if I'm wrong, but don't most authors go on tour? I assume a pregnancy would make that much more difficult. And down the road, how do you expect to find the time to write if you have a baby around who requires your constant attention?"

"I'm not saying there won't be hurdles. But that's where you come in."

"Avi, I'm already working two jobs, both of which I adore. I have no desire to change any of that."

"But see, I'll have more money now that I'm a published author. Granted, I've only been given a small advance for this book, but it will grow. Eventually, we'll be able to afford a nanny. Your house would be a perfect place to raise a child. I'm only thirty-seven. That's not too old to conceive a baby by today's standards."

"You're going to stop drinking?"

"What? Well, I mean, I know this may take sacrifice."

"*Can* you stop drinking?" Jane's cell phone rang. Retrieving it from the back pocket of her jeans, she saw that it was Cordelia. Feeling an acute need to step away from the Twilight Zone for a few seconds, she said, "I need to take this." She rose from her chair and crossed into the living room. Mouse was asleep on the couch, so she eased down next to him. "Hi," she said.

"I'm calling with an update," came Cordelia's voice. "Am I catching you at a bad time?"

"Not at all." Jane glanced into the dining room just in time to see Avi pour herself another glass of wine. "What's up?"

"I've got the name of the woman the police found behind the wall last night. It's Decca Foster."

"Doesn't ring any bells."

"Did for me. She was a reporter for *City Pages* back in the day. Since I had some free time, I used my awesome sleuthing skills to do a little research. Turns out, she was writing an investigative piece on the Deere family when she suddenly dropped out of sight."

"Wow."

"I ran into Red in the hallway a little while ago. Since you said he remembered so much about Stanislaw Melcer, I asked him about Decca. He said that she tried to interview him one afternoon while he was painting one of the offices on the second floor. He felt like she was trying to pull together a gossip piece, so he pretty much refused to cooperate. He also mentioned that last time he saw her, she was with Archibald Van Arnam. He had his arm around her and they were walking out the front doors. He said they looked very cozy. The plot thickens, does it not?"

"It sure does," said Jane. "Anything more on the ballistics?"

"Oh, right. That's the other big news. Turns out they found evidence that all three victims were shot with the same gun. Here, let me read you what the officer said." She paused. "Okay. Not that this means much to me, but it might to you. The gun was a nine millimeter, possibly a M973, made by IMBEL. Used a nine-by-nineteen parabellum cartridge. It's a Brazilian army pistol. Nine rounds in the magazine. Single action. Short recoil, semiautomatic. Black. It's rare."

"Can you text me that? Or just text it to my dad? He'll want to feed those specs to DePetro."

"Will do. Hey, where are you?"

"I'm at Avi's apartment. We just finished dinner."

"Everything satisfactory in paradise?"

"Just peachy."

"Sounds like we should talk. Stop by the Old Deep and Dark tomorrow. Out."

Jane returned to the dining room. The wine bottle was empty.

"I can tell you're not convinced a child is a good idea," said Avi.

"You're right."

"You've never wanted a child?"

"I thought about it when I was in my twenties," said Jane, sitting back down. "When Christine and I were first together. But no, neither one of us wanted a child. And believe me, if I didn't want one when I was young, I certainly don't want to take that on at my age."

"Age has nothing to do with it."

"For me it does. And remember, you're a writer, Avi, one who's just starting out."

"People can be more than one thing."

It was obvious she'd made up her mind, and equally obvious that Jane wasn't going to be persuaded. "So, we're at an impasse."

Avi pointed to the clock on the buffet.

It was ten to nine. The groomer was at least twenty minutes away. "I've got to run," said Jane, jumping up and looking around for Mouse's leash.

"To be continued," said Avi.

31

That night, Archibald took a cab to the police station in Minnetonka. It was a long way from his home in Prospect Park, a historic section of Minneapolis, where many professors lived. The ride cost him an arm and a leg, though it was better than allowing his car, a silver Audi Q5, to get rained and sleeted on. It was setting up to be a beast of an evening.

As he entered the station, he stepped up to a counter and waited for the uniformed officer behind it to finish his phone call. The man looked bored.

"Help you?" asked the cop, after placing the receiver back in its cradle.

"I need to talk to Neil DePetro."

"Not here."

"This is a matter of some urgency."

He pulled out a clipboard and studied it. "He's on tomorrow. Any time after eight in the morning."

"But I need to talk to him *now*. Call him and tell him that Archibald Van Arnam is here and needs to speak with him right away."

"Can I ask what this is about?"

"I'd rather speak to Sergeant DePetro in private."

"If you expect me to call him and interrupt his evening, you're going to have to give me a reason."

With his lips twisting in annoyance, Archibald said, "I've come to turn myself in. I'm the man who murdered Jordan Deere last Sunday morning."

The cop eyed him. "You're . . . turning yourself in?"

"That's correct."

"Uh-huh. Okaaay. Why don't you have a seat over there." He pointed to a series of chairs. "I'll give the sergeant a ring, see what he wants to do."

"Thank you." Archibald walked over and sat down. There were a few magazines on offer, though they all looked greasy and unappealing.

Twenty-two minutes later, DePetro arrived wearing jeans, a heavy red wool shirt, a long black raincoat, and a baseball cap. "Mr. Van Arnam," he said, motioning for Archibald to follow him into a back hallway.

In less than a minute, Archibald found himself in a small interrogation room, sitting at a round white laminate table. The room smelled like sweat and dirty gym socks. When DePetro sat down across from him, Archibald said, "You could use an air freshener in here."

"I'll make a note of it. Now, I'm told you're here to confess. You murdered Jordan Deere."

"That's right."

Drumming his fingers on the table, he looked at the digital recorder. "Oh, hell," he said, switching it on. "It's nine thirty, Wednesday night, October twenty-eighth. With me is Archibald Van Arnam. Mr. Van Arnam, could you take me through last Sunday morning?"

Archibald unbuttoned his sport coat and tried to relax. "It's common knowledge that Jordan Deere liked to do his morning run at Bayview Park. I confirmed this by following him there—"

"When was that?"

"Maybe a week ago."

"What do you mean, you *followed* him?"

"I . . . parked in the lot and waited for him to arrive, taking care to make sure he didn't see me. And then I followed him, at a distance, to see what route he took." Archibald tried hard not to stare at DePetro's enormous, almost grotesque, Adam's apple. He'd noted it the first time they'd met—at Kit's house last Sunday.

"You're a runner?"

"On occasion."

DePetro's gaze dropped to Archibald's big gut. "Uh-huh. How far did you run that morning?"

"A mile, maybe a little more."

"Pardon me, but you don't look like a guy who could run a mile without stopping half a dozen times to catch his breath. Or without falling over."

With icy correctness, Archibald said, "I saw which path he took. Maybe it wasn't a full mile. I simply needed to locate the path. Once I had that, I scoped it out at my leisure, decided where the best place would be to ambush him."

"*Ambush* him."

"Yes."

"Sounds like you've watched a lot of cowboy movies."

"It's really very simple. I hid in the bushes. When he came past I stepped out. He was surprised to see me. We talked for a few seconds and then I shot him."

"He didn't try to stop you?"

"It happened too fast for that."

"You shot him once? Twice?"

"Twice."

"Where?"

"The forehead and the chest."

More finger drumming. "When you stepped out, what was said?"

"Just . . . he asked what I was doing there."

"And?"

"I said I needed to talk to him. He rested his hands on his thighs to catch his breath. Wanted to know if it was about the family reunion. I said yes. And then I pulled out the gun and shot him."

"Where were you standing in relation to Jordan?"

"Right in front of him."

"How far away?"

"I don't know. A couple yards. Maybe a little more."

"Where was the gun?"

"In my jacket pocket."

"Did you get any blood blowback on your clothes?"

"Yes. I burned them."

DePetro cupped his hands and gazed languidly at his fingernails. "You weren't afraid someone would hear the gunshot? That you'd be found out?"

"I used a silencer. I had my escape route planned and I took off running right away. Nobody saw me."

"What kind of gun?"

"I don't know the name. I bought it illegally."

"Where?"

"In St. Cloud."

"Where in St. Cloud?"

"It was in a parking lot on the edge of town. I could probably find it again. The guy sold the guns out of the trunk of his car."

"How did you find out about him?"

"I refuse to comment on that."

"When did you buy this gun?"

"A few months ago."

"You were planning the murder that long in advance?"

"I was thinking about it, yes."

"Tell me more about the gun. What did it look like?"

"It was silver colored, with a black handle."

"You mean stainless steel?"

"I suppose."

"Small?"

"Yes."

"And the bullets?"

"They were gold. Other than that, I can't describe them because they were inside this piece of metal that fit inside the handle. The dealer showed me how to remove the safety latch and fire it. He told me I had seven bullets. I practiced, fired two or three shots out in the woods one afternoon. That seemed like enough."

"So you're not a marksman."

"No."

"You fired a gun and hit a man square in the forehead and then dead center in the chest. Must have been lucky shots."

"I wasn't far away."

"How did Jordan fall?"

"Excuse me?"

"On his back? On his stomach."

"I can't remember."

"On the path? Off the path? Did you pull him off the path, or leave him right where he fell?"

"I left him and I ran off."

"Did he say anything to you after you shot him?"

"He just looked surprised."

"Where is the gun now?" DePetro's freakishly large Adam's apple continued to bob.

"I threw it in a Dumpster on the way home."

"Where?"

"Is that important? It's gone by now."

"What part of the city?"

"Honestly, I don't recall. I was quite upset, Sergeant. I'm not a killer."

"Tell me why you did it?"

"To protect Kit. Jordan was going to leave her. He was planning to come out of the closet, which would have, in effect, made Kit look like a liar."

"She is a liar."

Archibald flashed his eyes at DePetro. "Until you've walked in another person's shoes, unless you know the full story, I believe it's best not to defame another human being in such a glib way."

"You see yourself as her savior."

"I wouldn't put it that way, but yes. I suppose, in a way, I do."

"You love her?"

"Without question."

"Are you infatuated with her?"

"What? No, of course not."

"Were you ever?"

"I don't see what that has to do with anything."

"I'll take that as a yes. Are you married, Mr. Van Arnam?"

"Not at the moment."

"But you have been."

"Several times. It never seemed to take."

"You were unfaithful?"

"As a matter of fact, no. I've never been unfaithful to any of my wives."

"They were unfaithful to you?"

"I'm not answering that. Could we, perhaps, get back to my reason for coming here tonight?"

"To turn yourself in, to admit to murdering Jordan Deere."

"Correct."

Folding his arms, DePetro, who looked seriously unimpressed, said, "You see, I have some problems with that. First, I think you're here to give yourself up in place of the actual guilty party."

"No. Absolutely not so."

"I think your story has so many holes in it that there's no chance in hell it would hold up in court."

"You're calling *me* a liar?"

"And here's another problem. We've come into possession of evidence connecting Mr. Deere's murder with three others. We believe the same person committed them all. Would you like to confess to four homicides, Mr. Van Arnam? You'll need to do that, and give me details, in order for me to believe you."

Archibald stared back at him.

"You said in an earlier interview that you were working with Cordelia Thorn at her theater, doing research on the history of the building."

"That's right."

"Then you must have heard about the bodies found buried in the walls. Can you tell me about those victims? How you did it?"

"Obviously, with a gun."

"And why?"

"That's my business. No comment."

"If you recently bought a gun to use on Jordan Deere, it couldn't be the murder weapon."

"I'm the one who should know. I shot him with it."

"The same gun was used in all four murders."

"How could you possibly know something like that?"

"It's called ballistics."

"Whatever. You have to take this seriously. I did it. I confess to everything."

"Okay, Mr. Van Arnam. You did your bit. But I've got better things to do with my evening than indulge your personal superhero fantasy. I suggest you leave now, before I arrest you for misdemeanor theft—of my *time*."

32

Booker turned over in bed the following morning and, for a moment, thought Erin had gone AWOL. Stuffing a pillow behind his back, he sat up and looked around. When he heard the water on in the shower, he smiled.

He had to give it to his old man. He'd spared no expense, paying for a full suite on the top floor for as long as Erin cared to stay. The night they'd spent together was everything Booker had hoped it would be and so much more. In his youthful dreams, of necessity, Erin had been a cipher. Now she was flesh and blood, and the difference was astonishing.

Relaxing under the blankets, he flipped on the TV to see what was happening out in the world. His intent was to remain apart from that world for as long as he could convince Erin to stay in bed. After finding a local news station, he picked up the room service menu and began flipping through the breakfast options. He'd pretty much decided on eggs benedict when he heard the news anchor say, "Breaking news on the Jordan Deere murder investigation. Let's listen in."

Turning up the sound, Booker watched a distinguished looking older man in a beautifully tailored suit step up to a podium. He'd been introduced as Dr. Daniel Woodson.

While dozens of cameras flashed, Dr. Woodson gazed out from the podium, giving the reporters time to take their shots.

"What's going on?" said Erin, coming out of the bathroom wearing nothing but a bath towel.

"I don't know," said Booker, patting the bed next to him. "Some doctor's about to reveal breaking news about my father's murder investigation."

"Good morning," said Woodson. He glanced around without smiling.

"He's nervous," said Booker.

"He's very good-looking," said Erin.

"But too old for you. I'm exactly the right age."

Woodson gazed down at a page of notes. "This past Tuesday, I contacted the police in Minnetonka. Not only did I give them a personal statement, but I offered significant evidence I felt would be important in bringing Jordan Deere's murderer to justice. I assumed this information would be released to the public right away. Since nothing seems to have come of my communication with Sergeant Neil DePetro, I decided to call a press conference to release the information myself.

"What I'm about to say may cause bewilderment, heartache, and even anger for some. I want you all to know that I'm aware of the possible repercussions, as was Jordan. It was his wish, as well as my own, for this information to be made public."

"Oh, God," said Booker, reaching for Erin's hand. "Here it comes. The bomb is about to be dropped."

Kit and Tommy sat in the family room, ignoring their coffee, riveted by the man on the TV screen. A friend of Kit's, a woman who worked for KTWN-TV in the Twin Cities, had called her shortly after eight to give her a heads-up about the news conference. Kit had immediately called Tommy. Because there was no cable in the beach house, she'd invited him to the main house so they could watch together. Beverly refused to leave the basement, where she was riding the stationary bicycle and reading a novel. She said she intended to stay in, stay warm, and keep her head down. Booker was gone, nobody knew where. That left only Chloe, and when Kit had approached her door she found it closed, with a taped note that said DO NOT DISTURB.

"Who is this Woodson guy?" asked Tommy. He looked a little more put together this morning. His clothes were clean and pressed, and he'd recently showered and shaved. She couldn't be positive, but she suspected that being arrested for murder had a way of focusing the mind.

"No idea," said Kit.

They fell silent as the man began his statement.

"Jordan Deere was a gay man," said Woodson, his voice firm and unapologetic. "He was my life partner. We'd been together for the past two years."

The press room erupted. More photos were snapped. People started yelling questions.

"Please," said Woodson, holding up his hands. "Let me finish."

"Did his wife know?" called one of the reporters.

"What about his kids?" called another.

Again, Woodson held up his hands for quiet. "Please," he said, flashes continuing to burst. Only when the room had finally quieted down did he continue. "For the last year and a half, Jordan has been working on a piece of writing, part novel, part memoir."

"Oh no," said Kit, feeling her heart begin to race. "That guy's read it. What if he has a copy?"

"I know that Jordan hoped it would be good enough to one day be published. I'm not a book critic, but I doubt that would have happened—unless he'd published it under his own name, which he refused to even consider. Still, I think the book should be read. I want to make it clear from the outset that the stories in this rather rough manuscript are fictional. Let me underscore that last word. They don't represent the specifics of Jordan's own life, and yet, in an important way, they do represent the emotional truth of what it was like to live as a gay man in the last half of the twentieth century while working in an industry that would never have let him get so much as the tip of his boot in the door if he'd been honest about his sexuality."

Again, the room exploded.

"Please," said Woodson. "I'm almost done. Just let me finish."

This time, the news room quieted more quickly.

"I have nothing but respect for the people in Jordan's life who have supported him and loved him. However," he said, pausing to search the faces staring back at him, "I also believe that one of those intimates murdered him last Sunday morning. It wasn't an accident, nor was it random. Someone who knew Jordan's routines was waiting for him in the park and took his life. I want that person found and dropped into the deepest, darkest, lowest reaches of hell. Jordan was the greatest gift I've ever been given. He was good and honest and true. And yes, he also lived a complicated life. I believe, fundamentally, what gave him the most joy was singing for all of you. When he was onstage, Jordan Deere was most himself. Onstage, Jordan never had any doubts about what was right and who he was."

Taking a moment to regain his composure, Woodson began again. "I've brought along with me today twenty copies of Jordan's manuscript. No one owns the rights except Jordan himself."

"We'll see about that," whispered Kit, outraged at the man's audacity.

"You'll find the copies on a table at the back of the room. If you want to make more copies, feel free. Jordan wasn't a trained writer, and yet, I think you'll find that his words touch you deeply. He was about to come out to the world, tell everyone the truth about who he really was. Before he could do that, he was cut down. I believe that his desire to finally tell the truth about himself was the reason for his murder. Unfortunately, his words died with him. All we have left is his music, the memory of his beauty, and that manuscript. I, for one, want to see it read. Thank you. I won't be taking any questions at this time."

"How noble," said Tommy under his breath.

Kit saw movement out of the corner of her eye. When she looked over at the door, she saw Chloe standing still as a rock, staring wide eyed at the TV.

"Oh, honey," said Kit, standing up to face her.

"It will all come out now, won't it," she said, her voice oddly flat. "The girl in the book, *me,* everyone will know how utterly dysfunctional I am."

"Chloe, that was years ago. You're not the same person."

"The shoplifting. The suicide attempts. The diagnosis. The mental hospital. Anorexia. Relapses. I don't know what that man on TV thought he was saying, but Dad didn't novelize *me.*" Turning her eyes on Kit, she screamed, *"Did he."*

"Honey—"

"Stop calling me that. You're useless, you know that. Totally and utterly useless." She turned and bolted toward her bedroom.

"Let me go after her," said Tommy, pushing out of his chair. "Maybe she'll listen to me."

"But what will you say?" asked Kit.

"I have no freakin' idea."

Kit let him go. There was a chance Chloe would talk to him,

and no chance at all Chloe would talk to her. The same deep sense of guilt that would occasionally sneak up on her throughout her married life, the one that could easily overwhelm her with the feeling that she was a terrible mother, was about to swallow her once again. She could never seem to forget what her own mother had told her: "Children come first. Then comes Daddy. Mom comes last. That's the way it should be, the way you will raise your own kids, not just because I'm telling you to, but because it's the way you'll want it to be. It's a natural impulse. You'll see, when you're a mommy yourself."

But that hadn't been the way Kit had lived her life. She often put herself, the needs of her career, her desire for romance and adventure, before the needs of her children and husband. Feminists would support her decisions, she used to tell herself. Her actions were grounded in the need for women to take some of their own power back. She saw friends, other women, allowing themselves a little selfishness. Men were given a pass when it came to work. Why shouldn't she be given the same break? It wasn't fair. And yet, no matter how hard she tried to turn off the tape inside her head, she couldn't.

If Kit *had* put her kids first, if she'd spent more time with Chloe and Booker, maybe they would have been happier children, become more balanced, more content with their lives. Jordan never seemed to second-guess himself. If he had things to do, places to go, he went. She never saw him agonizing over his role as a father. So why did she feel such guilt? Was she, in fact, a heartless monster, an utter failure as a mother, the reason her children were so screwed up? She fought against that conclusion, refused to believe it, and yet that little voice inside her head wouldn't go away. Surely she had the right to take some time for herself. Surely Chloe's problems weren't all her fault. Surely, if a woman married and acquired a husband and children, she didn't automatically, by her very nature, become an indentured servant. She had a solid political and philosophical basis for her decisions, and still . . . she feared those questions as much as she did the answers.

33

Jane wiped brick dust off her face as she returned to her office at the theater. She'd spent the last hour and a half going over the two crime scenes in the basement. Only one more to go. As she'd expected, the police had done a good job of sifting through what material there was, which meant she'd found nothing.

Dropping down heavily on her desk chair, she popped the top on a cold Red Bull and took a long sip.

"What's that in your hair?" came Cordelia's voice.

Jane looked up to find her friend standing in the doorway.

"Brick dust. I'm covered in it."

"Lovely." Cordelia was wearing what looked like a 1950s prom gown—a frothy, strapless coral concoction with a full skirt and an attached netted wrap. "I spoke to Daniel Woodson. He'll be here around three."

"I can't believe you actually got hold of him."

"It is axiomatic that when people see the name Cordelia Thorn pop up on their cell phones, they *take* the call."

"If I haven't mentioned this before, I'm glad you know everyone in town."

"Not everyone," she replied, with fake modesty. "But almost."

"Lovely dress."

"Oh, do you like it?" She twirled into the room. "I was feeling exuberantly femme this morning. I love the fabric. Not so sure about the color. I think it makes my skin look a little green. And," she added, lowering her voice, "as we all know, it's not easy being green."

"Funny. Not to change the subject, but do you hear water running? It's like someone turned on a faucet and forgot to turn it off."

"Ah, Gilbert and Hilda are playing tricks on *you* today. I'm usually their target of choice."

Jane refused to believe ghosts were the cause of the noise. "I think you may have a plumbing problem."

"I do, dearheart. It's called Gilbert and Hilda King."

"Since you're here, why don't you sit for a minute. I have a question."

"And I likely have the answer." She sat down on the folding chair facing Jane.

"It's about Avi."

"Of course it is. What is it this time?"

"Are you suggesting that Avi constantly presents me with problems?"

"Yes."

"Well, this one is a whopper."

"I shall brace myself."

"She wants to have a baby."

Cordelia shrieked, then hooted.

Jane waited for more. "That's all you've got to say?"

"I thought my response was quite eloquent."

"You think it's a bad idea."

"Duh."

"Why?"

251

"*Why?* How does she intend to support this child? Oh, I see. That's your job."

"No, she thinks she'll make good money as a writer. She'll hire a nanny."

Another shriek. "Does that woman live on the same planet that we do? Okay. Let's take this slowly, one question at a time. Are you on board with this? I mean, are you even considering signing on with Avi and child?"

Jane shook her head. "But what worries me is that, whether or not I'm part of the equation, she's still full steam ahead. She believes firmly that a child will fill a void in her life that nothing else can."

"I'm not going to argue how much the love of a child can bring to your life, but it's not for the faint of heart, for heavy drinkers, or for starving artists—not if your primary goal is the happiness and safety of the kid. If you start out thinking that the kid is there to do something for *you* . . . you're already ass backwards. Feel free to quote me."

"So give me some advice. If it were you, what would you say to her?"

"One little phrase: 'Good-bye and good luck.'" Looking as if she wasn't completely sure that Jane was convinced, she added, "Listen to Auntie Cordelia. It is *not* your responsibility in life to make everyone happy."

"I know that."

"Do you? Earth to Jane? If you want to be nice, tell her it's her dream, not yours, and you want no part of it. And then run. Fast. Now." She rose regally from the chair. "I must attend to other matters. As a parting comment, let me just say this: Refuse to darken the door of any sperm bank and tell Avi to do the same."

Jane muttered to herself as she finished her Red Bull, nursing it, not really wanting to brave the third crime scene, but knowing she couldn't leave loose ends. She also needed to get back to her office in time to clean herself up a little before Woodson arrived. Slinging a messenger bag over her shoulder, she took the elevator up to the third floor. As she came through the theater on her way backstage, she saw that the new curtain was about to be installed.

Cordelia and Octavia had argued, of course, about the color. Octavia wanted a bright red-orange. Cordelia insisted on a wine red or, failing that, a rich royal blue. Since they were at an impasse, and Jane was the third person on the board—the tiebreaker—she chose the color she liked best, the blue. She was glad to see that it went so beautifully with the gilded ceiling, the chandeliers, and the lovely pastel colors on the plaster carvings around the stage.

Pushing through a curtain, she ducked backstage and walked briskly to the dressing room along the rear wall. Once inside, she took out a flashlight and slipped sideways through the opening in the bookcase, making her way carefully down the wooden stairs to the murder room. Washing the flashlight beam over the interior, she saw that the trunk had been removed. She set her bag down, slipped on a pair of latex gloves, and began her search. The walls came first. She felt ridiculously Sherlock Holmesian when she used a magnifying glass, but it remained a good tool, even if it was low tech.

Once again, she understood that it was unlikely she'd find anything. After examining all four walls, she was about to get down on her hands and knees to inspect the floor when she heard the sound of footsteps. Backing up, she hit the wall as the beam of a flashlight hit her square in the eyes, blinding her.

Twisting her head away, she demanded, "Who's there?"

"It's just me," came a familiar voice. Red turned the flashlight on his face, which helped her identify him, but also made him look like a ghoul. "What are you doing in here?" he asked mildly.

"Building an intercontinental ballistic missile," said Jane, trying to dislodge her heart from her throat. "You scared me." Didn't this guy have anything else to do but prowl around?

"You need a hand with anything?"

"No. Thanks."

"Okay. If you change your mind, you know where to find me." With that, he walked off. Moments later, she heard a door close. And then the unmistakable sound of a running faucet started up again. Why couldn't Cordelia have bought herself a nice, new, unhaunted theater somewhere in the boring burbs?

Easing down on all fours, Jane began running her flashlight beam across the cracks in the floorboards. She was almost done when she found something odd. Scooting over to her messenger bag, she removed a pair of tweezers, then moved back and carefully eased a folded piece of paper out of the crack. Holding the flashlight in her mouth, she opened it. When she saw what it was, she felt a pure adrenaline rush.

It took a few more seconds for the dread to set in.

"That's . . . quite a costume," said Daniel Woodson, smiling at Cordelia. "You always seem to find the most . . . unusual . . . clothing. Makes me feel like I'm at my senior prom. I think my palms are even sweating." He'd taken a seat on the uncomfortable Savonarola chair in Cordelia's office. "You know, this feels good. I don't think I've even cracked a smile all week."

Jane, who was half sitting, half leaning against a red lacquered trunk, thanked Woodson for coming. In person, he looked years younger than he had on TV. She asked him what he did for a living—what the "Dr." in front of his name meant.

"I'm a cardiothoracic surgeon," he said.

"You're a heart doctor," said Cordelia. "One of the premier heart doctors in the great state of Minnesota."

"At the moment, I'm hiding out," he added. "After that press conference this morning, the phone at my office has been ringing off the hook. Same with my cell. I can't go home because my house is surrounded by camera crews and reporters. I keep thinking this is all a dream and that I'm going to wake up."

Jane gave him a few seconds. "Are you okay with answering a few questions?"

"Sure, that's why I'm here. If you're trying to figure out what's going on, I want to help."

"Where did you meet Jordan?" asked Jane.

"At a party. Since we both love golf, we got to talking. A few days later, he called and we played nine holes. And then we had dinner. I guess you could say that our relationship took off from there."

"Cookies?" said Cordelia brightly, waving her hand over the plate of Russian tea cakes on her desk.

"Um, no thanks," said Woodson. "I don't have much of an appetite."

"This may not be a cookie kind of conversation," said Jane.

"Really?" murmured Cordelia, fingering the glass beads at her throat as she glanced longingly at the plate.

"Did Jordan ever talk about his family?" asked Jane.

"Oh, sure, constantly. For want of a better term, he called them his 'circle,' since they weren't all, strictly speaking, related."

When Cordelia thought nobody was looking, she inched the cookie plate closer and tapped one off into her lap. Palming it, she lifted it to her lips and took a nibble, smiling innocently until she saw Jane watching her.

"From what you said this morning," continued Jane, "it seemed to me that you believe one of them is responsible for his murder."

"I do."

"Who's at the top of the list?"

"Well, at first, I assumed it had to be Tommy Prior. He's been so sullen, so angry with Jordan, and so erratic because of the drinking. I thought he'd finally snapped. I figured that he knew Jordan was seeing someone and that it was serious, so he bought himself a gun and made his plans."

"But you've changed your mind?" asked Cordelia, wiping a tell-tale crumb off the side of her mouth.

He drew in a breath. "As I said before, I'm not a fan of De-Petro, but in this instance, it seems to me that Kit did have the most compelling motive."

"The divorce," said Jane.

"Not just the divorce, but everything that came along with it."

"Such as?"

"Jordan's need to be honest with his fans about who he was, which meant Kit's willingness to participate in Jordan's sham life would've come out. And then, tangentially, her sex life would be out there on the table, fodder for tabloids. Think about it. All the fraudulent interviews. The fake husband-and-wife photographs. I don't care how she tries to shape-shift it, those would be huge admissions for a woman who's been out there peddling the 'Deere family values' for years."

"You know, I think this *is* a cookie kind of conversation," said Cordelia, snatching another Russian tea cake, this time openly, and taking a defiant bite.

"Tell me," said Jane. "Other than Kit, is there anyone else in the family you think could be responsible?"

"Beverly Elliot," he said without hesitation. "Jordan made it clear that Beverly never liked him. I don't honestly think it was Jordan she disliked as much as it was the fact that Kit would never even consider her as a possible lover and life partner. Believe me, I understand those feelings. I was in love with my best friend in high school. I knew he was completely oblivious to how I felt, and it hurt like hell. Whoever Kit's husband was would have been a target of Beverly's hostility."

"You think she hated him enough to murder him?"

"Let me clarify: I don't think she would have committed murder simply because she hated Jordan, but more specifically because of what he was about to do to Kit. From what I understand, she's always been fiercely loyal to Kit, and I also believe, deeply in love with her. Apparently Kit has amazing charisma, or charm, or whatever you want to call it. At heart, I believe she's shown herself to be a good, generous, warmhearted woman. But she can also be selfish and imperious."

"Nothing wrong with imperious," mumbled Cordelia.

"I think Beverly, if she is guilty," continued Woodson, "might have been trying to prevent what she considered a greater tragedy than Jordan's death."

"Last Saturday night," said Jane. "The night Jordan left his house and didn't return. Can I assume he stayed with you?"

"Yes, he did."

"You picked him up from the Heidelberg marina?"

"That's right. I live near there."

"Your car is black? An Audi?"

"A black Lexus. Boy, you've done your homework."

"Can I also assume that Jordan kept some clothes at your house? That's why he had on different clothing on Sunday morning."

He nodded.

"So, how did that work? Did he take your car to Bayview Park?"

"No, I dropped him off. He said to give him an hour, that he'd meet me back in the parking lot. I drove into town, did some errands. By the time I got back, the lot was filled with police cars and medical vans. They weren't letting anyone in or out. I asked one of the officers what was going on, but he didn't have any information. I couldn't find Jordan anywhere and I started to get this sick feeling in my stomach. I waited around until the police began directing traffic away from the site, so I was forced to leave. I called his cell over and over, but never got him. I assumed he'd left the park and somehow made his way back to his house, that he'd been swallowed up by his family problems and couldn't find a moment to get away to call me. It wasn't like him, but it was the only explanation I could come up with. That evening, when I was listening to the local TV news, I found out what happened."

"How awful for you," said Cordelia.

Woodson swallowed hard.

"Are you up for one final question?" asked Jane.

"Sure."

"Before Jordan's death, did he receive any notes, possibly on typing paper, with the letters of his name—or part of his name—printed in the center?"

"How could you possibly know that?" he asked, looking stunned. "Yes, he did. Every few days. And with each note he received, one more letter was missing. There was always a little black crow drawn at the bottom. Jordan hated crows. Or, more accurately, I think he was terrified of them."

"Why?" asked Cordelia.

"He told me that when he was a kid, he was outside playing one afternoon when several crows started dive-bombing him. They flew at him and flew at him, pecking and cawing and flapping. He has a scar, right next to his eye, where one of the beaks connected with his face. Later in life, he said he assumed that a crow baby was probably on the ground and that they were trying to protect it, trying to chase him off. But that attack made a big impression on a small boy."

"Heavens," said Cordelia. "A true Alfred Hitchcock moment."

"Do you remember when Jordan received the last note?" asked Jane.

"Saturday afternoon. He had it with him and showed it to me on Saturday night. In fact, he'd brought the entire folder of notes with him. He'd saved every one."

"Did you ever show them to the police?"

"Sure did. DePetro looked them over, didn't say much. I got the impression he thought someone was having a little fun with Jordan."

"What did the last note say?"

"Just the letter 'J.'"

"And the next day Jordan died."

"You think it's connected? Because, I have to tell you, it was really starting to bother him. Jordan was superstitious—especially about the crows. He said it felt like it was some sort of hex."

"Excuse me," said Red.

Everyone turned to look.

Rubbing his hands down the sides of his overalls, he said, "Cordelia? I'm leaving in a few minutes. I wanted to tell you that I've found two guys I want to hire as maintenance staff. Do you want to see their résumés?"

"Just hire them," said Cordelia. "Make sure they stop off at the business office and fill out the necessary forms."

"Will do. Hi, Jane," said Red, smiling a bit sheepishly. And then he nodded to Woodson.

"You look so familiar," said Woodson. "Mr.—"

"Red," he said. "Call me Red."

"Have we met?"

"Not that I recall. Well, I'm off. Sorry about the interruption."

"Huh," said Woodson, shaking his head as Red shuffled away. "That guy is so familiar. Drives me crazy when I can't place a face."

Jane found herself staring at the spot where Red had been standing. Staring and . . . wondering.

34

Kit was relieved to find Chloe in the living room later that afternoon. She'd shut herself away in her bedroom after the press conference and refused to talk to anyone, even Tommy, who'd stood at her door for a good half hour trying to get her to open up.

"Chloe? Can I get you something to eat?"

Standing at the window, looking down on the beach, Chloe shook her head. "I'm not hungry."

Kit felt a pain deep in her bones seeing how pale and thin her daughter looked. "Some hot tea, then?"

"Do you think it will ever stop raining?"

"I know how you feel," said Kit. "It's such a cold rain. The damp gets inside you. Let me find you a sweater." All her daughter had on were jeans and a thin cotton T-shirt.

"No, I'm fine."

Stepping over to the wall thermostat, she turned up the heat in the house. If she couldn't warm her daughter one way, she'd do it another.

"I had to turn my cell phone off," said Chloe, keeping her back to her mother. "It never stops ringing. I don't want to talk to anyone. I mean, what am I supposed to say?"

"It was your dad and me," said Kit. "None of this is on you. You and Booker were innocent bystanders."

"Not according to that manuscript."

"Chloe, please. That man, that doctor who gave the news conference this morning, he said several times, even underscoring it, that the story your father wrote was fiction. It was."

"Not all of it."

"But nobody knows that. Only those involved, and that's such a small number. Doctors are constrained by confidentiality issues, and Ray Lawless was able to get your police record wiped clean. Nobody in the family will say a word. I think you're reacting to a catastrophe that will never happen."

Turning around, Chloe's eyes fastened on her mother. "Where's the key to Dad's gun cabinet?"

"Why?"

"Because I want a gun."

"No way. Not happening."

"This is my house now. I own everything in it. I want the key."

"You don't own it yet."

"When it's mine, you know what I'm going to do?" She stepped a few paces closer. "I'm going to call a real estate agent and sell it. I never want to set foot in this place again."

"Chloe, honey—"

"And if you don't stop calling me honey, I'm going to burn the house down with *you* in it. Do you get it now? Do I make myself clear?"

Kit had no desire to talk to Ray. She didn't want to talk to anyone. In a matter of days, the life she'd loved so much had disappeared forever. And yet, when he'd phoned, she agreed to meet, mainly because he said he had some important news. Her one proviso was that, if he intended to drive out to the summerhouse, that they had to meet in his car. She couldn't chance upsetting Chloe any more than she already was.

As Kit sat in the passenger's seat, heavy rain beating down on the windshield and mercifully obscuring the house, she couldn't help but wonder if all the good times she'd spent here with her family had been part of the same lie as her marriage.

"It's all gone," she whispered. "And nothing can ever bring it back."

Ray sat silently behind the wheel, offering no words of encouragement.

Rousing herself, Kit said, "You have information. And questions. I have one, too. That man—Woodson. He said he had every right to release Jordan's manuscript, that it belonged to Jordan, and now that my husband was gone, he had the right to offer it to anyone who wanted to read it. Is that true? Shouldn't the manuscript be considered part of Jordan's estate?"

"I assumed you'd ask that," said Ray. "The quick answer is, yes, most likely what he did was illegal. I suggest you contact Joji Mura. He may have better, and perhaps more specific, answers for you. That said, there's no way to undo what he did. Taking Woodson to court, if that's what you're thinking, might win you the right to prevent further distribution of the manuscript, but again, the horse is out of the barn." He waited a few seconds, then went on. "We had a breakthrough yesterday, one that will have an impact on the case DePetro is building against you. That's why I'm here. The cold case unit of the MPD was able to connect Jordan's murder with three other murders that took place years ago at Cordelia's theater."

She looked up sharply. "Connected how?"

"The same gun was used. William Edward Chapman. Stanislaw Melcer. And Decca Foster. I understand you knew all three. May I ask how?"

Her eyes rolled toward him, then away. "Well, let's just guess, shall we? The men I slept with. The woman was a disgusting worm of a journalist looking for dirt on Jordan and me."

"It never seemed strange to you that they all disappeared?"

"No, Ray, it didn't."

"Let's take Chapman. Were you still sleeping with him when he went missing?"

"We hadn't been together in weeks. I assumed he'd left his wife and taken off for greener pastures. He wasn't happy in his marriage."

"So your relationship with him wasn't serious?"

"Hardly."

"And Melcer?"

"I ended it. He was angry, or hurt—or both. He went around blustering that I was a witch and a bitch and a ballbuster. Beverly had a little talk with him. It doesn't mean, by the way, that she murdered the guy."

"How long after she talked to him did he disappear?"

"Honestly, Ray, I have no memory of that." Kit jumped at the sound of a rap on the side window. Locating the power switch and rolling the window down, she found Booker standing outside in the rain.

"Hey," he said. "Oops. Am I interrupting something?"

"Of course not. We were just talking about DePetro. Where have you been?"

He grinned. "Is Chloe home?"

"In her bedroom. Go to her, okay? We had kind of a blowup."

"Will do. Hey, Ray." He waved, and then took off running up to the house.

"He's in a good mood," said Kit, as she rolled her window back up. "I'm glad someone in this family is."

Ray spent a moment adjusting the heat.

Kit spent the same moment watching him. "I wish there was more I could tell you."

"At the very least, this new information will slow DePetro down."

"So I'll still end up in jail, it will just take a while longer. You know," she said, stretching her arms, "sometimes I think I should just pack up a few million dollars, get in that Learjet and have my pilot find me a nice warm little country that doesn't have an extradition treaty with the U.S. You could even join me." She glanced over and saw the horror in his eyes. "I'm joking." Though, in truth, she wasn't.

"That would be an admission of guilt, Kit."

"What's the difference? I didn't murder anyone and I'm probably going to spend the rest of my life in a six-by-eight-foot cell."

"Is that Booker up on the porch?" asked Ray. He rolled down Kit's window. "Can you hear what he's saying?"

"Mom," came Booker's scream. "Come here. Quick."

In an instant, she was out of the car, rushing toward him.

Booker ran out to meet her. "It's Chloe. She's unconscious, facedown on the bed. I found these next to her." He held up a pill bottle. "It's Xanax. I don't know how many she took."

Kit grabbed the bottle and read the words "Sixty pills" out loud.

Ray was right behind her, already on his cell phone. He gave the house address to the 911 operator and then added all the important details.

"Thank you, Ray. Thank you, thank you. What would I do without you?" The next second, she was on her way to the front door, in the hallway that led to her daughter's bedroom, careening off walls, shattering a mirror, nearly falling. This couldn't be happening. Not Chloe. Not her little girl. "Get them to send an ambulance right away," she screamed. "Now. Right now."

35

Jane sat in front of the fireplace in her living room, feeling warm for the first time all day. As the fire snapped and the birch logs shifted in the grate, she ate her dinner—a bowl of buttered popcorn. Her dogs had hunkered down next to her, their eyes moving in lockstep with her hand, back and forth as she lifted the popcorn from the bowl to her mouth. It must be like watching a tennis match, she thought to herself. Except that, in this case, the ball was edible. She'd been calling her father ever since Woodson had left the theater. Knowing what she did now, she was worried about him. The fact that he hadn't returned any of her calls only increased her uneasiness.

"I suppose I could call Avi," she said to her dogs. Watching Mouse's reaction, she said, "Yeah, I agree. Not a good idea." She didn't want to talk to Avi, which was a real switch. Something besides the logs in the fireplace had shifted.

When the doorbell rang, Jane got up and set the popcorn bowl on a table by the windows. She looked through the peephole and saw her father outside.

"Come in," she said, helping him off with his soggy raincoat and hat and then giving him a long, extra-strong hug.

"That was nice. Why do I rate?"

"I'm just glad to see you."

Rubbing his hands together, he said, "It's freezing out there. Mark my words. We'll have snow before morning."

"I've got a fire going."

"I can smell it," he said, slipping off his wet shoes. "What a night."

"Would you like something hot to drink?"

"You know, honey, after the day I've had, I could really use a whiskey."

As he bent down to greet the dogs, Jane went into the kitchen and came back with a bottle of Jameson and two shot glasses.

Ray stood by the fire for a few minutes, warming his hands. "I got your messages while I was at the hospital. I thought, instead of calling, I'd stop by instead."

"Why were you at a hospital?" She sat down on the couch and poured them each a shot.

Lifting the glass from her hand, Ray said, "Chloe Deere tried to commit suicide this afternoon."

"Oh, God. Is she okay?"

"Thankfully, Booker found her not long after she'd swallowed the pills. Yes, it looks like she'll be fine. Kit, on the other hand, completely came apart. She blames herself—and Jordan. I can't say that I disagree." He sat down on the rocking chair next to the hearth. "My but this fire feels good on a cold night. Hate to think about going out again."

"Don't," said Jane. "Stay here tonight."

"Right. You want me to hide until all the crazies who leave notes in my mailbox fade away."

"Listen, Dad. I found something this afternoon. I want you to see it." She rose and went back to her study, returning with a plastic bag and a pair of latex gloves. Slipping the gloves on, she removed the page from the bag and held it up so her father could see it.

"What is it?"

"You see the letter in the center of the page?"

" 'S.' Yes, I see it."

"I found this at the theater this afternoon—between the floorboards in the room where Stanislaw Melcer was buried." She waited for him to make the connection. "Melcer must have had it with him when he was murdered. Somehow, the murderer didn't see it and it worked its way between the floorboards."

"Are you suggesting the notes I've been receiving are linked to that?"

She explained what she'd learned from Daniel Woodson about the notes Jordan had been receiving before his death.

"You talked to Woodson?"

"This afternoon."

"Wow, you're quick."

"I had to be, because I think we're running out of time. The day before Jordan was murdered, he received a note that said 'J.' The first letter of his name. I'm guessing it was the same with Melcer, Chapman, and Foster. I believe the killer was saying their time was up. Since you've been receiving the same kind of note, I think you're his next target."

Ray downed the Jameson. "Seems rather silly. I mean, why me?"

"Why any of them?" said Jane. "I see a connection between Jordan's death and what he was about to do. But as for the other three homicides, I'm in the dark. All I know is that the Deere family is at the center of it. Since you're representing Kit, you've apparently made yourself a target." She paused to let her words sink in. "When did you receive the last note?"

"Today. This morning before I left for work."

"And what did it say?"

"R."

It was what she'd dreaded hearing. "You can't go home tonight. You have to stay here."

"Jane, I can't let this . . . whatever it is . . . chase me out of my house."

"No, but . . . just for me. To be on the safe side? Can't you stay here one night? I've got a security system. Sometimes I forget to use it, but I'll make sure it's on tonight. You know I have a comfortable bed upstairs for you because you've slept in it."

"Pour me another and I'll think about it."

"If I pour you another, you're definitely staying."

He held out his glass. "Did I ever mention that you're a lot like your mother? You not only look like her, but you have the same facility for persuasion." Once he'd settled back into his chair, he said, "Kit, Tommy, Beverly, and Archibald. One of them is our killer."

"I think we have to add someone else to the list. A man you don't know. Red Clemens."

"Who is he? And why would you include him?"

"He's worked as a janitor at the theater since he was a teenager. He had a crush on Kit when he was young, and I think it's possible he still does. He's a celebrity freak—likes to have pictures of himself taken with famous people. He's the one who knew about the hidden rooms in the theater. He learned about them because he saw Kit disappear from her dressing room back in the late seventies. He'd been watching her through a keyhole. I actually kind of like the guy, but I don't think we can rule him out. He makes a point of knowing everything that goes on around his place of employment. It's his universe. His own personal daytime drama."

"Okay. You make a good case. Clemens should be on the list."

For the first time since talking to Woodson, Jane felt herself relax. Her father was safe, at least for the moment. "I suppose it's possible for a woman to drag a dead body behind a wall, or lift one into a trunk, but that woman would have to be strong."

"With adrenaline comes strength," said her father. "And we all know a woman can use a gun as easily as a man."

"But in this specific case, Kit is a small woman. I just don't think she could have managed it."

"I'd be happy to cross her off the list," said her dad. "On the other hand, she could have hired someone to do it for her—or asked a loyal member of her extended family. Based on what we know, it's difficult to eliminate or accuse any of them. We need the same thing DePetro does. A key piece of evidence. A smoking gun."

If they couldn't catch a break, Jane's father might be the next victim. He might want to put a less dramatic spin on it, but she couldn't.

"You know, Janey, this feels good, just sitting here with you, relaxing by the fire." He wiggled his toes. "Even if we are talking about a murder investigation, it's . . . nice."

"Are you really doing okay?" she asked. "I'm sure you miss Elizabeth."

He smiled. "Peter was sure I was going to dissolve into a puddle when she left. Honestly, Jane. I don't know how to account for it, but it was like somebody reached up and turned off a switch inside me. One minute I thought I was in love, and the next . . . everything looked different. Felt different. I've never had that happen before. When your mother died, I grieved for years. Hell, I'm still grieving. When Marilyn and I broke up, it was terribly hard. I didn't talk about it much, especially with you and Peter. I don't want to make my problems your problems. But with Elizabeth, it was different. Maybe I'm growing shallow in my old age. Has anything like that ever happened to you?"

"I'm not sure," said Jane.

"I looked at Elizabeth one minute and I thought she was beautiful. The next, I didn't even find her attractive." He shrugged. "I'm too old and life's too short to overanalyze it. So, to answer your question, I'm fine. A little lonely around the house at night, but that's nothing new. Actually, during the last couple of months Elizabeth and I were together, I'd never felt lonelier than when I was with her. The human heart," he said, shaking his head as he held his drink up to the light of the fire. "As the Bible says, 'Who can know it.'"

Jane helped her dad get settled upstairs, putting out some clean towels in the bathroom and making sure the bed linens in the spare bedroom were fresh. She opened the door on a closet full of Peter's old clothes. Her brother had stayed with her once for several months. It had been many years ago, when he and Sigrid had separated for a time. He'd never entirely moved out. She kept telling him that he had clothes at her place, but he never seemed to come by to pack them up, and then, after washing everything and storing them away, she'd forgotten about them.

Her dad and Peter were approximately the same size. Not only was Jane able to produce pajamas and a bathrobe, but there were socks and even clean underwear in a drawer. Tomorrow, he would have his pick of several sweaters, a couple of oxford cloth shirts that Jane had ironed, even half a dozen ties. Pants would be a problem, unless her father was willing to wear jeans.

They said their good nights just after eleven. Jane drifted back downstairs to the living room, where the dogs were still sleeping, and after tossing a couple more logs on the grate, fell asleep herself in front of the fire.

A little after two A.M. the sound of a text scissored into her sleep.

Opening her eyes, she saw that the fire had gone out. Fumbling to dig her cell phone out of her pocket, she flipped it open and saw that it was from Cordelia.

I'm outside. Open up.

Jane ran a hand through her long, tangled hair as she stumbled into the foyer. She turned off the security system and pulled the door back.

Cordelia barreled inside. "What weather." She flung off her cape and tried to fluff the sleet out of her hair. "I saw your dad's car outside, so I decided not to ring the doorbell."

"Good call," said Jane. For Cordelia, two A.M. was the middle of the day. "What's going on?" She switched on a couple of lamps in the living room.

"I know who murdered Jordan and stuffed those bodies in my theater."

"You do?"

"It's so simple. I don't know why I didn't see it the moment you and Woodson mentioned those notes. It's *I, Claudius*. Pure Robert Graves." She spotted the popcorn bowl on the table. Grabbing it and hugging it to her stomach, she sat down on the rocking chair. "It's Germanicus. You remember him? The John F. Kennedy of ancient Rome?"

"I don't think we ever met," said Jane, crawling back under her quilt.

"And Caligula. He was the real culprit. Well, I mean, it's probably not literally true, but it's from Graves's book—and the BBC TV show. You remember it? I rewatched part of it tonight. Didn't you just love Derek Jacobi? What instincts that man has. I'd love to direct him. But back to the notes."

"The notes?"

"Yes. That's what I've been talking about. Haven't you been listening?"

"I thought I was."

"It's those notes," said Cordelia, popping some popcorn kernels into her mouth. "Who would know about those notes? They were supposed to frighten Germanicus. Apparently, he was deeply superstitious. Okay, so maybe it wasn't Caligula. It could have been his mother, or even Tiberius. But somebody poisoned him. And before they did, they tried to scare him to death. In the room where he died, they found the remains of human babies, tablets with curses on them, anything and everything they thought could scare the wits out of him. And, again, the notes."

"What about the notes?"

"Just like the ones that were sent to Jordan. To Ray. To Stanislaw Melcer."

"How does that tell you who the murderer is?"

"It's *Roman* history," said Cordelia. "Who do we know who's a Roman scholar?"

"Archibald?"

"Of course, Archibald. Bingo. Strike. Score." She pumped her fist in the air. "We have our man."

"I'm not sure that's proof."

"You don't know him the way I do. He's arrogant. Thinks he's smarter than everyone else. If it was his work, he'd want to sign it. That crow? He knew the image of a crow would rattle Jordan. Those notes were Archibald's signature. Who else would have that piece of information at his fingertips? You'd have to be some kind of wacko Roman historical nut job to know about it."

"Otherwise known as a one-time professor of Roman history."

"Exactly. He was playing with his victims. Honestly, I might like the guy, he may bring fabulous wine to my parties and love to gossip, but this would totally be his kind of MO."

"This theory of yours would never hold up in court."

"Maybe not. But with so little to go on, and so many potential suspects, we're looking for *probability*. The notes point to someone—and probability says it's Archibald."

"What else? What was his motivation?"

"He loves Kit. Almost worships her. Initially, he probably wanted to collect her. He has always been drawn to 'the fascinating among us,' as he says. Somewhere along the line, his feelings deepened."

"You think he's *in* love with her?"

Cordelia turned up her nose. "Can't quite imagine that pairing. He's not exactly Ryan Gosling."

"Hope springs eternal. Think about it. Maybe everything he's done was to protect her. In the process, why not knock off a few rivals? Chapman. Melcer."

"Your father."

Feeling suddenly cold, Jane pulled the quilt up to her nose. "We have to find concrete proof, otherwise it means nothing."

"We have to get him to admit what he did."

"The thing is, he already did. He went to DePetro and confessed to Jordan's murder."

"In an effort to protect Kit. Everything he's done, in his own twisted way, was because he loves her. That confession should have scored him some points."

Jane considered it. Sitting up, she said, "Dad told me that, initially, Archibald only admitted to Jordan's murder. When DePetro mentioned the bodies found at the theater and connected them, he admitted to those, too. But it was a lame confession. DePetro never believed him for a minute because he screwed up the firearm details."

"Brilliant reverse psychology. If he admitted to the murders

274

and was laughed out of the interrogation room, what better way to prove his innocence."

Jane wasn't convinced.

Cordelia dug energetically through the popcorn, looking for the pieces with the most butter. "So, back to my initial point. We need to get him to admit what he did—this time, in real, believable terms."

"How?"

"That's what we have to figure out."

"You willing to work on this?" asked Jane. "Now? For as long as it takes to come up with a plan?"

"You never butter your popcorn enough. We need sustenance. Brain food. I'll make us two of my world-famous omelets." Rising to her full height, she charged off into the kitchen with the dogs trotting after her.

Sometimes, when Cordelia came to the house in the middle of the night, Jane had the sense that the Marines had landed—in every sense of the word.

36

Without an alarm clock to wake him, Jane's father slept until almost ten on Friday morning. When he dragged himself into the kitchen, wearing his son's striped bathrobe, rubbing the sleep out of his eyes and yawning, Jane and Cordelia were still working at the kitchen table. Jane had gone out earlier to buy fresh bagels, cream cheese, and lox for their breakfasts. After returning home, she'd thinly sliced a tomato and a red onion to go along with it, and made a pot of coffee, strong and black.

"You two look like the cats that ate the canary," said Ray, pouring himself a cup.

"Dad?" said Jane. "Are there any local judges who owe you a favor?"

He scanned the food on offer. "Yes. Probably. Why?"

It all tumbled out, mostly from Cordelia. How she'd put it together that Archibald was responsible for the notes, and if that was true, it followed that he was the murderer. Ray talked over their ideas with them, did his best to poke holes in their arguments, but in the end, agreed that Cordelia had made a significant connection. And then, hesitantly, Jane sketched out their strategy for trapping Archibald. "All you'd have to do is call the judge," said Jane. "Archibald's already admitted to Jordan's murder. I think that was a significant error in judgment. Cordelia and I are fairly certain he never intended for DePetro to believe him and actually arrest him. It was just one more way to muddy the waters and prove to Kit that he was her hero. But," she said, getting up to pour herself more coffee, "it gives DePetro probable cause to search his house."

"Good thinking," said Ray. "Yes, you can leave all that to me."

"Promise you won't go back to your place today," said Jane. "I'll handle everything on that end. We don't want to tip our hand."

After giving Jane his word, her father headed upstairs to shower. Jane and Cordelia were left alone in the kitchen.

"Can we really do this?" asked Jane.

"There will be only one seriously dangerous moment. And you won't even be there. It's all on me. Cordelia M. Thorn, private eye."

"Last chance to back out."

"No way." She searched through her digital address book until she found Archibald's number.

"Put him on speakerphone so I can hear, too," said Jane.

She made a couple of taps, then set the phone down on the table between them.

"Hello," came Archibald's voice.

"Hey, babe, it's Cordelia. Have I got an invitation for you."

"You do?"

"Are you free tonight?"

"Actually, I'm not. I have plans."

"Look, Hattie will be with me at the theater until seven thirty or so. Could you come after that? Eight? Even nine would work. You've been so incredibly helpful with all the research you've done. Since you don't want money, I thought this might be a way to give you something—an experience you'll never forget."

Jane thought she was laying it on a bit thick.

"I'll even throw in a bottle of chilled Cristal," said Cordelia. "To add to the celebration."

"Celebration? Can you give me a few more details?"

"I don't want to spoil the surprise. Let's just say this will be mind-blowing, especially for a theater lover like you."

"It does sound intriguing."

"More than intriguing. This will be a first. A debut. And you'll be in on it. Part of history in the making."

"Oh, hell, why not. I can get my business done by nine, I'm sure of it. Consider it a date."

"Splendid," said Cordelia, her arms shooting up like she'd just scored a goal.

While Cordelia drove back to her house to change clothes and make a few more phone calls, Jane headed back upstairs to change into dark clothing. For what she had to do tonight, she needed cover.

On her way up the stairs, she met her father coming down. He'd changed into one of Peter's shirts and sweaters, and had on a pair of his jeans. "You look great in jeans," said Jane. "You should buy yourself a pair."

Her father gave her a sidelong glance. "Thanks. Not really my style."

He was carrying his laptop under his arm.

"Can you work from here today?"

"That's the plan."

On an impulse, she sat down on one of the steps and patted the space next to her. "Can we talk—just for a minute?"

He sat down next to her. "Having second thoughts?"

This close, Jane could smell that he'd even borrowed some of Peter's Old Spice. "No, not at all. I think our plan will work—

with a little luck. What I wanted to say was that . . . I appreciated you opening up last night about your feelings for Mom, for Marilyn and Elizabeth. It helped me sort through some of my own issues."

"Nothing in life is ever easy."

"I agree, but has it ever occurred to you that we have similar romantic trajectories? We both got it right with our first partner, though after that, we've been less successful."

"There certainly is a parallel, Janey. But a parallel isn't a prophesy."

"No, I know that."

"Problems with Avi?"

"Like you said last night, I don't want to make my problems your problems."

Turning to her, taking her hand in his, he said, "I never want you to feel that way. I'm here for you, sweetheart, as you are for me. That's one reason I like the idea of us working together. You have an absolute right to your privacy, as do I. We both have active, busy lives, but those lives, more often than not, take us away from each other instead of bringing us closer together. Maybe that didn't bother me so much when I was younger, but it does now. If you ever want to talk something over, I'm here to listen. The more you're around, the more chances we'll have to listen to each other. There's nothing more important to me than that."

"Oh, Dad," she said, tears welling in her eyes. She couldn't imagine a life without him in it.

"I can tell what you're thinking," he said, squeezing her hand. "I won't be around forever. That's simply the way of the world."

She rubbed an arm across her eyes.

"I remember the last time I saw my mother. She was old and ill. I'd come over to her house to help her get some lunch. I kissed her before I left and then walked over to the door. When I turned to smile at her, the look on her face was so intense, it stopped me. She was trying to memorize me, Janey. That was a hard moment. I realize that I sometimes look at you and Peter that way now. I don't want to forget a thing." Again, he squeezed her hand. "Don't worry about those notes, honey. I'm going to be around for a long time."

"Promise?"

His smile was gentle. "Promise."

Later that morning, Jane drove across the river to her father's home in Saint Paul. She took a couple of passes past his house to make sure Archibald wasn't watching the place. Convinced that he was nowhere around, she entered through the back door and quickly pulled the shades in the living room. After turning on a couple of lamps, she made sure the patio door leading out to the back deck was unlocked.

Finally, in her father's office, she placed his daily calendar in the center of the desk, circled the date, and wrote, in big block letters, "Overnight Trip to Chicago." She wanted Archibald to be able to get into the house easily and see that her father wouldn't be home until tomorrow. Armed with that misinformation, he would be free to join Cordelia at the theater.

On her way back to Minneapolis, where she intended to spend the bulk of her day at her restaurant, she decided to stop by Avi's apartment. She figured she owed it to her to be honest about her intentions. It would likely be a difficult conversation. Thinking that this was already a day for hard conversations, she pulled up outside the apartment and headed up the walk.

Avi welcomed her in, this time with both a kiss and a generous hug.

"Am I interrupting your work?" asked Jane.

"No, this is great," said Avi. "I made us a pot of soup."

"I can't stay," said Jane. She felt like a coward for using such a trite excuse. It wasn't that she *couldn't* stay. She didn't want to.

"Okay," said Avi. "Can you at least sit down for a few minutes?"

They sat in the dining room. Jane sensed a tension she'd never felt around Avi before.

"Have you thought any more about what we talked about the other night?" asked Avi, getting right to the point. "About having a child together?"

"I have."

Taking Jane's measure for a few seconds, her eyes fell to the kitchen towel in her hand. "You don't have to spell it out. I can see what your answer is."

"I'm sorry."

"Sure." She pushed her sweater sleeves up her arms. "So. Does that mean we're over?"

"I don't see how we can go on when we have such different needs."

"What if one of my needs is you?"

"Honestly, Avi. I don't know what to say. This sort of thing is never easy."

"You mean telling your girlfriend you don't want to have a baby with her. You've done that a lot, have you?"

"You know what I'm saying. This is hard for me, too."

"Spell it out."

"I could never ask you to choose between me and a child. So, yes, I think we're over."

Avi seemed to be about to say something. At the last second, she thought better of it and stayed silent.

"I only want what's best for you," said Jane. "I hope you give this idea of yours more thought. It's a huge decision."

"You think I don't know that?"

"You're right. It's your business, not mine."

"Just leave."

"Avi—"

"What?"

"Will you stay in touch?"

"Oh, screw you," she shouted, looking up defiantly. "Get the hell out of my apartment before I really lose my temper, you useless, self-righteous . . . old woman."

Under other circumstances, Avi's stinging rebuke might have upset Jane. Today the words seemed simply flailing and feeble. She rose and stood over Avi for a few seconds, wishing she could touch her, though understanding that she'd lost the right. She remembered Cordelia's words. She hadn't been put on this earth to make everything right for Avi, especially when it had all become so terribly tangled and wrong.

"Bye," said Jane, closing the door quietly on the way out.

37

As the light faded from the sky, Jane sat in her CR-V, a quarter of a block from Archibald's home, waiting for him to come out and get down to the business of murder. She listened to an old Eurythmics CD. As the song "Sweet Dreams" came on, he appeared. He walked resolutely out of his front door dressed all in black, carrying a briefcase. She let him drive off, then, when he seemed to be heading in the direction of the freeway, she allowed him to pull a block ahead.

The silver Audi eventually took the Lexington Avenue exit. Jane stayed several car lengths behind until they were two blocks from her father's home. Archibald drove past the house several times. Jane hoped the lights she'd turned on inside would give the impression that her dad was there. She needed Archibald to go in and find the calendar entry.

Parking half a block away, he slipped out, no longer carrying the briefcase, and darted through one of the front yards toward the alley. Jane drove past his car and turned the corner. She pulled a U-turn in the middle of the street and parked. From the angle she'd chosen, she could see her father's back deck.

Archibald took his time. He stayed out of sight for several

minutes, no doubt casing the exterior, finally emerging in the backyard. He edged swiftly up the deck stairs to the sliding doors. A second later he was in.

Jane switched off the music so that she could concentrate fully on her anxiety. Five minutes went by. Then another five. Growing frustrated, she began to drum on the dashboard. She stopped when she saw him creep back outside. He rushed down the steps and headed through her father's front yard straight for his car. She waited a full minute, then inched her SUV forward.

Turning the corner, she saw the Audi's red taillights speeding away in the darkness. She followed, again at a distance, as the car headed back to I-94. She assumed, since it wasn't yet eight, that he'd phone Cordelia from his cell to tell her he'd be able to come over earlier than expected. But just as they were about to pass one of the U of M exits, he pulled off and appeared to head back to his house. She wondered if something had gone wrong.

Parking in the driveway, he got out and carried the briefcase inside. In less than a minute, he was back outside and driving off. This time Jane didn't follow him. Instead, she called Cordelia.

"Speak to me," came Cordelia's voice, low and somewhat muffled.

"Where are you?"

"If I told you I was hiding under my desk, would you believe me?"

"Listen up: Archibald's heading your way. With the traffic on the freeway, I'd say maybe fifteen minutes to the theater."

"Was I right? Did he go to your father's house?"

Jane had known, from the moment Archibald had stepped outside dressed all in black, that Cordelia's theory was a home run. "You were right."

"How on earth could I have enjoyed having dinner with a serial killer?"

"Are you all set on your end? Is Tommy sober?"

"Seems to be. I didn't do a Breathalyzer."

"Good luck."

"We'll both need it. Out."

Jane left her car feeling a welcome hit of adrenaline. One of Nolan's tutorials had covered lock picking. If she did say so herself, over the last couple of years, she'd gotten pretty good at it.

After snapping on her latex gloves, she examined the lock on the back door and saw that it was old, an easy in. She couldn't believe people protected their homes with such crappy locks. It was denial, really. And that denial, tonight, worked in her favor.

"Close your eyes," said Cordelia, feeling the earth drop away under her feet as she and Archibald sped upward in the elevator.

"This isn't going to hurt, is it?" asked Archibald, making what he thought was a joke.

Little did he know, thought Cordelia. "Are those eyes closed?" The doors opened on the upstairs theater lobby.

"I know where we are."

"Are you ready to be awed?"

"Always."

She passed her arm through his, revolted that she had to stand so close to him, and led him up the center aisle toward the stage. Halfway to the front, she stopped. "You can open up now and behold." She spread her arms toward the new theater curtain. "Isn't it breathtaking?"

Archibald seemed genuinely impressed. "What a perfect color. You have astonishing taste."

"I do. You're the first person, other than the workmen, to see it hanging there in all its perfect blue glory. Just think how many productions will begin with that curtain going up."

"It sends chills through me. It really does."

"Want to see it raised?"

"Yes," he said eagerly.

Cordelia motioned to the tech booth. "Let 'er rip."

The curtain moved slowly, pulled by wires one foot apart, to form an arch over the stage.

"Gorgeous," said Archibald, clapping his hands together. "Absolutely glorious."

"A new piece of history is about to begin for the Old Deep and Dark."

"Honestly, I can't wait."

As the lights in the auditorium dimmed, lights came up on the stage.

"Are you already in rehearsals?" he asked, eyes narrowing.

Four chairs faced the back of the stage. One chair, ringed by a spotlight, faced the audience.

"A rehearsal of sorts," said Cordelia, feeling a different kind of chill run through her. She moved away from Archibald as Tommy rushed toward him from the rear of the auditorium. Archibald didn't turn around until it was too late. Tommy pulled his arms behind his back and cuffed his hands. It all happened so fast that Archibald hadn't even struggled. In fact, he seemed to think it was all part of Cordelia's show.

"What now?" he said laughing. "A little S and M."

"Let's go up onstage and find out," she said.

Seemingly annoyed by Tommy's presence, Archibald whispered to Cordelia, as if Tommy wasn't right behind them, "I don't know why *he* has to be here. It spoils the moment."

"All will be revealed," said Cordelia. She strode out onto the stage, momentarily dazzled by the lights. Motioning to the single chair, she nodded for Archibald to sit.

In the spirit of fun, he sat down.

"Archibald Van Arnam, this is your life!" She was improvising.

He was old enough to understand the reference to the long-ago TV show. And in a way, it was true.

From stage right, Kit and Beverly walked out and each took a chair facing Archibald. Tommy took the third chair. Cordelia the fourth.

Showtime.

Jane paused in Archibald's study to phone her father. "It's me."

"What's the word?"

"Our theory was correct. Are you with DePetro?"

"Yes."

"He's got the search warrant from your friendly judge?"

"He does."

"And you've briefed him?"

"I have."

"Okay, just listen. I'm in Archibald's house. If it takes DePetro and his men more than five minutes to find the gun—and it is the murder weapon we've been looking for—then Minnetonka needs a new police force. I'm out of here." She clicked off the phone, took one last look at Archibald's briefcase, made sure she hadn't left anything out of order or any trace that she'd been inside, and then hightailed it through the back door.

Archibald wasn't smiling anymore. "What's going on?" he demanded. Glancing up at the spotlight, he squirmed in his seat. "Enough, okay? Tommy, you can take the cuffs off now. I am not amused."

"Never expected you would be," said Tommy.

"Cordelia? Is this some sort of game?"

"I think I'll let Kit take it from here." She couldn't believe they'd gotten this far without their plans going up in flames.

Standing, Kit stepped a few paces away from her chair, glancing down as if she were searching for her blocking. She, too, took a moment to look up at the spotlights, though the light on her was less intense than the hot white glare Archibald was bathed in. "I really only have one question. Why did you murder Jordan?"

His features contorted ever so briefly, then composed. "I would never hurt Jordan. He was my friend. And frankly, I think I've more than proved my devotion to you over the years. I don't deserve to be treated like this."

"Please, I truly need you to make me understand."

"If you had any evidence against me, I wouldn't be talking to you and your band of sycophants, I'd be talking to DePetro."

"If it were up to me," Beverly piped up, "I'd shove his chair—accidentally, of course—off the stage into the orchestra pit."

"I've had enough of this," said Archibald, struggling to his feet.

"Sit *down*," shouted Tommy, standing with his fists clenched. "You're not going anywhere."

He sat down hard.

This was great theater, thought Cordelia. If it hadn't been a matter of life and death, and if something couldn't still go wrong, she'd really be enjoying herself.

"What's the point of this little drama?" demanded Archibald. "Even if I admit I murdered every last one of those people, it wouldn't be admissible in court."

"Just answer my question and we can be done with this," pleaded Kit.

He studied her.

"Archibald, please."

"I get it. You want me to admit to murdering Jordan, but you don't want me to tell the entire story. You want the punch line without the joke."

"This isn't getting us anywhere," said Kit, turning to Cordelia. "I think we should call it a night and go home."

"For instance, why don't we discuss Eddy Chapman? We all know who he was. Why did he need to disappear, Kit? Did you ever ask yourself that?"

She turned around to face him. "If you ever loved me—"

Cordelia couldn't believe he'd given in so easily. Then again, he was partly right. Without proof, none of this could be used against him. Still, people with secrets were *always* dying to tell them. In this moment of revelation, with little at stake, he actually seemed to be enjoying himself.

"You were pregnant," he said. "Chapman was the father."

"That's a lie," screamed Kit.

"Let's put it all out there for this eminent kangaroo court to consider. Cordelia, as head kangaroo, you can make the final judgment about guilt or innocence. I place myself in your hands." He cleared his throat. "Why don't we start at the beginning, when Kit and Jordan made their fateful bargain. He would marry her to help him hide the fact that he was a homosexual, and in return, he would make her bastard baby girl legitimate. Believe me, it wouldn't have happened if Eddy had stayed in the picture. He was a small-minded, nasty little man. He would have blown Kit and Jordan's story out of the water just because he could. That is, if I hadn't stepped in. He was a womanizer, too, in case you didn't know that, Kit. You think he was faithful to you before he shuffled off this mortal coil? He was trying to bed every woman who didn't run away fast enough."

"None of this is true," said Kit. "He's making up a story just to hurt me."

"You think Jordan didn't confide in me? How many years were we friends? You think I don't know it all?"

"Listen," pleaded Kit. "If he's admitted to one murder, he's admitted to them all. Let's stop right here. We have what we came for."

"What about Melcer?" asked Archibald. Beads of sweat had formed on his forehead. Without a free hand, he couldn't wipe them away. "Jordan came to me. Told me Melcer had taken nude photos of you during one of your trysts. My God, woman, but you can be stupid. I tried to pay Melcer for the negatives, with Jordan's money, of course, but he wouldn't take it. He needed leverage because he wanted you back. You know, Kit, quite honestly, I felt sorry for him. How do you do it? How do you make men think you're some sort of goddess?"

"I'm not a goddess," she whispered.

"Yeah. Tell me about it. And yet, even now, I still want you. If there was a way out of this maelstrom, a way to be with you, I'd take it and never look back."

"Archibald," she said softly, pleadingly.

"And Decca? You were the one who put me on to her. She was sniffing out the truth about Jordan. She would have gotten there, too. She was clever, and dogged. Didn't you ever wonder what happened to these people?"

"Eddy . . . he left town. Couldn't face his wife. That's what I thought. And Stan? I didn't know he was blackmailing Jordan. You're right, I am a fool. I've always been a fool. When he disappeared, I thought he'd taken off because his business was failing. And Decca. When she evaporated, I simply turned away and thanked my lucky stars."

"You should have thanked *me,* Kit. You still don't get it, do you? Everything I've done was to protect you."

"Oh, no. No, no. You can't put your actions on me."

"You loved me once. The time we were together was the happiest few months of my life. Why did you have to end it? What did I do? I never understood. I thought—I've always thought—there was a chance we'd find each other again. If nothing else, for Booker.

All I ever got to be in his eyes was his godfather. You don't know how much I wanted to claim him as my own."

"Did you tell Jordan?" she asked weakly.

"He already knew. He wasn't stupid. He could see the resemblance, even if no one else could."

Cordelia flapped air into her face. This was the *National Enquirer* and *Inside Edition* on steroids.

Beverly sat with her head bowed. Tommy had turned away, refusing to look at Kit.

"But what about Ray?" asked Cordelia. "Why were you targeting him?"

Archibald's face flushed a deep red. Narrowing his eyes at Kit, he said, "It was *my* turn. You should have come to *me,* not another pretty boy in an expensive suit. I saw the way you looked at him, how you touched his hand, tilted your head, smiled, and cooed. You pulled away from me and showered all your warmth on him. Why? Am I so grotesque? Why is it that you could never see *me.* I've been there for you my entire adult life. Why doesn't Archibald ever merit one of your loving looks? Ray Lawless was nothing. He didn't believe in you, or care about you. He would have left you just like every other man you've ever loved. I couldn't stand to be in the same room with him. Kit, I'm done putting up with your faithless, cheating ways. There will be no more men in your life. Only me."

From the back of the hall, uniformed officers began to filter down the aisles.

Cordelia stood as Neil DePetro entered stage left and brushed right past her. He held up his badge as he approached Archibald. As he read him his rights, he glanced at the handcuffs, then back at Cordelia.

She waved and tittered.

An instant later, Jane appeared next to her. "I can't believe it," she whispered.

"They found the gun?" Cordelia whispered back.

"You were right. Archibald suffers from terminal arrogance. Must've thought he was too smart to get caught. He never even tried to hide it."

As two uniformed officers led a furious and sweating Archibald away, DePetro walked over to Jane and Cordelia. "You two think you're pretty clever."

Cordelia was good at looking innocent. "You talking to us?"

"Where did you get those handcuffs?"

"An army-navy surplus store?"

"He let you put them on him willingly?"

"He's kind of kinky. Or perhaps he saw it as a joke."

Scowling, DePetro favored them with a stern look. "Some joke."

"I've always thought humor was a rather personal thing," said Cordelia.

"You two are a real pair."

With one last hard look, he left the stage.

"We did it," said Jane.

At what cost, thought Cordelia, seeing Tommy, his shoulders sagging, walking up the aisle all alone. Beverly continued to sit with her back to Kit. Nobody would come out of this feeling like a winner.

38

Jane paused next to the empty box office window to watch Cordelia and Booker, arm in arm, talking animatedly, make their way across the first floor theater lobby toward her. Three days had come and gone since Archibald had been arrested on four counts of murder. Almost every national and local news outlet was covering the story 24-7. Jane was so sick of hearing about Archibald and his lawyer's various spin moves that she refused to turn on the TV, read a paper, or listen to the radio.

Her work with her father was done for the moment. She was glad that she could return to her restaurant, content in the knowledge that when it counted, she hadn't disappointed him. She looked forward to working with him again, as long as it wasn't until after the holidays. It would be lonely this year without Peter and his family, and especially lonely without Avi. But Jane pushed those thoughts out of her mind, unwilling to let them bring her down. She was in too good a mood.

Cordelia had met with Booker, hoping to get him to commit to taking a job with the theater. Judging by her buoyant expression, Jane assumed she'd closed the deal. Kit stood across the room next to an open door that led into the new indie bookstore—Fitzgerald's. She was with an odd-looking man sporting an oversized gray beard and leaning on a silver-handled cane, someone Jane had never seen before. After everything that had happened, Jane was a little surprised to see her out and about, obviously enjoying the bearded man's company.

"Afternoon," said Cordelia, nodding pleasantly to several women who sailed past her. The first floor was no longer off-limits to the public, mainly because the bookstore and the Italian deli had finally opened. People wandered in and out, curious to see what was happening inside the new Thorn Lester Playhouse. They couldn't get upstairs just yet, but were able to watch the murals on the first floor being restored to their former glory.

"Janey, meet our new set designer," said Cordelia, beaming at Booker as if he were a shiny new toy.

"You took the job," said Jane. "Congratulations."

"Had to." He shot a guarded glance toward his mother. "My girlfriend wrote the play."

"You and Erin are together?" Cordelia enthused. "How . . . utterly fascinating. A new rock-star theater couple has been born."

"No thanks," said Booker. "I like living in the shadows. So does Erin."

"Who's the man with your mother?" asked Jane.

"He wants to write her authorized biography. He's already got the go-ahead from Simon & Schuster. Mom said he's done a number of other biographies, so he's legit."

"My stars and garters," said Cordelia, pressing a hand to her chest. "I would think your mother has had enough media attention to last the next hundred years."

Booker tried to cover his look of disgust with a shrug.

"She's a survivor," said Jane. "You have to give her that."

"How's Chloe doing?" asked Cordelia.

"Good," said Booker. "Actually, there's a new man in her life. When he found out what had happened, he flew here from California to be with her. He's taking her home today. He was so overwhelmed by the thought that he might have lost her, that he asked her to marry him. The wedding will be next June."

"That's terrific," said Jane. At least something good had come out of it.

"Well, listen you two, I gotta bounce. Erin's leaving tomorrow, flying back to Seattle. I intend to spend every minute I can with her. I head back to New York tomorrow night."

"What about your mom?" asked Cordelia, nodding obliquely in her direction.

"Her new biographer can take her home." He gave Cordelia a kiss on her cheek, then turned and gave one to Jane. "Adieu, ladies. To be continued."

Jane liked Booker, and was glad to hear he'd be back. As she watched him push out through one of the glass doors, she caught sight of a familiar face inside the bookstore. She moved a little to her right to get a better look. Red Clemens was sitting at a table, dressed in a dapper suit and tie, signing books for half a dozen people who waited in line. "What's all that about?" asked Jane.

Cordelia looked over Jane's shoulder. "Oh. I forgot to tell you. I found out yesterday that Red's a published poet. He's quite well known."

"I've never heard of him."

"He doesn't go by Red Clemens. He writes under his real name, Philip Powell Clemens."

"*He's* Philip Powell Clemens?"

"Apparently, people come from all over the country to meet him here at the theater. Just think of it, a poet janitor. Then again, didn't Ted Kooser sell insurance most of his life?"

"Incredible," said Jane. So he wasn't a celebrity freak after all. The celebrities came to meet *him*. "Will this place ever stop surprising me?"

Cordelia put her hand on Jane's back and walked her toward the elevators. "Not to dwell on the obvious, but another case has been successfully completed. Thanks to *moi*."

"I have to agree. You deserve the credit."

Two middle-aged women cut in front of them. The shorter of the two said, quite loudly, "Did you see how old she looked in person?"

"What's her first name?" asked the taller one.

"Kit. Kit Deere. She must be seventy years old. I used to think she was so beautiful. I saw her onstage last winter and she looked twenty years younger. How is that even possible?"

"Must be her husband's death."

"He's another one," said the shorter woman. "I went to one of his concerts at the state fair two years ago. Believe me, in person, he looked nothing like the hunky guy you see on TV. He was downright puny."

"Funny, isn't it," said the taller woman. "It's like that super handsome guy who plays in all those action movies. I don't know why I'm blanking on his name, but I've had a crush on him for years. When I was in New York last summer, I walked right past him on the street. He wasn't more than five feet tall. I towered over him."

Jane and Cordelia exchanged glances.

"Guess that old saying is true," said Cordelia, pausing as the elevator doors opened.

"What saying?" asked Jane

They walked on, turning and standing next to each other.

As the doors closed, Cordelia whispered, "Get on your knees every night and pray that you never meet your heroes."